'Intense, gripping, scary . . . exactly what a thriller is

 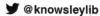

John Connor left his job as a barrister to write full time. During the fifteen years of his legal career he prosecuted numerous homicide cases in West Yorkshire and London. He advised the police in numerous proactive drugs and organised crime operations, many involving covert activity. He now lives in Brussels with his wife and two children. His novel *Falling*, a part of the Karen Sharpe series, was shortlisted for the prestigious Portico Prize for Literature.

Also by John Connor

Phoenix
The Playroom
A Child's Game
Falling
Unsafe
The Vanishing
The Ice House

The Opposite of Mercy

JOHN CONNOR

ORION

First published in Great Britain in 2011
by Orion,
as *The Opposite of Mercy* by Tom Winship

This paperback edition published in 2019
by Orion Fiction,
an imprint of The Orion Publishing Group Ltd
Carmelite House, 50 Victoria Embankment
London EC4Y 0DZ

An Hachette UK Company

1 3 5 7 9 10 8 6 4 2

A CIP catalogue record for this book is
available from the British Library.

ISBN 978 1 4091 8886 5

Typeset at The Spartan Press Ltd,
Lymington, Hants

Printed and bound by Clays Ltd,
Elcograf S.p.A.

www.orionbooks.co.uk

For Anna, Sara and Thomas

With very special thanks to Sara O'Keeffe.

Thanks also to DI Jon Hoyle, Ray Dance, Det. Sup. Max Mclean, Phil Patterson.

And to Fia Nordman and Felizia Grindefjord.

1

Saturday, 29th May, 2010

It took them just over an hour and half to get there, Paul driving fast, well over the limit all the way. It was still dark as they left Halifax – a chill, cloudless night with a full moon – but the sky turned grey around four thirty, and by the time they were past York it was blood red out to the east, shading into daylight above them.

The light made things worse. It had been about fourteen hours since the beating, leaving Paul's face bruised, one eye closed and a tooth broken. Despite that, and because the roads were empty, they had made good time on the motorways up to York, only having to slow on the narrower, twisting road across the moors.

The twenty miles across the tops, from Pickering to Whitby, then north to the tiny village of Silton, took an eternity, the huge bare hillsides stark in the periphery of his restricted vision, all his concentration tight on the thin band of tarmac. As they came out of Silton, dropping towards the coast, they sank into a thick fog, blotting out the weak dawn light. Paul switched the fog lights on and kept his eyes on the twisting stream of gleaming cat's-eyes.

Nearer the house, as they came over a rise, the fog thinned enough for them to glimpse the chimneys and bunkers of the chemical works, off to the left. So he knew he was on the right track. There was a mine, on land which had once been part of the Rathmore estate, and next to it a small industrial complex owned now by a multinational. Eight years ago, when Paul had first come here, the place had still belonged to the Rathmore family and had been operating at full capacity. Even at night he could remember it spewing out a yellow gas, polluting the darkness with halogen light and the grinding noise of heavy machinery. The *real* Rathmore. In darkness it had looked like a vision of hell – belching flames and fumes. Now it was all but shut down, in the process of being sold again, or decommissioned.

The road fell away from it about two miles out from the house and climbed another hill, up towards woods. They took a dirt track running between high hedges shrouded in mist. If the hill hadn't been there then you would be able to see the entire chemical plant from the front of the house. As it was, the hill and woods screened everything off, making the house difficult to find if you didn't know it was there, even with a car. Paul was navigating from memory because the satnav showed nothing but a blank space.

The main building stood by itself, isolated, woods to both sides. From the end of the dirt track it looked empty and unused, looming at them out of the fog. The woods were over four hundred years old, a mix of conifer and oak, towering over the gables so that the place was buried in their shadow. No lights on, no signs of life. Paul stopped the car in the gravel semicircle beyond the front door and stepped into the cold, damp air. He could smell the sea.

He waited for his eyes to adjust, at first keeping his torch switched off and concentrating with his ears. Past the edge of the gravel, where the neglected flower beds straggled into the woods, he couldn't see much. No movement though, no indication there was anyone out there besides himself. There was enough light for him to see that the front door was wide open. That set his pulse off.

It had been eight years since he had last stood where he was now and he'd been with Chris and Lara then. They had all been sixteen years old. The place looked only a bit smaller than he remembered. The central part, with the flight of eighteen stone steps up to the gaping door, gave onto two symmetrical wings, which curved back towards the woods. Twenty bedrooms over four floors, everything made of Portland stone. There were tall ornamental pillars either side of the door and according to the stone above one of them, they'd been there since 1826. Chris always called the place Rathmore − just the single, simple name − but the words carved by the date above the door were actually *Rathmore Hall*.

Paul switched the torch on and looked behind him to where the policeman − DS Andy Macall − had got out and was standing by the open passenger door of the Focus. 'They're not here,' Macall said, voice too loud, disappointment obvious. 'No one's here. The place is deserted.'

'The car could be round the other side,' Paul said, whispering. 'You check. I'll do the house.'

He set off without waiting for agreement. He should tell Macall about The Boat House, he knew − warn him. But in his head he was still trying to work out whether he was going to let Macall go down there. He was still trying to work out whether he could trust Macall at all. If Chris and Lara had come back here then they wouldn't be in *this* place − the collapsing nineteenth century pile − they'd be down below, at the bottom of the cliffs, in the newer place.

In 2001 − when they'd first come here − only the ground floor of the great house was still accessible. The structure was already decaying, plaster coming off the walls, ceilings sagging, the roof leaking, weeds growing up the exterior, some of the windows broken. It looked worse now. The ground floor windows were boarded up, the upper floor window panes broken, graffiti low down on one wall. There was a prominent alarm box to the right of the door, but it couldn't have been working. Phil Rathmore – that was Chris's dad's name, the same name as the house and the chemical companies – had wanted to sell the place as soon as his elder brother was killed, but there were complications to do with tax liabilities and grants. Meanwhile he had let Chris use it every now and then. Part of the price of buying his silence. At least, that was how Chris had put it. Maybe that had been true, maybe not, but that's how they ended up there: Chris, Lara and Paul. Three sixteen-year-old kids from suburban Manchester let loose on an abandoned country manor. Absurd. Maybe Chris and Lara had been used to it, but Paul had felt like a burglar just standing in the hall.

Out the front, beyond the terrace and lawns, there was a twisting path through a mile of woods to cliffs, then rickety wooden steps down to a cove with a short private beach and a boat house. That's what they called it – The Boat House – though there were no boats there. It was a proper house, with five rooms, but it was a thirties' design, partly on concrete piles – like a pier – extending towards the beach. That was where they had stayed. There were beds and cooking facilities, even a bar. The beach was rocky and boulder-strewn, sloping away at a steep gradient, but the pier part of the house ended right over the edge of it, so that the tide would come in at night and if it was really high the water would be close enough to wake you.

Paul got his mind back to the open front door. He had an

irrational feeling of dread as he went up to it. Enough to stop him and make him look back at Macall, still fumbling in the car for the other torch. Then, as he turned back to the opening, the smell hit him – faint traces of it reaching his nose before he could even see inside. Not something over-powering, but a very particular smell.

A freaky juxtaposition. Standing in North Yorkshire, in that place – a place he knew so well – but with a smell like Afghanistan in his nose, the noise of his heart in his ears. He stepped up and moved the torch beam through the space beyond the door, but he didn't need it – it was gloomy inside, but there was enough light to see *this*. He switched the torch off. He felt the ice run into his blood.

An unmistakeable, disgusting, stinking mess. The mess that killing leaves behind – at least *that* kind of killing – hands-on, protracted, violent. It took time and strength to put someone down like that. He could read how much time and strength it had taken by looking at the trail left behind: spattered up the walls, across the carpets and sheeting, foot-prints smeared through it, finger marks clawing at the walls and floor where the victim had tried desperately to escape. And all the time the heart pumping out blood – litres of it; a slippery, congealing slime of black and red that even after a few hours begins to reek enough to make you gag.

But this was fresh. What he had in his nose was the spe-cific smell of a stricken human who had *recently* bled to death. Pulse racing, heart in his mouth, he picked out the trail, took a deep breath, then stepped over the threshold. Ears straining into the silences, he followed the trail through the cavernous, empty rooms.

The path of spilled blood led right up to a shape lying at the very back of the place. Whoever it was had managed to get through the hall and two rooms, right to where a set of tall, arched, glass doors opened onto a terrace with a view across an ornamental lawn. Maybe they'd thought to get out there, to smash the glass. There were streaks of blood down the pane, as though a hand had slipped across it. Paul looked through the glass. Outside the fog was shifting and stirring. He began to shiver, then tried to step forward.

But he couldn't move, couldn't get any nearer.

He was terrified. Because in his head all he could think was that it must be Chris, or Lara. He started to take huge, gasping breaths, his heart pounding furiously. He was caught in a split second of suspended time, with all the chaos and insanity of the last seven days rushing around him. This was where it all led. To this moment. To Chris, or Lara, to one of them lying here.

He had a sudden, unwanted image of them as they had been eight years ago. Down by The Boat House, still alive and laughing. They were sitting on the rocks, the tide out, drinking the mad cocktails that Chris invented, chatting, reading, listening to music. They had the limitless sense of time that only young people can have. He could *feel* it, as if he were actually back there, in the skin of the person he had been. The room around him faded, the sun flashed into his eyes. The weather was fantastically hot, high summer heat, the kind you only get in distorted memories. The water was the North Sea – always too cold to swim in, unless you were really out of your head – but Lara was standing at the edge of the pebble beach in a white swimsuit, threatening to try it, shouting for Chris to dare her. Paul was on a deckchair, back near the house. He was just sitting there, watching her, completely fixated by the way she was standing, the way she held herself. It was the first time he had seen her in a swimsuit, the first time he had seen so much of her. He was transfixed. The complete lack of self-consciousness, the open, easy way she laughed. That morning they had walked along the beach and she had held both their hands, Chris and he, one each side of her. He could still feel her hand now, feel its tiny warmth against his fingers.

The stench jolted him out of the past. The image cut and his feet moved. He walked forwards like an automaton. Then stopped again, a few feet short of the body, his mind desperately searching the empty, aural space surrounding him. Had he heard something behind him? He turned and looked, moved the torch across the high, ornate ceilings, the crumbling stucco. Nothing. He stepped over to the corpse, legs trembling. He bent over and looked.

It wasn't either of them. Not Chris, not Lara. It was a man – middle-aged, dark skin, lank hair, slightly fat. He was on his front, head twisted sideways, jaw open, loose, broken and hanging from the rest of the face, smashed teeth sticking out, eyes swollen shut, nose crushed flat.

Paul heard the breath rushing out of his own lungs. Relief. This wasn't anyone he knew. He started to laugh about it, out loud. But then his stomach turned and he retched, the bile coming into his mouth before he could stop it. He swallowed hard. The battered head was resting in a thick pool of jellied blood, exposing the fatal injury. Behind the ear there was a wound so devastating there were shards of skull jutting through the clot-soaked hair.

Automatically, Paul stooped and touched the skin on the back of one of the hands. The warmth went through him like electricity. He recoiled. Only minutes ago this man had been alive, crawling, desperately trying to get away. Which meant Paul had walked into the middle of something, something that was still going on.

He caught his breath and looked frantically around him. They had to be here. Not here in this room, not here in this

7

building. But somewhere near. Down there, by the sea, in the other place.

That meant *he* was here also. Pasha. He was *already* here. That was all it could mean. He had been here when Chris and Lara arrived. He had been waiting for them.

Paul stood and started to run, out through the echoing rooms, back to the open front door. As he came out into the diffuse light he started to shout for Macall.

2

Saturday, 22nd May, 2010

Seven days before, Paul was in London, where he'd been living since getting back from Pakistan in mid April. He was still trying to adjust to the odd mix of convenience and discomfort, still trying to convince himself he somehow belonged in this suffocating crush of commodities and people. He found himself missing things he had once hated – the desert, the heat, the interminable views to distant mountains. At the time the jagged peaks had seemed like a wall, hemming them in a killing zone full of unidentifiable threats.

That Saturday, like any other since he'd got back, had started early: out of bed and into a cold shower, just after five. The boiler was faulty – he'd complained already – and could just about manage to get the water hot by midday, but Paul couldn't lie in bed that long. Force of habit. He needed coffee in his system and his eyes wide open by six.

He was living in a one room apartment in Bow, not much more than a bedsit, but it was way above the standard of accommodation he'd become used to – luxury compared to sleeping in the back of a Humvee in northern Pakistan, which was where he'd been just over a month before. The flat came as part of a job. After leaving the army he had passed a year doing private security 'in theatre' and then another six months in Pakistan, but this was his first job since coming home. The man he was working for was living in a new development about a mile away; a gated, guarded and more exclusive place. It was close enough for Paul to get there on foot, in under thirty minutes, which he was required to do on demand, in an emergency, and by ten o'clock each and every morning, seven days a week.

The building Paul was in was a converted townhouse and the remaining floors were taken by three eastern European families, each with a swarm of kids and an unceasing stream of new arrivals burdened with massive wheeled suitcases. They were connected to his employer in some way, since he owned the block, but Paul was trying to keep a blind eye to all that.

The job was a straightforward security job, organised through an agency that specialised in placing ex-soldiers, and it wasn't any of Paul's business to work out what his client did. Cheap foreign labour, drugs, prostitution, people trafficking? It didn't really matter, provided he didn't see any of it. All he had to do was drive the man around and watch his back. He'd been told he was there because of a 'general criminal threat'. It wasn't a professional level of information to work on, but then Paul didn't regard this kind of work as professional. If they came at the car with guns, or in numbers, he'd be the first to leg it. A higher level of dedication would require a higher level of remuneration than one and a half grand a month and a shitty bedsit with a broken boiler.

Today, the change in tempo started with one of those vivid memory episodes that now periodically disrupted his waking hours. He was passing Bow Road tube, just after nine thirty-five, on his way to the client. He had the earphones in and the iPod working through a playlist of recent D'n'B material he'd put together online, without paying a penny. The track was something by Breakage, from a new album. He was wondering whether he wasn't too old for this drumfunk thing—— when the memory slotted right in there, out of nowhere. Then he couldn't hear the music at all. His mind was a million miles away. Or several thousand. In a tent, a long way behind the notional front line, a laptop on his knees, programming the movements of an unmanned recon drone with a wireless controller not very unlike the sort of thing kids used on an Xbox. Except this wasn't a game. He had just identified a set of structures and delivered co-ordinates. The drone had been on station all morning and the process had taken him forty-seven seconds. A record for him. The result – six minutes later – had been a one minute barrage from three howitzer batteries dug in over eight miles away. He couldn't see them, but he had heard them clear enough. The morning had been full of that sound.

There were twenty-two casualties, thirteen killed instantly. In one minute. The most accurate piece of observation he had ever pulled off, and it was all done with an eight-hundred-thousand-dollar remote machine that was not much larger than the RC planes he had played with as a kid. At the time he had thought of it with satisfaction. Seven minutes forty-seven seconds from request to ordnance delivery. There had been lots of backslapping and handshaking. The drone was a relatively new resource for his spotter unit and it had worked. It had been less dangerous than crawling around in the dirt to get a line-of-sight fix.

Thirteen dead. The word, and the number, meant nothing said just like that – out loud, whilst standing in the middle of a London street, the sweat pouring off him, people looking at him as if he were mad. It meant nothing as he had looked down on it all afterwards from two thousand feet, through the drone's powerful twin lenses. He had been able to see the bodies then, the 'civilians' running with them, the frantic struggles to get people out of the devastated structures.

But now he was here, two years later, trying to understand it. He had brought a set of cross hairs over a complex of buildings in some unknown village – just one little stage in a bigger battle plan. Someone in the field – an officer with a squad pinned in crossfire – had put in the request and he had responded. He had pressed a button to send information to an artillery system. Just grid references, computer images and automated tasks. Sitting in a tent full of sand and dirt and cabling, stripped to his faded beige T-shirt with other people constantly moving around him in the insufferable midday heat.

He had killed thirteen people.

Or was it the gunners? Or the officer who had radioed the request? He stared at the London street and tried to get some sense of reality into it. He watched the cars and people moving around him – the people *for whom* he had pressed that button – faces and shapes as undifferentiated as the rows of body bags they'd lined up afterwards.

At the time – throughout his time in theatre, in fact – he had thought nothing of this action. Nothing at all. There had been too many other moments crowding it out, some so closely fought and terrifying that he still had nightmares about them. Most of his second tour had been spent as an artillery spotter, and that had frequently meant operating from forward positions. Sometimes their plans had come unstuck. He was twenty-four and there was already a lifetime of horror burned into his brain. But this was the first time he had remembered a remote action like this.

Suddenly, and inexplicably, he had to fight back an urge to cry. They had moved through the village later that day. That was when he had walked through the results of his little video game, when it had become a reality. Two of the body bags had been tiny. The size of children.

The break beat thudded on in his ears, the people in the street flooded around him. There were enough people converging on the tube entrance for his presence to be an irritation to them. He was a lump of static flesh, an obstruction. But not one anyone was going to shout at. He was far too big for that. Six foot five, and muscular. The cropped hair, the physique and the bearing made it an easy guess that he was either a squaddie or a bouncer – but the hair and the unusual size distracted from a face that had more sensitive features. The eyes were shy – an attractive, grey-green the eyebrows fine. His nose had never been noticeably broken and his jaw didn't jut aggressively. Instead he had a cautious, sideways manner of looking at things that betrayed a thoughtfulness it was easy to miss. It was the same when he spoke. The voice was predictably deep, but the delivery was careful and slow.

He'd never worked at his shape, never did anything deliberately to keep fit. The physique was a genetic 'gift'. It was a mistake people had made all his life that they assumed he was stupid, that all he could do was fight and make trouble. And after all, he was Big Eddie Curtis's son. Joining the army was exactly what was expected of him.

Not that the army was what his father had wanted. When alive his dad had done everything he could to keep him away from violence – including getting enough of a regular income to pull Paul out of the local gutter-comp he had himself attended as a kid. The alternative was expensive: a relatively new private day school – still very definitely local, but with a name for good exam results. Eddie Curtis thought he was setting his son up for life, but in Chorlton – the nondescript Manchester suburb where Paul had grown up – everyone knew the kinds of people Big Eddie worked for, knew where the money was coming from. And anyway, Big Eddie was dead before Paul's fifteenth birthday, murdered. If Paul had been inclined to forget them, there was no more effective way to rub in his roots, to stamp them right through his character like a name in candy rock. When Paul looked back on his school days, mostly it felt like a failed experiment in social mobility. He hadn't even got rid of the Manchester accent.

He brought a hand up to his eyes and rubbed them, then took deep breaths. And at that moment the second thing happened. Out of the corner of his eye he saw movement by the kerb. He turned slightly to see a big black Merc SUV pull in right beside him. Even before it stopped the doors were opening and he had fight-or-flight screaming through every vein in his body. If this was six weeks ago he'd be on autopilot by now, ducking, going for his weapon. Or running. If cars came at you like this in Peshawar, or Pindi, it was either a kidnap or a hit. But this was London. He forced himself to recall that. He held his breath, turned towards the car and waited.

The man coming out the front passenger side was white, unarmed. Everything about his look and manner said police. Paul didn't like the police, didn't trust them. It had been that way all his life, another gift from his dad. Behind the first man was a bigger guy: darker skin, shades, bulky clothing, arms loose in the way you held them if you were going to pull something from under your jacket. Paul let his breath get back to normal, reached up and slipped the earphones out. The noise of London traffic came at him.

'Paul Curtis?' the first one asked, stepping towards him. Unmistakeably official voice. Paul nodded, looking down at him. Ordinary middle-aged face, smart suit. Nothing to worry about. Not physically, anyway.

'We need you to come with us,' the man said. 'Just a short detour.'

Was something going down with his client, he wondered? A search, a raid, which meant they wanted him out of the way first? He considered asking, but it didn't really matter. The client meant nothing to him. By contrast, the man standing below him was showing him official ID. Paul nodded, without scrutinising it. Back at the Merc the other was standing watching, hands at his sides.

'OK,' Paul said. He let the army reflex kick in – obedience to authority, unless that was absolutely impossible. 'You going to tell me what it's about?'

'Of course.' The man was leading him back to the car now, a gently persuasive arm on his elbow. Paul had to resist the urge to brush it off.

3

At that moment, DS Andy Macall was hunched over a computer monitor in a shabby office block in Acton. The block was one of several nondescript buildings SO15 – the Counter Terrorist Command – used to house electronic surveillance processing teams. At that moment half of Andy's six-man team was deployed in front of screens in the same room. The room, like the building, was nothing special: a set of desks with four computers beneath them and four keyboards on top, four identical nineteen-inch computer monitors arranged in front of the four available chairs, strip lighting flickering uncomfortably, a whiteboard covered with scrawled notes and diagrams, shelves sagging with copies of paper logs and transcripts; all in a space no larger than one of the kid's bedrooms in Andy's house. The atmosphere was close and unpleasant, the ventilation poor, the walls lined with soundproofing tiles that, over the three years the facility had been up and running, had already become covered with a staggering variety of lewd graffiti. The surveillance operation Andy was running from this room was part of a larger enquiry that had been given the random codename HAKA.

This morning it was Mike Luntley who had worked the night shift. A stocky twenty-eight-year-old from Nottingham, with a thick mat of red hair and a matching moustache, he was one of Andy's best investigators, a man with a good combination of intelligence and intuition. Luntley was at the desk opposite Andy and the two detectives slated to relieve Luntley – DCs Gordon Graham and John Haldane – were standing by the remaining monitors, which were still booting. The handover should already have taken place, but hadn't, because as Graham and Haldane had come in with their coffee cups something interesting had started to happen on Luntley's screen.

The computer screens were each split four ways to be able to show different camera angles or different rooms, but in this case they only had two cameras up, so only two of the boxes were live. In one of them Andy could see their target – a man called Pasha Durrani – moving around in his bedroom.

'The sister's here,' Andy said to Graham and Haldane. 'Sit down. Something might happen.'

'He's moving onto camera two,' Luntley said. Camera 1 covered the bedroom. Camera 2 covered the main ground floor room of the house. The house was a substantial property in Richmond, part of a gated and walled-off plot consisting of an eight bedroom residence plus indoor pool and outhouses, the lot worth about eight million.

'She's already screaming at him,' Luntley said, rubbing his eyes and looking suddenly more alert. 'This could be fun.'

The target's sister had now come into view on the main camera, gesticulating wildly about three feet in front of her brother. Graham and Haldane sat quickly by their screens, fitting earpieces as they took their jackets off. 'What's it about?' Graham asked. But Andy didn't reply. All his attention was on the screen and the audio feed.

Over the last two months they had amassed enough

information on Lara Durrani to know that if sparks were going to fly then something interesting might be said. Pasha Durrani was typically careful. He was reluctant to talk business inside any building, more comfortable using a mobile in an outdoor environment. Often they knew he was about to say something significant because he stepped outside the Richmond house to take the call. These precautions made little difference because for over two weeks they'd had facilities running on three of the five mobile phones he used, but they were sure he didn't know that. Nor did he know the house was wired, as was his mother's house, and his cars and several phones and properties of close associates. He took ineffective evasives when he was out and about, but that wasn't because he actually suspected that there was a team on him. It was just the normal operating protocol for criminals at his level. But two months was a long time to keep up your guard and he had slipped often enough even before they'd hooked most of his comms routes. Mostly when he was angry. He had met his sister only twice during the last two months, and both times had led to arguments, errors and valuable information. Given that D-Day for Durrani, and for their operation on him, was now only ten days away, Andy expected today might yield more.

Luntley had put together an extensive file on Lara Durrani, mostly culled from legwork up in Manchester, where the family came from. She was three years younger than her brother, and on the face of it a clean sheet. She'd gone to an unremarkable private school in Manchester until the age of sixteen, at which point her father – a GP in Rusholm – had committed suicide and precipitated a family financial crisis. They'd only come through that because of Pasha Durrani's criminal activities in London. He'd been so successful that his sister had eventually been sent to finish her schooling at St Paul's, had gone on to read law at Nottingham, and was now a junior barrister, handling mainly criminal work out of a new set of chambers off Gray's Inn Road. That was ironic, and interesting in itself – rich potential for conflicts of interest, depending upon her exact relationship with her brother. But they knew since Durrani's last meeting with her that she was into his schemes much deeper than that.

Andy watched her shouting now, trying to make out the words, and thought again that neither of them looked Asian, or, at least, not obviously so. The technical equipment was state-of-the-art and provided an incredible level of resolution for a gadget that must have been about as visible as a pinhead, but it had its limits. Figures right beneath the device were very clear, but as they moved away there was distortion. The sound suffered similar limitations. Nevertheless he could see that both the target and his sister were relatively tall and pale-skinned. Pasha looked white in their high-definition covert mugshots, the sister looked like she had a very light olive tan.

Andy worked for an organisation that was latterly obsessed with political and religious correctness, and such niceties were not without impact. In court, incorrect terminology could give enough credence to the habitual allegations of racist bias to mean the end of a case. Luntley had discovered that the Durrani family tree was complex enough for them to designate Durrani and his sister as 'mixed race' in all the documentation. The name – Durrani – was most common in the east of Afghanistan, but somewhere back in the family tree there were marriages into wealthy English families with interests in Pakistan and India. The father and mother were, in fact, both born in Pakistan, but had spent nearly all their lives in the UK and had dual nationality. They both came from influential Pathan families from north-west Pakistan, with extensive links across the border in Afghanistan. The link to Pakistan accounted for nearly everything Pasha Durrani was now doing, where his money came from, and the reason why SO15 was looking at him. Out east he was connected to some major players in the world of drugs and fundamentalist terror funding.

Right now Pasha was dressed in jeans and a black T-shirt, with bare feet. Lara was in her work clothes – typical barrister's black and whites: a smart white blouse, pressed black trousers, dark shoes with no heel, a jacket she had placed carefully over the back of a chair.

As usual, the target looked confident and walked like he could handle himself and wanted to advertise that, even within his own home. There was a hint of suppressed aggression about his movements. She had more grace and was strikingly attractive – tall and slim, with an elegant physique and fine features to her face. Luntley said often that she looked like something out of a fashion magazine. Her hair was dark, Andy guessed coming down to below her shoulders but held up now in a pony-tail. If he hadn't known her ethnicity Andy would have thought her Spanish, perhaps. She had a hint of fire to her as well, the way the head moved suddenly, the chin high, the pony-tail bouncing. He heard her shouting at the target now: *'You're totally off your head, Pasha. You're mad.'* Andy saw the brother walk off-camera, towards the kitchen, and heard him reply: 'I warned you. I warned you many, many times. You have only yourself to blame, Lara.' Andy watched as Lara followed off-camera, leaving them just the sound feed to focus on.

They were brewing to a big one, no doubt about it. Deprived of images, Andy concentrated on the words.

There were just two voices, sometimes shouting, sometimes low and urgent, often unintelligible across the equipment.

'Why are you with him?' It was the brother asking, speaking in a forceful hiss. 'What are you doing with him? I'm not the one who is mad . . .'

'It's nothing to do with you. Nothing . . .' Her voice was higher, the words lost beneath his.

'It has everything to do with me,' he said. 'You know what it means to me. You know what you're doing—'

'It's between me and him, Pasha. It's nothing to do with you.'

'Shut up. Don't be stupid.'

'Don't tell me to shut up—'

'I will tell you exactly what I want to tell you. You're my sister, my responsibility . . .'

She began to laugh, but it sounded desperate. 'Are you mad, Pasha? Are you fucking crazy?'

'Don't speak like that. Don't swear. You sound like a slut.'

'A slut? How dare you.'

'I dare because I have to. Everything you do reflects upon me.'

'It has nothing to do with you. I'm an adult. For fuck's sake, Pasha. I'm a fucking—'

There was a sudden clatter of noise from the probe and the woman's voice raised in alarm, almost a scream of fright, then a momentary silence, followed by a slapping sound. He heard the woman exclaim, in surprise, or pain, then the same sound again.

'I think he's hitting her,' Luntley said.

In the kitchen, out of view of the tiny lens of the surveillance camera, Lara Durrani was stunned. She stood, leaning back against the kitchen counter, with her cheek throbbing and tears starting in her eyes. Her brother was right in front of her, blocking her in, his hand raised to slap her again.

'You going to do it again?' she asked, amazed at how calm she sounded.

'If I have to.' His eyes were burning with rage, his face shaking.

She looked straight at him, forcing him to look at her, then slowly shook her head and looked away. 'This isn't you, Pasha,' she said, very quietly. 'What's happened to you?'

She was surprised to find herself unafraid. He had hit her twice with his flat hand, hard, both times on the same side of her face. She could taste blood in her mouth. She reached her hand up to her smarting skin and rubbed it gingerly. It felt hot, so it would swell up too. How would she explain it at work? *If* she got in to work today. Thank God she wasn't in court. And it was Saturday, so the barrister she shared an office with wouldn't be in.

'Nothing has happened to me,' she heard him say, still right in front of her. 'I am who I am, who I've always been. It's you that's changed.'

She shook her head again. 'No. You weren't always like this.' This was new. *Striking her.* He had ruptured something between them, but he hadn't even noticed, it seemed. She took a breath, trying to control her reactions. 'This isn't you, Pasha,' she said again. 'It's not—'

'This is me. This is precisely who I am.'

'You were never like this when we were younger. There were none of these medieval attitudes . . .'

'There's nothing medieval about it. You are my responsibility, my sister.'

'Is it a religious thing? Is that what it is?' She looked up at him again.

'I am a Muslim, a Pakistani,' he said. 'I can't avoid that. But it's more than a question of religion. It's to do with an entire culture. You can't get away from what we are, Lara. You can't choose your family, can't choose your roots. We are from *that* background. *That* is where we belong—'

'Bullshit,' she said, wiping the back of her hand slowly across her mouth, then looking at the blood. 'My grandmother is a white woman. English. That's your grandmother as well. Your father's grandfather was white. Also English. Have you forgotten that? Where does that leave you – about one third Pakistani? They were from here, for God's sake. From London. Not from some terrorist shit hole in Pakistan—'

'I think you'll find there are quite as many "terrorists" in London as Lahore.' His voice had a smirking tone, but at least he turned away from her now. 'And though it's true I have white blood polluting me, the Asian influences are stronger.'

'*Polluting* you? I thought you couldn't choose your roots?'

'That doesn't make them any less toxic.' He walked to the other side of the kitchen. 'It's the influence of that white bastard that makes you behave like this.'

'It's the grown, independent adult that I am. I am a grown woman . . .' She stopped, not wanting it to continue, not wanting to inflame him further. He was still her brother. No matter what he had said or done, he was still her brother, her *Pasha*. 'Listen, Pasha.' Her tone softened. 'We can forget this. You got annoyed, you exploded. You always had a temper—'

'I'm not annoyed.'

'You wouldn't have struck me if you weren't angry.'

'I struck you to bring you to your senses. I don't want to forget it. It was what I should have done a long time ago. What I need you to do now is obey me. Do you understand that?'

She felt the chasm opening again. Maybe he *was* mad. How did he get to speak like this suddenly? Once they had loved each other, been children together, had a sibling bond that had seemed unbreakable. Her head was filled with only good memories of their childhood, of how he had played with her, protected her. He had been her best friend for so long. How could he now behave like this?

'Obey you?' She said the words as if she didn't understand them. She didn't.

'You must sign the papers.'

'I won't sign anything.' She heard her voice tremble as she thought about it.

'You will.'

'It's your mess, Pasha. I can't help. I can't have anything to do with it.'

She saw him take a deep breath. 'You have no fucking idea,' he muttered. 'No fucking idea at all.' He had disclosed to her a month ago that he had 'bought some properties and put them in her name'. How he had done that without her she had no idea. Some species of fraud, no doubt. Now he needed to sell them urgently and wanted her to sign the transfer papers on Tuesday the first of June, in ten days' time. He'd bought them years ago, he said, without her even knowing. It was part of some dirty laundering scheme he was running. She knew it without asking him, but she had still been too afraid to request more details. It terrified her. He was going to drag her down with him, drag her into the mud he was crawling through. If anyone heard about these properties, if anyone at work heard . . . God, she couldn't even think about it. 'It will ruin me, Pasha,' she said, almost in tears. 'I can't go near it. It has nothing to do with me. It's your problem . . .'

'You will sign and there won't be a problem. Easy. That's number one.'

'Number one?' She laughed bitterly. He was going to list his instructions to her, speak to her like he spoke to his low-life flunkies on the mobile.

'Yes. Number one. Number two, you must stop seeing that *ganda gora* Chris Napier. That *white filth*. Stop at once. At the moment only I know about it. But you are flouting it. A week ago I saw you holding his hand, in full view.' Was he having her watched? Could he be that mad? She had no recollection of ever seeing him whilst she was out with Chris. 'I cannot have that,' he continued. 'We have an arrangement. So it must stop.'

The arrangement. That was, of course, what it all came down to. She swallowed hard. It was like some nightmare. Like confronting someone stuck in a time warp. Without even consulting her, he had made an arrangement with someone from out there when she was just sixteen years old, when she was a mere child whose father had just died. Some bearded freak – now in his late thirties and living, no doubt, in a concrete compound in some shitty, dirty village near Peshawar – some man she couldn't even recall had looked at her and decided she was 'for him'. Just like that. A piece of property. And to force her into *this*, Pasha had sent two thugs to jump Chris, two days ago, in Camden High Street. A deliberate attack – to send the message to her. He had been threatening her with it since she had started seeing Chris again. And now he had done it. That was why she was here. Because this all had to stop. The delusion Pasha was living had to end. 'I'm not marrying Shamsuddin Asuri,' she said firmly. 'I'm not doing that, no matter what you do. You know that. It's what I've always told you and it will never change.'

His eyes flared immediately. He was coming at her again, marching across the kitchen at full speed. She pushed herself away from the counter. She should get out now. She had said it, so now she should get out. She would have to go to the police about him, take the consequences. But even as she thought that, even with him coming at her with fists clenched, she knew she could never do it. Because he was still family. And you didn't take your family to the police. Not ever. She walked quickly away, hands up to ward him off, then started to run, out of the kitchen and into the main room. If she could get to the door she could run out into the garden, shout for help . . .

'They're back,' Luntley said.

'Fuck. He's really going for her.'

The sister didn't so much run into view as stumble, her brother close behind and lashing out at her back and head. She was shouting something at him, the words not clear, her voice high with fright and panic.

'He's using his fists,' Graham remarked quietly, from next to Andy. 'Northern scum. They're all the same. He's in a multimillion-pound gated property, but he's still scum from Manchester . . .'

She was on the floor now, right beneath the camera. They were screaming at each other, too loud to make out any of the words, wrestling around the living room floor, knocking furniture out of the way. Durrani was trying to pin the woman and she was hitting out at him, trying to defend herself. Andy felt the sweat start on his back, the adrenalin

26

in his blood. 'Christ! He might really hurt her,' he muttered.

The target managed to knock her onto her back, then he was sitting on top of her, holding her down. They couldn't see where his hands were, but she was thrashing around, her legs kicking out, the shoes fallen off, the beads from her necklace dancing across the parquet floor like spilled marbles.

'What's he doing? I can't see his hands . . .' Andy said.

'They're around her throat, I think,' Luntley said. 'He's throttling her. His own sister.' He sounded unmoved by it all.

But Andy was beginning to panic. 'We can't let him kill her,' he said.

'He won't kill her. Don't worry . . .'

'How do you know? It looks serious. She's slowing down. She's losing consciousness.'

'He won't kill her. He's attacking her because he wants her to marry someone. He needs her alive for that.'

'He might go too far.'

The woman was lying still now, the man rolling off her.

'She's out,' Haldane said. 'You're right, of course. He could have misjudged it. But too late now . . .'

'I'm going to call the locals.' Andy reached his hand over to the phone.

'Too late, boss. She's either dead or unconscious. By the time the boys in blue get there it will be over, either way.'

'Fucking hell.' Haldane was right. But how would they explain this later, if she died? He had to call. He picked up the phone.

'Look at him, now,' Graham said. 'Fucking freak.' The man was lying down next to the prone woman, stretching out beside her, panting heavily. His head was on one elbow, his face very close to hers, his free hand stroking her hair like she was a pet animal.

'What's he doing?'

He was whispering something to her, but too quietly for the gear to pick it up.

'Muttering sweet nothings,' Graham said.

'Her eyes are still closed,' Luntley said.

'Her feet are moving now, though. And her chest. She's alive.'

Andy paused with the phone. The man was still stroking her, still speaking softly. Now it looked for all the world as if they were watching some scene with two lovers, or at least two people who loved each other. No. That was wrong. She was still out of it. Her feet were moving, her eyes fluttering, her chest heaving, but she had no choice in this.

'I think he's whispering sorry to her,' Luntley said, listening intently. 'He sounds like he's crying too . . .'

The woman convulsed, then rolled over and began to retch. Andy held onto the phone. 'If it starts again, I'll have to call,' he said.

Graham laughed. 'It's over. He got what he wanted.'

'Which was?'

'To scare the shit out of her.'

4

Paul ended up on a half hour ride into Belgravia, with no more explanation forthcoming. As the minutes went by he began to think the journey wasn't going to end in some police station, charged with something he'd forgotten he'd done. Something else was going on. Which meant he could spend the wait wondering what *was* going to happen, or let it come. As a teenager he'd been the kind to brood on things, but the army had knocked that out of him. So much of his six years had been spent waiting that it had become second nature to just put up with it. If you tried to guess the future you ended up a nervous wreck, discharged with ulcers and irritable bowel syndrome.

Finally, they pulled into an underground garage beneath one of those exclusive, whitewashed Georgian terraces and he was led up back stairs to a room that was like something out of a BBC costume drama – all wood panelling and big oil portraits.

'Sit here and wait,' he was told. 'Don't touch anything.'

He waited another twenty minutes before a gaunt, white-haired man finally appeared, holding out his hand, smiling like he was a long lost friend. 'Paul. So nice to see you. Thanks so much for coming.' Paul went along with it, shook his hand. He had no idea who it was. He started searching through his memory.

They went into another room, a kind of office, done out in similar style. There was no mention of the police escort, no sense that Paul had been virtually frogmarched here. He assumed that was meant to confuse him. The man had tea already laid out on a silver tray placed at the edge of a table that was long enough to be in a divisional officer's mess.

The man poured tea with delicate, fastidious gestures. 'It's Assam, I'm afraid,' he said. 'From an estate we have in Bengal. It's all I can drink for breakfast these days, but it's rather sharp. Please say if you would prefer an ordinary tea bag of something more blended.'

Paul left the tea but followed him to the coffee table, trying to look as if the whole thing wasn't like something out of *Alice in Wonderland*. They sat opposite each other. His host looked comfortable, but Paul's legs were too long for the little chairs and he felt the urge to stretch out. There were some magazines arranged on the table top. The common theme seemed to be police and crime. He started guessing the man was a politician of some sort.

The guy was about sixty, maybe a bit more. He had very white skin, unnaturally so, but didn't look bad for it. The grooming was immaculate. It looked like there wasn't a hair out of place on his head. He was perfectly shaved and there was a delicate suggestion of aftershave hanging in the air around him. He had on a charcoal grey suit of lightweight material, not very rumpled, shiny black shoes, a posh white shirt with a removable collar, like the officers used to wear to ceremonial dinners, and huge cuffs, held together with links with some kind of black and red heraldic motif.

'I've heard so much about you, of course,' the man said. 'I feel I know you quite well.'

Paul nodded. 'That right? I don't know you at all.'

The man smiled a little, not unpleasantly. 'I'm so sorry. I assumed you did. You don't recognise me?'

'You're some bloke who had me picked up by the police. I'm waiting to find out why.'

'I'm Phil Rathmore. Chris's father.'

And so it began. The exchange that followed had a surreal quality to it, because on the one hand it was suddenly like any other professional discussion Paul might have had with a prospective client – there had been two in Pakistan that had met him just like this, over a coffee table, trying desperately to look relaxed and in control – but on the other hand it was about Chris, Paul's childhood friend, and this man sitting here was actually Chris's father, whom he'd often wondered about as a teenager, but never met.

'When did you last see Chris?'

'Maybe six or seven years ago. In Manchester.' It wasn't the last he'd heard from him though. There'd been good contact – mainly by email – for about a year after Paul left school. Then he'd been posted east and Chris had moved to London. Contact had died off quite quickly then. New priorities. Maybe that had been the natural thing to happen, but Paul hadn't wanted it. He had mailed Chris a few times in the period between, but had no replies.

'A long time ago,' Rathmore said. 'But he still speaks highly of you. As he did back then. I think he really trusted you, Paul, and he hasn't trusted many people in his life. You were his greatest friend. No doubt about that.'

Paul shrugged, not sure how to respond. He did feel confused now, now he knew who the man was, now he had the idea of Chris planted in his head out of the blue. Chris had certainly been *his* best friend. Chris and Lara both, but his feelings for Lara had been more complex. Thinking about Chris brought on an urge to see him again, a pang of longing for those days. Not for the things they had done, or the sense of youth that had been so violently drained from him over the last six years, but for the friendship, for that feeling of closeness to someone else. He hadn't had that since, not even with his friends in the army. Working together under fire certainly forged close bonds, but it was different. Not the easy thing he'd had with Chris. In the army there'd always been the feeling the friendship might be cut short.

'Has something happened to him?' he asked.

'No. He's doing well,' Rathmore said. 'With his music, I mean. He has a very successful band now.'

'Really? That's good.' Music had been Chris's obsession. Music and Lara. For as long as Paul had known him Chris had been in a band, writing songs, planning the big move to London. That was when everything was going to come together for him. If that had happened then Paul had missed it, and he was an obsessive consumer of popular music, so it seemed unlikely. If Chris Napier was big somewhere in the UK music scene Paul was sure he would have known about it.

'They are about to start a little tour,' Rathmore continued. 'Just of UK cities, mainly London. But it's progress, I think.'

'I'm sure it is. What's the band called?'

That stumped him, apparently. He thought for a bit. 'I could find out,' he said, looking toward the desk. Paul had the impression then that he might have a file on his son, lying there.

'Is the name important?' Rathmore asked.

'I might have heard of them.'

'Of course.' A pause for tea. 'You like that kind of music, then. That's helpful.'

What kind of music? And helpful for what?

'You don't ever think about him?' Rathmore asked.

'How do you mean?'

'Do you ever think about seeing him again?'

'Of course. Sometimes. But I've been busy with other things, and times have changed. You know how it is.'

'Yes. But perhaps you would like him still. Perhaps it could be like it was before.'

Paul shifted uneasily, not sure where this was going. Chris would be an adult now, after all, not the man's six-year-old kid in need of a playmate.

'He's living in Camden Town,' Rathmore said. 'It's a rather grotty place, near the canal. I would put him somewhere more pleasant, but he won't take my money, won't even hear of it.'

'Uh-huh.' That didn't surprise Paul.

'It wasn't always like that.' Another pause for another sip of tea. 'When he was younger we were closer, ironically. I'm not sure how much you know about the circumstances . . .'

How much did Paul know? He could remember two versions of the family history. Version one: Diane Napier was an ambitious, university-educated, middle-class woman who was employed by Rathmore when she was younger, as a researcher. Rathmore was then – as now, Paul assumed – some kind of big hitter in the Tory party. And titled – a peer, or a Lord, or something he never mentioned, because that wasn't fashionable, or wouldn't serve his political interests. They had an 'affair' in the eighties. How long had it lasted? Paul had no idea. She got knocked up, though, hence Chris. Rathmore then dropped Diane like a ton of bricks, leaving her to bring up their kid alone and in disgrace, in darkest Altrincham, the affluent Cheshire suburb she hailed from. This was more or less Diane's version, swallowed whole by Chris when he was little. Paul wasn't told, but had assumed that Rathmore had a nice upper class wife and legitimate offspring in the background, down south somewhere.

Version two was a little sadder, in some ways. It was what Chris told him as he gradually got some contact with his 'dad'. Rathmore was married, but he had no other children. Through most of Chris's early years he had been desperate for contact with his only son, but Diane Napier had forbade this. His mother had insisted on moving away from Philip Rathmore, sending her son to a local Manchester school – the New Academy – the same institution Paul's dad had saved so hard to send him to, which was how someone like Paul had got to be friends with someone like Chris, and where they had both met Lara. Rathmore had been offering Chris a place at the family public school – Winchester, or Westminster, or Wellington, or some such. Diane got Rathmore to pay for the Academy, but that was it as far as taking his money. She had *pride*. Too much, Chris came to think.

As Chris got older he started seeing Rathmore without telling his mum. Rathmore let him use the family pile in North Yorkshire for illicit weekends with Lara, now his girlfriend. The plan throughout Chris's childhood had been that Rathmore was going to go through some legal process to 'legitimise' Chris, so that Chris could inherit the family title. But political expediency – and Rathmore's wife – kept getting in the way. The affair with Diane Napier was a potential source of scandal, a family secret. So Chris had never been 'recognised', and evidently that had soured things a little.

'I can't really get to see Chris very easily these days,' Rathmore said. He looked genuinely miserable about it. 'I don't think you have children, Paul. Not yet, anyway. Is that right?'

Paul shook his head.

'It's an interesting experience being a parent.' He smiled, as if everything were now explained, then moved his hand elegantly through the space in front of him, brushing away some irritating thought. 'You'll learn one day, perhaps.' He moved forward in the seat, eyes firmly fixed on Paul's. 'I love my son,' he said. 'That's why you're here.' A tinge of colour came to his cheekbones as he said the word 'love'. 'I want to make sure no harm comes to him, but I'm at a loss as to how I might best do that when he won't even agree to see me, won't even speak to me by telephone.'

'You don't seem short of resources.'

'You mean the police who brought you here? I'm a part of the new government . . .' He smiled whimsically. 'A small part. I have the usual official protection that goes with that. But those officers are not at my personal disposal. A quick favour is one thing. Watching my son on a full-time basis is quite another. I've used private agencies, of course, but that's not really what I need. I can *spy* on him, yes . . .' He licked his lips as if the word 'spy' had a foul taste. 'But that's not very pleasant, or ethical, perhaps. And there are limits to what that kind of outside vigilance can achieve. Besides, it's not the kind of involvement I wish for. Times are very delicate right now. The general election and all the subsequent uncertainty . . .' He looked meaningfully at Paul, as if Paul would understand what he was suggesting. In fact, Paul had paid very little attention to the recent election and couldn't have been less interested in politics. 'It's a coalition administration,' Rathmore explained. 'It's fragile, despite appearances. And my position is extremely vulnerable. Family complications are unwelcome, to say the least. So I need something more discreet.' He smiled again, opening his hands to indicate Paul. Paul noticed his forehead had become a little damp as he spoke about his position. Rathmore dabbed at it now with a handkerchief produced from his top pocket.

'Something more discreet,' Paul repeated. *To say the fucking least,* he thought. If Rathmore was in the new government then he could imagine how well this stuff would go down with a tabloid. 'You mean you want *me* to spy on your son?' he asked.

'Of course not. Weren't you listening?' A hint of annoyance. 'I want you to hook up with him again.' He said 'hook up' as if it were in inverted commas, a piece of teen jargon he'd been told about. 'I want you to renew your friendship. There can't be anything bad in that. I will pay you to do so.'

'Why pay me? It would be great to see Chris again, if that's what he wants. Just tell me where he lives.'

'That's what I'd like on the surface, yes.' He moved further forward, eager now. 'But I want you to get close to him. Let's not call it a bodyguard, or anything silly like that. Just as a friend, a close friend. Be with him as much as a close friend would be. That will be enough.' He sighed, and looked away. 'I realise that these things don't always go to plan. Perhaps you two won't "hit it off" again. Who knows. But I would like you to try. He's led a sheltered life, I fear. He's vulnerable. Of course, I'm probably just being a silly old man. He is my only son and misfortune has dogged our family, and that has made me cautious, perhaps overcautious. But the world he moves in – the drugs, the lifestyle, the whole music thing – I worry about it.'

Worry about the bad publicity, Paul thought, *were it ever to come out*.

Rathmore looked sideways at him. 'You've grown into a

decent young man, Paul. You have an exemplary military record.'

'Exemplary?' It was news to Paul. There weren't any decorations, no acts of valour, no mentions in dispatches.

'You know what I mean. I mean I believe you are trustworthy, or I wouldn't have asked you to meet me. You had a poor start in life. We can agree on that, I think. Your father . . . all that terrible business with your father . . .' He let the words drop off. Paul held his eyes. 'And all that earlier stuff with the police and courts. I've read about that, of course. You were a tough, rebellious kid. You had to be.' He said it as if it were a point of honour. It was a reference to Paul's convictions for theft and assault. Juvenile convictions. Part of the reason his dad had arranged the change of school. 'But you put it behind you,' Rathmore said. 'You moved on.' He smiled slyly. 'But not that far, I'll warrant. You're different to Chris, I think. You are who you are and no need to be ashamed of it. Our society needs all kinds of people to flourish. I would guess, looking at you, that there's still a gutsy Mancunian street kid inside you. A fighter. Someone who knows the world, who can look after himself.'

Paul sighed and moved unhappily in the seat. Too many crawling clichés. 'Someone who can look out for your son, you mean?'

'Precisely.'

'And how does this job work? I just walk up to Chris and tell him you're paying me to protect him?'

'Of course not. It wouldn't work at all then. He wants nothing to do with me. I told you that. And this is above all a delicate matter. It has to be strictly between ourselves. Completely confidential.'

For a moment they sat staring at each other. Paul could

hardly believe the proposition being put to him. He opened his mouth to tell the man where to go, but at that moment Rathmore looked down at the floor and coloured bright red. The effect was so sudden, and so unlike his normal pallor it looked like tiny spots of blood had appeared on his cheeks. He cleared his throat. Paul closed his mouth. 'Please don't make me beg, Paul,' Rathmore said quietly. His voice was hoarse with emotion. 'I'm desperate. I'm really desperate. You're my last chance on this. Really you are. I'll give you seven thousand a month, after tax, plus accommodation. Do it for three months. See if it works. That's all I ask.'

5

Tuesday, 25th May, 2010

Late Monday afternoon DI Snowden – Andy's immediate boss – had been told that Charles Stanesby wanted an urgent briefing on operation HAKA – the larger operation that Andy's target, Pasha Durrani, was part of. Stanesby was the commander in charge of the entire section, at least two grades above Snowden, so the request put Snowden and his chief super, Liz Hemmings, into a panic. It was assumed there was a fuck-up somewhere if a commander wanted an urgent briefing.

Snowden had two detective sergeants running the two teams investigating Pasha Durrani – Andy and Karen Exeter. But of the two, Andy's team was the only one that was 100 per cent dedicated to Durrani, so it was Andy who was told to present the progress report to Stanesby. Stanesby had only been in post three weeks and Andy had never met him. That made him nervous. The meeting was scheduled for midday today, Tuesday. He needed to be up bright and early to prep his side of it.

Waking early was no problem – the kids guaranteed that. Bright was a different matter. Andy wasn't good at getting up. It hadn't always been like that, but at thirty-nine years old, he found it increasingly difficult to get his brain going before eight thirty or nine in the morning (and certainly not without a couple of strong coffees to assist), a luxury he had rarely enjoyed during the last four or five years. These days it was a rare thing not to be woken at five by one of the kids.

Andy had two kids. Sophie was two years old and very much her mummy's baby. She slept in her own room, next door to theirs, but still woke at least once in the night, taking Helen away from him and onto the mattress next to Sophie's cot. As compensation – if that's how these things could be put in the balance - he was usually joined in the bed by Magnus, some time before six o'clock. Magnus was four, his first child, and through a combination of circumstances and psychology Andy had by far the strongest feelings for him. He recognised this as a fact he had no control over, but not without guilt for the sake of Sophie.

This particular morning was no different. Helen disappeared from the bed sometime around four – he woke just enough to hear Sophie crying for her – then he awoke again at five thirty, with Magnus sticking his bony little knees into his back and snuggling into him. As always Andy rolled over sleepily and put his arms round his son, then they slept like that – Magnus tight against him – until six, when the light poking through the curtains brought Magnus to life like a switch had been thrown.

They tiptoed downstairs and he left Magnus in the living room watching a DVD, then struggled in the kitchen to complete a series of simple tasks made frustrating by his morning clumsiness. Cutting bread, opening packets of cereal, pouring milk – how often did he slip up and cut himself, or spill the milk, or rip the packets apart in frustration, spreading cereal all over the floor? He had never drunk much when younger, and barely drank at all now, so it couldn't be that he'd already pickled his reflexes. He was sure it was age, the first signs of his body deteriorating, accelerated by the experience of worrying about children, the chronic sleep-loss, the strain of having his mental space constantly in demand, at work and at home.

He managed to get some cereal together and placed it in front of Magnus, then sat beside him with his coffee. Magnus opened his mouth to start asking questions about the film, but Andy held a hand up, then pointed to his coffee cup. They had a long-standing agreement that Magnus wouldn't bother him until he'd finished his first coffee. So they watched the movie in silence for a while, Andy leaning back with his arm over Magnus's shoulders. This morning Magnus had picked *The Incredibles*, an animated comedy about crime-fighting superheroes. Andy had watched it with him about twenty times, though despite that, the gags would normally have him laughing too. But today he watched without really seeing the images. His mind was already on the meeting with Stanesby.

The teams met in a conference room in New Scotland Yard. A standard room with a long table, low ceiling, whiteboards and projectors. The view from the windows was onto Victoria Street. Andy sipped the tepid coffee provided and stared at the traffic whilst they stood around waiting for Stanesby to enter. The others discussed in hushed tones what they thought the problem might be, who might be to blame.

When they got going there were eight of them around the table. At one side was Stanesby and a couple of assistants – one taking notes, the other shuffling briefing papers and occasionally placing sheets in front of his boss. At the other side was Chief Super Hemmings, DIs Snowden and Pearce and their two detective sergeants, including Andy. The seating and atmosphere made it seem like some kind of court proceeding, with Stanesby cast as judge. He looked too young for the role, Andy thought, definitely not much more than thirty-five, obviously a fast tracker, tall, thin, inscrutable. He didn't smile – there wasn't time for that kind of thing. 'Who's first?' were his opening words. No handshakes or pleasantries.

DS Dev Johal started, seated and talking in a low voice, uncharacteristically cowed. Andy could barely hear his words, but he knew it all anyway. Pasha Durrani was just one part of operation HAKA. Snowden's counterpart, DI Pearce, led two teams who were focused on the target who had originally been the sole interest of HAKA – a man called Raheesh Khan. Pearce had brought Johal with him to talk about Khan.

Raheesh Khan and Durrani were related through various family links in Pakistan. In terms of the pecking order, Khan was an infamous big fish in the north-west of England, and in the drugs pond alone he was much juicier than Durrani. Johal had been looking at Khan for over two years, working with the Serious Organised Crime Agency and Greater Manchester Police. Pasha Durrani was only a recent addition to HAKA, a minor offshoot.

But Stanesby wasn't interested in Khan. Johal had barely got through his introduction before he was interrupted; 'I think I know all this,' Stanesby said. 'What about Pasha Durrani? Can anyone tell me about him?'

'That's me, sir,' Snowden said. He was sitting beside Andy. An ex-Harlequins prop forward who always looked squashed in behind a desk, he didn't react well to pressure. Andy thought he looked ready to burst out of the chair and headbutt someone. His forehead was shiny with perspiration. He turned to Andy now and introduced him clumsily. Stanesby glanced at Andy, raised an eyebrow. At the other end of the table Dev Johal was already folding his paper-work away, a smirk on his face. Andy could see the tension leaving DI Pearce too. Obviously it wasn't *their* fuck-up.

'Tell me about him,' Stanesby said, 'this Pasha Durrani.'

Andy cleared his throat. 'We've been looking at Durrani for two months,' he said. 'He was originally a protégé of Raheesh Khan. He's independent now—'

'Are they competitors?' Stanesby asked.

'No. Same criminal family, with real family links back in Pakistan. In any case, Khan is a drugs importer and shifting drugs isn't Pasha Durrani's speciality. He provides financial services, including to Khan. He layers and moves funds, invests and banks proceeds. He's a bright middle class boy from Manchester – not quite the profile for a drug dealer. His father was a doctor, his sister is a barrister. The father committed suicide when he was a teenager and the family moved to London. Through a Pakistani uncle Durrani briefly ended up on the edges of some groups we now watch very closely – the TTP, for example' – this was the *Tehrik-e-Taliban Pakistan* – 'but we weren't watching them so closely back then. And Durrani was only a kid. He quickly moved off it. So he looks clean, no convictions. Which is not to say his set-up is much different from the norm. He behaves, lives and acts like a middle tier drugs importer; he has a coterie of crooks around him, five or six of whom work directly for him on a full-time basis, and he treats them like a private army. They have access to firearms. I'm sure he imagines he's big enough to be untouchable, but he doesn't take unnecessary risks to prove that. He's been under the radar, in fact, until we started looking at him two months ago—'

'And this was because of the informant?'

'Yes. Simon Parker.' The informant name was a code-name.

'And *you* handle Parker? You're his designated handler?'

'Yes.' Andy paused, unsure how to continue, how much to say. If security procedures had been followed then he was the only person in the room who knew Parker's real identity. That would be normal enough, were there not a personal connection between Andy and Parker. Parker's real name was Mark Johnson. And Mark Johnson was a close friend of Andy's, probably his closest male friend. An ex-police officer who now ran a private security agency in the north-west. He had come to Andy just over two months ago with the information that had got them interested in Pasha Durrani. Andy had shunted the information up the line, expecting an informant handler and controller to be allocated in the normal way. But Mark had insisted that he would only provide further information directly to Andy. Andy had expected this request to be refused but, surprisingly, someone had authorised the arrangement. 'We think,' he continued, 'that Durrani currently holds or controls three high-value properties which were bought with money belonging to a man called Mahmood Asuri—'

'Does Durrani have a property company? They're not in his own name, surely?'

'No companies for these three properties. Everything personal. They are held in his sister's name, in fact. She wasn't told she was the registered freeholder, but has recently found out, and isn't happy. She's a barrister, and has a lot to lose if this comes out.'

'Tell me about the properties. Their location and value.'

'They are all roughly similar value detached private residences, one of historical significance. They've been valued at over eight point five million each.' He paused, but there was no reaction from Stanesby. Maybe his own house was worth that much. 'Two are in Richmond, one outside Brighton.'

'Does Durrani have legitimate interests, also?'

'Not legitimate, sir. Everything he has and does sources back to drugs transactions. The start-up money at least came from drugs. But he has a multitude of companies that he owns or controls and uses to wash and layer money on behalf of Khan and the Asuris, amongst others, we believe. We've only been up a couple of months and have just scratched the surface. We know of two companies dealing in lesser value property transactions, and several involved in investment – small investments, but at high volume – perfect for rinsing drugs cash. One of the property companies has a substantial turnover in legitimate property lettings in the north of England. On the surface Durrani doesn't touch it much. An associate runs it for him.'

'And where does Durrani live?'

'He has no place of his own. Not as far as we can determine. A company he controls is in the process of buying a nineteenth century mansion in North Yorkshire which we think might be intended for his private use. But at present he lives between two of the houses held for the Asuris – one of the ones in Richmond, and the one in Brighton.'

'I see.'

'The Asuris are more a tribal block than a family. Mahmood is the present figurehead. They are very significant players in—'

'I know about the Asuris.'

Andy stopped, as if reprimanded. He looked at the notebook open in front of him, trying to decide where to go next. But Stanesby spoke again: 'There was information a few months ago that Bin Laden was being sheltered on Asuri land, in Orakzai.'

'Yes.' It was one of the flunkies at his side who spoke. 'High grade information, in fact.'

'Had you heard about that, Sergeant Macall?'

Andy shook his head. 'Durrani's personal connections are mainly to the Asuris,' he continued. 'We're not sure of the exact family nexus, but we do know that there is a marriage arrangement between one of the younger Asuri sons – Shamsuddin – and Durrani's sister – Lara Durrani—'

'The barrister?'

'Yes. She's refusing to go along with it.'

'Is the arrangement of significance?'

'We think so. We think it's a way that Pasha Durrani can further connect himself with Asuri patronage—'

'Obviously.'

'Yes, sir. Obviously. But we also know that he expects a very high transfer of funds if the marriage goes ahead.'

'Personal funds – payment for himself, personally – like some kind of dowry? Or business funds – more cash to layer and wash on behalf of the Asuris?'

'Payment to him. Personal funds. We don't know why yet. We don't know why the marriage would release such a high amount.'

'What kind of amount?'

'Nearly three million dollars.'

Stanesby cocked his head on one side, as if considering this. 'Can't just be the marriage, then,' he said.

'No, sir. We think a property transfer of some sort over in Pakistan. Something connected to the marriage that the sister doesn't even know about.'

'Does Durrani have property there?'

'Nothing that we can find. There's a possibility that the sister does, however, or his mother. We're still waiting for further information from the Lahore office.'

'OK. And in a week's time – the first of next month. Is that the date this marriage happens?'

'No. That's the date for the finalisation of sales on all three Asuri properties. They need the money quickly. They've instructed Durrani to sell the properties and liquidate the monies. Matters are desperate in Pakistan. There are army operations against the Asuri powerbase. They need weapons and men. This was the original information the informant Simon Parker brought to us and this is what we've focused on, with some success.'

'Will the sales go through?'

'It depends upon Durrani getting his sister to sign. The solicitors for all three sales are straight-up, honest. They need the registered freeholder – the sister – to appear and sign in person. She refuses.'

'He'll force her?'

'Or use some subterfuge. Someone using his sister's identity. He's taken steps to arrange that already, though at the moment he's bringing a lot of pressure on the sister. To get her to sign would be the surest way.'

'And we're on top of all this?'

Andy nodded. 'Yes. We know first tier destination bank accounts for all three sales.' He realised he was speaking with some pride. They had put a lot of work into this. 'There are three Swiss accounts. The money will be in there for about a millisecond before being split between forty-two different accounts in eleven countries. We presently have no co-operation from the Swiss end, and don't expect it, but we have full co-operation at this end, from the buyer's banks.'

'And you intend to what?'

'Block the transfers and arrest him. All on the first of June.'

'And what then happens to Raheesh Khan?' Stanesby's eyes moved to DI Pearce, then Dev Johal. 'All your work in vain, gentlemen? A two year operation blown . . .'

'Not so, sir. We intend to isolate the—' It was Chief

Superintendent Hemmings who started to speak, but Stanesby held up a hand to silence her.

He looked at the table in front of him and slowly shook his head. 'It's not possible,' he said. 'There's no way I can see Khan maintaining his present operations if Durrani is taken down in ten days' time. If that happens then Khan will know that we are into him also. Operation HAKA will be blown. I'm sure of that. And Durrani is just a sideline – significant, but not the main player. We mustn't lose sight of that. Khan is the main target here.'

Andy saw Johal trying his best to suppress a smile.

'It was your predecessors' decision, sir, to arrest Durrani.' Hemmings said. 'Commander Bailey wanted a result.'

'Too short-term.' Stanesby dismissed Bailey's decision without a blink. And why not? Bailey was out of it, retired. Hemmings would go next year too. What was she . . . nearing fifty-one now? She looked frumpy across the table from Stanesby. She'd been thick with Bailey, but it didn't look like it was going to work that way with Stanesby. Maybe she hadn't been to the right school. The country was being run by public schoolboys now, an old-Etonian in Number Ten. Stanesby was from that kind of background. The future belonged to them, bizarrely, not to some working-class time-server like Liz Hemmings.

'We can't let nearly twenty-five million pounds' worth of funds get to the end users in Pakistan,' she said now. Her voice had gone up a tone. 'You don't want us to do that, sir . . .'

Stanesby looked down at his pen, moved it deftly through his fingers. 'We'll find another way,' he said. 'We need to co-ordinate the arrests of Khan and Durrani, which means delaying the arrest of Durrani, which in turn means ensuring he does not finalise these property sales in ten days' time. I suggest we place pressure on the solicitors handling Durrani's deals. Get them to back out—'

'Christ above.' Andy heard the words slip out of his mouth, almost a whisper, but Stanesby looked straight at him. 'I think he'll kill someone if the pressure gets notched up any further,' Andy said. 'He's losing it already. He attacked his sister . . .'

Stanesby shook his head. 'He needs her to sign the paperwork. He won't kill her.'

'He might seriously harm her, sir. I think the boyfriend, Chris Napier, is also in danger. The informant has already told us that Durrani has made contact with someone we suspect is a contract killer, and that Napier's name was mentioned. Napier's a threat to the entire deal Durrani is arranging. It might look like an easy way to solve a couple of problems to kill Napier. It will clear an obstacle to her marrying Asuri and make sure she knows what her brother is capable of.'

'You think he's that amateur?'

'There is strong information that he was involved in the murder of two drugs couriers at the very beginning of his criminal career, eight years ago.'

'He's moved up a bit since then, though. A clumsy murder won't get him anywhere now.'

Andy closed his mouth. Stanesby had already decided, it seemed.

'You will need to cover the boyfriend and the sister though,' Stanesby said. 'Just to be safe. If it looks like Durrani is serious – if it really looks like Napier is in danger – then you'll have to do something. But for God's sake don't blow it all by being jumpy.'

6

Paul was impressed. He met Rathmore on the Saturday and two days later he was moving into a paid, furnished apartment in Camden Town, not fifteen minutes from where Chris Napier was living. He was on four weeks' notice with the client in Bow, but that wasn't going to get in the way of seven grand a month, plus a ninth floor flat in a clean, modern block that had a view across the rooftops to the canal. If he could hold the position for a year, living as frugally as at present, he stood to save in excess of fifty grand, enough to give him options he didn't presently have. At the moment that outweighed his misgivings about the job. If Chris and he got on again, he realised, it wasn't going to work like that. But for now he would run with it. He called the agency and quit on the Saturday, right after meeting Rathmore.

Chris wasn't hard to find – his father had supplied details of his home address and his day job – but he proved a little bit harder to watch than Paul had imagined. Paul spent most of Monday shadowing him and it didn't take long to work out that Chris was nervous about something. He stopped frequently to look around him, scanning the traffic, the people behind him, even peering a considerable distance back. Paul was a good head above most people, and stood out even if you weren't looking hard, so it was challenging to make sure Chris didn't spot him. It was the first thing that made him think there might be more to this than a silly, rich old man worrying about recreational drugs.

He had been a little afraid that he wouldn't recognise Chris. Rathmore had given him no photo. But in the end the man who exited the address and crossed the street about twenty feet ahead of him was very little changed from the image Paul held in his memory. Just about the only thing different was that Paul was almost sure he had a black eye. Off went another little warning light.

At five seven, Chris was a little shorter than average, with nothing very distinctive about his clothing. During the evening he wore jeans that were baggy and frayed from trailing on the ground, plain T-shirts, a scuffed up brown leather jacket and red baseball shoes. By day he was only fractionally smarter, changing into chinos, black shoes and an open-necked shirt. He hadn't put on any weight in seven years and still had a good physique. Nothing overstated, but he was solid enough. Good looking too. That hadn't changed. His hair was very distinctive, blond almost to the point of being white, exactly as his father's had been, cut neatly above his ears and neck.

By the time Paul shifted his stuff on Monday – a single flight case of clothes and toiletries, plus his laptop and a handful of books he'd read twice already – he was confident it wouldn't be hard to 'bump into' his old friend the following day. Like most people, Chris's movements were probably the same every day of the week. He had an admin job with Westminster Council and used the tube to get there and back. That was enough to work on.

Paul found Camden dirty and disturbing, too densely packed by a long way. The air smelled persistently of the junk food on offer all over the place, mingled with rotten market produce from around Inverness Street, and then the stink created by the incessant crush of people, a vast mix of the weirdly dressed – all young, all wanting desperately to make statements about their identities – and the tourists who came to look at them. By night the place changed only by adding multiple competing sources of loud music and the stench of stale alcohol into the mix. The flat Rathmore had found him was a little way up Kentish Town Road, far enough off to be quiet. Beyond the square mile or so given over to 'the Camden experience', the area was no different to any other part of central London.

On Tuesday Paul anticipated that Chris would stop for a coffee at a little Italian place, on his way back from work, because that's what he'd done the night before, so he parked himself at a table there and waited. Sure enough, just after six, Chris came through the door looking breathless. Immediately inside he turned and paused, looking out into the street. He waited like that for a few moments, until someone leaving had to push past him to get out, then turned to walk over to the counter. Up close Paul saw that his right eye was definitely bruised – the remnants of a shiner that had to be about a week old. And he looked troubled.

But if he was afraid that someone was following him, it didn't last long. In no time, over at the counter, he was chatting to the owner in fluent Italian. He hadn't picked that up at school, where French and Spanish had been the only languages forced on them. Obviously a regular, he was given coffee and a small slice of fruit cake without having to ask. Then he leaned against the counter and resumed his gazing at the outside world. He hadn't even bothered to glance around the faces inside the place.

Paul sighed, stood up as if to leave, walked until he was level with Chris, then paused, looking down at him. Chris glanced up and frowned. The frown turned into a wide-eyed smile of recognition just as Paul said: 'Chris? Chris Napier?'

'Fuck me! Paul fucking Curtis!' He turned from the counter and stood looking stunned but pleased, unsure whether to offer an embrace or a handshake, perhaps.

Paul smiled at him. 'I thought it was you, Chris.' He held his hand out. 'How nice to see you again . . .'

'Nice? It's fucking brilliant, man.' Chris knocked the hand aside and stepped in close to hug him. 'Where've you been, Paul? Man, it's so good to see you. I've tried to reach you so many times.' Still the same Cheshire accent – the posh, just-south-of-Manchester variant. 'Shit! This is brilli-ant . . .'

'Ditto, Chris. Good to see you. I tried to reach you too. We must have had the wrong addresses, or something . . .'

'I tried the address you gave me, man. I thought you must have been blanking me . . .'

'I thought the same . . .'

Chris shook his head. 'I can't believe it. What? Seven years, is it?'

'About that. Yes . . .'

'I would never blank you, man. Never. They told me you were in the army' – a glance at the cropped hair – 'you look the same. Same haircut.'

'I was in the army, yes . . . out now . . .'

'That's great, Paul. Great. Great you got out, I mean. That's bad shit all that mess over there . . . But what?' He glanced around them. 'Were you in *here*? Amazing. This place is my favourite place. I live near here. Just round the corner. Amazing. I can't believe it. Why are you here? I mean why *here*, in *this* place?'

'Getting a coffee. I've moved here . . .'

'To London? Brilliant . . .'

'To Camden. Not far from here. You say you live close?'

'Just round the corner, man. It's crazy, eh? One of those London things. I'm always bumping into people I thought I'd never see again. Shit. This is great, Paul. You finished your coffee? You want another?'

'Not another, no.' He tapped his head with a finger. 'Already had too much caffeine today.'

'You're right. Let's get a drink. I know a great place. Very close. You got time?'

Paul smiled. 'Of course, Chris. Of course I've got time.'

'Or better still – why not we go back to mine? It's just over the road – I can cook you something. I'm hungry. You eaten yet?'

'No. But that's cool. You can cook now?'

Chris laughed. 'I could always cook, man. It was you that didn't know how to fry an egg.'

'That right? I remember that time at Rathmore you bought a frozen chicken and put it in the oven without defrosting it . . .'

'No. Don't remind me.'

'Then dropped it on the floor . . .'

'OK. OK.' He looked hard at Paul. 'Rathmore? Shit. You remember all that?'

'Of course.'

'So do I. So do I. But I thought it was *just* me.'

Paul smiled. It couldn't have been going better if Phil Rathmore himself had scripted it. Within five minutes he had an invite back to his son's flat and they were getting along as if they'd never lost touch.

The flat was a four room place – living room, bedroom, bathroom and kitchen. It was small, but looked comfortable, like

Chris had been there a while and grown into it. In what should have been the living room there was barely enough space to move. This was obviously where he did the music thing. There were three or four different keyboards, plus amps and mixers, speakers, PA systems, a couple of guitars, an old-style turntable and records – real vinyl records, some scattered across a table. On a smaller table Paul saw music paper, scribbled all over, along with an assortment of letters and junk mail. There were boxes of unpacked IKEA bookshelves leaning against the wall next to the pile of books meant to go in them.

'Sorry about this.' Chris grinned, looking back at him. 'This is where I work. Let's go through to the kitchen. I'll get you a glass of wine. Let's sit down and drink first. I can do some food later. There's a curry in the fridge from yesterday. You like curry still?'

Paul nodded. It was just about all he'd eaten for the last year and a half.

The kitchen was clean, modern. Not enough room for a table, but Chris was already opening a door onto a small balcony. 'We can sit outside,' he said. 'It's nice out there. Best bit of the flat.'

Paul watched him take a bottle of cold white wine from the fridge, then struggle to open it with a bent corkscrew. He couldn't pull it. He passed it to Paul, then got glasses from a cupboard. He was talking all the time, small talk, nonsense about the flat and Camden and life here. He was genuinely excited to have met Paul again and the enthusiasm was infectious. Paul suddenly felt lighter than he had in years. It began to dawn on him what was happening – he was talking to Chris again, laughing with him, smiling. It was exactly like it had been seven or eight years ago – the same feeling of instinctive trust, of being with someone who understood him. Whatever thing had pulled them together then was doing it now, just the same. He pulled the cork and stepped outside to look at the view back towards the Lock. There was a small metal table and two chairs. 'I can't believe this,' Chris was saying again. 'I just can't believe it. Paul Curtis. Alive and well. I've missed you, Paul. I've really missed you. We both have.'

'Both?'

'Lara and me. Both of us.'

Paul did a double take. 'Lara? You mean *Lara*? She's here?'

'She's here,' Chris continued. 'In London. A fucking lawyer. She looks absolutely gorgeous. Better than ever. You'll kick yourself, man. You won't believe it when you see her.'

'She's what? She's . . . you two . . . I mean . . . are you . . . ?' He stopped abruptly, confused.

'We're together,' Chris said. He was grinning from ear to ear. 'That what you mean?'

'Together? What – all this time? Eight years?' He'd imagined vividly what Chris and Lara might have been doing in the eight years since they'd last met, but none of his guesses had included them being together again. Lara and her family had left Manchester before Paul had left school. Chris had stayed on at school another year after that. But he'd lost contact with Lara whilst Paul was still there.

'No. Not eight years.' Chris laughed. 'A few months though. You wouldn't believe how I hooked up with her again. Man, first Lara, then you. It's a full set. The old crew. It's fucking amazing. I have to tell you about it. I was playing a gig in Kentish Town . . .' He was starting now, starting on the story of how he and Lara had ended up together again. Paul took the wine he offered him and realised there were unwelcome feelings muddying his mood. Chris and Lara were together again. He should be happy about that. But he wasn't. 'Playing a gig?' he asked, interrupting.

'A gig. The band. It's my whole life. That and Lara.'

'I saw the gear,' Paul said, nodding back towards the flat. 'I thought you must still be doing something like that.'

'Turn Again.'

'Sorry?'

'That's what we're called.'

Paul was astonished. 'I know Turn Again. I can't believe it. I've actually heard you without realising. *You're* Turn Again? Really? You're not shitting me?'

Chris beamed. 'That's us.'

'You just put out a single, right? "Watching Love Grow"?' It was on his player, in fact.

Chris nodded, delighted. 'You've heard it? Fantastic.'

'I love it. It's on my iPod. I can't believe this. How come I didn't suss?'

'The name, maybe. I'm Chris Alexander in the band . . .'

'Chris Alexander! That's right. Now I get it.'

'It's my middle name, remember?'

'I do now. But I hadn't thought . . .' He couldn't believe he'd missed it. He'd listened to the single maybe five times in the last two weeks, but hadn't recognised the voice at all.

'If you'd watched the video we did you would have known. It's up on YouTube.'

'I haven't watched it. But I've heard nearly everything Turn Again have put out, I think. I like it all . . .' He was still surprised. He caught himself blushing, trying to stop himself from being too effusive. 'I can't believe it. That's you?' He began to laugh about it.

'The title comes from a Joy Division lyric. The band

name too. But you probably knew that. Your dad was into Joy Division. I remember you telling me that. Shit! I might never have listened to any of that old stuff if you hadn't said. So that's something I owe you. I'm nowhere near that standard, of course, but it's all my own stuff, at least. I write everything, words and music.'

'It's great stuff, Chris. I mean it.'

Chris shrugged, but he looked delighted. 'That's my life. The music. That and Lara.'

Lara again. Paul felt his spirits sink a bit. This was what it was going to be like. Up then down. A little rollercoaster. He had to get used to it. Why? Because he was being paid to do this, paid to be here. That thought stopped him in his tracks. He licked his lips and drank a large gulp of wine. Could he still do this? It already felt wrong. He'd just met Chris again and already he was lying to him. His very presence was a lie. He wanted rid of that complication. He wanted it to just be what he was pretending it was – a chance meeting that was working for both of them. He wanted to be Chris's friend, not his father's spy. He shivered. The sun was low in the sky, obscured by cloud. The evening was cold, he thought, too cold to be out here drinking wine. 'You make money from it?' he asked. 'You're doing well, right?'

'Money? I don't know about that. Maybe one day. It's mostly net exposure so far, which makes you nothing. But that's not the point. Screw the money.'

'You in touch with your dad, then?' He felt so dishonest asking the question his cheeks started to burn again.

But Chris didn't notice. He sneered. 'Fuck that. I have a job for money . . .' He waved his hand through the air, exactly as Rathmore had done, dismissing the unsavoury thought. 'But that's not important. It's the music I live for.

The job just keeps me in food. You know me. It's always been that way.'

Paul nodded, then smiled. He did know. All that idealism. Chris had been like that for as long as Paul had known him. No concern for money. Just the music. Paul had been so long without coming into contact with ideals that didn't kill you that it was like a curtain opening on something brighter. He felt his mood slip back a bit, then managed to listen to the story of how Chris and Lara had met again. Chris told it breathlessly, eyes off in the distance, one hand fiddling with a little twisted rope of coloured string around the other wrist.

He'd played a venue in Kentish Town and she'd been there, brought there by some guy from the record company they'd just signed to. She knew him through a friend of a friend. The guy brought her backstage afterwards to meet them and there she was, just standing in front of him again after all those years, as if it were the most natural thing in the world. Pure chance had brought them together, in a city of thirteen million people. 'It was totally devastating,' he said. 'I can't even begin to explain it. All these years she's all I ever wanted. I thought about her every single fucking day after she left us – back then, I mean, when she was sixteen. I was desperate when she left. I'm serious. I kept it from you, kept it from everyone. I've never met anybody like her in my whole life. I thought I'd never see her again, and here she was, right in front of me. And the most incredible thing? It was all there still, right between us, just like it used to be. Everything. You see what I'm saying, Paul? We *still* felt the same about each other. All those years and we had gone through the same experience in isolation, each never thinking we would see the other again. Then it happened. I'm not sure I can explain it to you.' He took a deep breath. He was staring dreamily into his wine glass, a private smile playing at the corners of his mouth.

'So you met again,' Paul said, summoning some enthusiasm. 'And then what? I mean, how's it going with you two now?'

'Fantastic. We've been back together for nearly three months now. I couldn't ask for more. The band getting signed. Lara. It's all I want, man. It's perfect.' He looked up. 'And now you. It's like someone must be watching over me.' Paul almost flinched. Chris reached out a hand and clasped his. 'It's so good to see you, Paul. I can't wait to tell Lara. She's gone up to a friend's place in St Albans for a few days, she said. But she'll come back to town for this. I'll text now. She'll want to see you. I meant what I said – we've both missed you. Talked about you loads. Big Paul Curtis!'

Paul laughed. Chris slapped his back, too hard, so some wine spilled. 'Big fucking Paul,' he said again.

So they were together. Chris and Lara. That was that. It didn't need to spoil anything. It wasn't what he'd expected, but it was familiar territory. 'And what's that?' he asked, pointing to the black eye. Nothing had been said about it. 'Is that just what happens when you live in Camden Town?'

Chris's face clouded. 'Did I say things were perfect? Life's never like that. There's always some shit in the ointment.'

'Which is?'

'That tosser brother of hers.'

Paul had to think for a moment. 'Pasha?'

'Yeah. Fucking Pasha.'

Paul waited for more. But Chris was saying nothing.

'You going to tell me about it?'

'Not now. I'm too happy to see you again. I don't want to think about all that crap.' He shook himself – like the thought might fall off him – and gazed out over the canal.

Then looked back at Paul. 'Forget that,' he said, voice bright again. 'Let's celebrate.' He raised his glass, and grinned. 'Cheers, mate. Here's to you!'

Paul smiled. He was trying to remember Lara's brother, but not much would come to mind. He'd been a geeky kid with glasses. A swot. It had been expected he'd end up a doctor or some such, like his father. 'Here's to you!' he said, raising his glass to clink it gently against Chris's. 'To both of you.'

7

That afternoon, just after two, Andy had got a text from Mark Johnson – aka Simon Parker, their informant. Andy had been on his way back to the Acton facility, still struggling with the instructions from Stanesby, when the phone beeped. The message had a flavour of panic about it, which was uncharacteristic of Mark. He wanted a meet immediately, with no prior phone contact. It ended: 'Between us only – essential.' The meet he was proposing was at Woolley Edge Services, on the M1 near Sheffield, a good two hundred miles away. Andy had cursed to himself, but the text was so unlike Mark he had to take it seriously.

To get to Woolley Edge Services by ten that evening, as Mark had requested, he had aimed to leave by seven. During the rest of the day he had checked in with Snowden, ignoring Mark's injunction on telling anyone else, then held a quick meeting with his team, passing on Stanesby's changes. The rough battle plan had been that they would put a mobile team on Christopher Napier and Durrani's sister, commencing that evening. At the same time, Andy was to try to prime Mark to get more information on the contract Durrani was rumoured to be considering putting on Christopher Napier. Separately, one of Pearce's teams was going to devise a way of giving Durrani's solicitors – there were two sets – a heads-up on Durrani's criminal status. Possibly they would call the solicitors and pose as someone else, one of Durrani's business partners, for instance – then spill the beans about Durrani's drugs connections. Something like that – enough to frighten the solicitors off Durrani without compromising the wider operation. Once that happened Andy thought things would start getting a little out of control. He wasn't looking forward to it. Emergencies meant compulsory overtime, which meant less time with Helen and the kids.

He ate at home, then helped get the kids to bed. Which meant it was eight thirty before he could get going. He lived in Harrow. They had two cars – a Toyota Verso, for transporting the kids and all their stuff – and an older Audi that he used to get into work if he couldn't face the tube. He took the Audi and drove fast. But he was still running late. It was almost ten thirty, and dark, as he neared Woolley Edge Services, on the M1 in West Yorkshire.

He drove into the main car park, as Mark had asked him to, pulled into a space, cut the engine and waited. Within seconds his mobile was ringing. He listened to Mark's voice, the familiar heavy Manchester accent speaking quietly, urgently: 'I'm in a blue Range Rover, I'll drive past you. Wait a couple of minutes then follow me. I'll be in the slow lane headed north.' Before Andy could say anything he'd cut the line.

It took about four minutes for the Range Rover to appear, so Andy guessed Mark had called him from inside the services, on a public phone. He was being very careful, enough for Andy to begin to worry what the danger might be. There'd been times in his career, long in the past, when he'd been placed in actual personal danger. But that was a young man's game. He didn't like it now. If it came to something physical he wouldn't have a clue. He'd spent too many years staring at surveillance gear to go back to the hands-on approach.

He waited exactly two minutes then followed. The motorway was quiet and it took him less than that to catch up. They came off at the next junction together and followed signs for the A636. Aside from being somewhere in West Yorkshire, Andy now had no idea where he was. He reached over and switched on the satnav.

The road curved past some factory units and a motel, then turned south, went under an old railway bridge and into open country. In the distance the land rose towards a dark mass of moor – topped by a huge radio or TV mast. He scrolled the satnav to identify it but just then the road entered a wood and Mark began to slow.

Andy could see no other cars ahead, none in his mirrors. Mark turned onto a gravel track without indicating, his taillights bumping into the trees. About one hundred yards into the enveloping darkness he killed the lights and engine and got out, leaving the driver's door open. Andy pulled in behind him, keeping his headlights on. All around he could see nothing but trees, mainly pine, which effectively obscured whatever moon there was. The place was dark, isolated, hidden.

He had known Mark since 1994, when they had met on the induction course at Hendon. After that they had both started as constables in Southall and quickly become close. The relationship had persisted when Mark had transferred to Greater Manchester Police, six years later. Now they saw each other about four times a year and spoke by phone or mailed frequently. They had a long weekend holiday together over the late May Bank Holiday that had become a regular fixture, sometimes going walking in the Lakes, more often on beer tours over the channel. This year they had a plan to do Prague again, but work commitments meant it would happen in June, not May. Helen instinctively didn't like these trips, of course, but she'd got used to them.

In 2001, about a year after Mark had moved to Greater Manchester Police, he had told Andy that GMP had accused him of planting drugs and were investigating him. Andy had not been too surprised. Mark was a rare combination – a man with a sharp, investigative intellect and reliable intuitions, who also had a clear mission statement hard-wired into his character – *protect the vulnerable, get the bastards who prey on them.* In the Met his investigative acumen had functioned untroubled by the niceties of criminal psychology. A suspect was a *scrote* – a specimen of sub-human low-life to be hunted, caught and incarcerated. By contrast, Andy had always felt substantially less convinced about the utter blackness of the bad guys, the helpless innocence of everyone else. And he had worked with Mark long enough to realise that the zealot streak was a fault line. It was only a matter of time before Mark would overstep himself and get caught.

When the inevitable happened Mark had been realistic enough to cut a deal. He had left GMP without a charge, or a pension, and immediately set up a private security business, milking what contacts he had to the max. That had been six years ago. The business had grown and done well, but the nature of it had led Mark in uncomfortable directions. The best clients were wealthy and had something to hide or protect, usually something illegal. Through the years Mark had squared this with himself by providing a useful flow of information to a variety of agencies. The present job was the first time he had come to SO15 though.

Andy cut the motor, leaving the lights on. Mark was already at his passenger door, knocking on the window.

Andy flicked the switch releasing the lock. Mark got in and immediately leaned over to switch off the headlights. 'We're trying to be inconspicuous,' he said. He sounded agitated. He had a tall, rangy frame, and had to slide the passenger seat right back to fit in. He looked worried. The keen, piercing blue eyes flicked over Andy and focused on the rear-view mirror.

'You think someone's tailing you?' Andy asked quietly.

'Yep.' Mark's eyes stayed on the mirror.

'There were no other cars on the road.'

'I know. I lost him earlier. I hope.'

'Who is it?'

Mark took his eyes from the mirror and fixed them on Andy.

'Pasha Durrani knows,' he said. 'He knows I'm looking at him.'

Andy frowned. 'You sure about that?'

'Absolutely. He's found out somehow. I don't know how. I'm working on that.'

Andy was involved in operation HAKA because Mark had come to him, two and a half months ago, with the information about Pasha Durrani being forced to sell three properties fast, combined with the suspicion that the purchase monies were destined for the tribal areas of Pakistan presently so high on the agenda of all agencies involved in counter-terrorism. But Mark had come across this information because his security company had been retained by Raheesh Khan, the original HAKA target. At that point Andy had had nothing to do with HAKA, hadn't even known it existed.

On the surface Raheesh Khan was a legitimate and successful businessman, well known in the Cheshire area – the sort of luminary who was regularly invited to civic events, who gave generously to local charities. What Khan had wanted Mark to do was investigate an associate: Pasha Durrani. Khan suspected Durrani was running a scam on him. He didn't know what it was. He had asked Mark Johnson's agency to find out. It was whilst doing that that Mark had heard the rumour about Durrani selling properties belonging to the Asuris, and come to Andy. But Mark's actual business with Khan was to try to find out if Durrani was fleecing him.

'Let me get it clear,' Andy said. 'You think Pasha Durrani knows that Raheesh Khan has retained you to investigate him?'

'I know he knows. I've been tailed for four consecutive days now. And other things. I've seen people outside the offices, outside my house as well.'

'Have you confronted them?'

'I've tried to.' Mark laughed quietly. 'They've been a bit slippery, so far. They're professionals. Yesterday they used three cars in relay. I thought it must be your lot at first, but they were all Asians.'

'And you're sure about this?'

Mark looked hard at him. 'I'm not an idiot, Andy. This morning I set a little trap and almost caught one of them. Didn't make it, but I saw him well enough. It was Ram Ali. He works for Durrani, does security for his Manchester operations.'

'What's the point? Why would Durrani tail you?'

'He wants me off his back.' Mark chuckled to himself, then seemed to relax a little. He sat back in the seat, let his eyes stray from the mirror. 'He's not having me tailed to find out about me. It's a threat, a warning. And I hear it loud and clear. He's telling me he knows I'm onto him, knows where my offices are, knows where my family live.

He's telling me to back off. He's frightened. And that makes me frightened. He's a fucking killer, Andy. A killer with a lot to lose. If it was just me I'd probably laugh in his face, see what happened. But I need to be careful. I've got Kevin and Rita to think of.'

'Of course.' Kevin was Mark's eight-year-old boy. His mother was Rita, a nurse from the same area of Manchester as Mark.

'And you want me to do something about it?' Andy asked. 'That's why I'm here?'

Mark shook his head. 'I look after myself, mate. You know that. I know how to deal with this kind of thing. You don't need to stress on my account. You're here because I trust you. Because I don't want to blow things for you without giving you a heads-up on it.'

'Blow things?'

'The reason Durrani is worried enough to threaten me – despite my connection to Khan – is that he's got wind of where I've been putting my nose. He doesn't know what I know yet, because if he did he'd have hired someone already to deal with me.'

'And what do you know?'

'I've found out what Durrani's scam is.' He looked pleased with himself. 'It's taken me this long because he's good. But I'm onto him now. I'll have him stitched up by next week, I believe. That will end my problems pretty effectively.' He smiled.

Andy felt suddenly tense. 'What do you mean?'

'Khan asked me to look into Durrani because he thought he was fleecing him. If he is I haven't come across it. But what I have found out is that he's about to fleece the Asuris, who are way more powerful and scary than Khan. In about ten days I'll have enough evidence to report this to Khan –

not court evidence, but the sort of information Khan will appreciate. And act on. He'll pass it to the Asuris.'

'Tell me more.'

'Four years ago Durrani was given three high-value properties belonging to the Asuris. I've told you this already.'

Andy nodded. Mark was aware that Andy was involved in an operation on Durrani arising out of that very information, though he had no idea as to the scale of it, or the details.

'All he had to do,' Mark continued, 'was sell these properties, buy three others with the purchase money, hold on to those until asked to sell them and move the funds again. A fairly normal drugs money layering exercise. The point being to make it seem that the Asuris have nothing to do with the properties, by putting distance between their organisation and the original purchase monies. The Asuris want their money liquid now, so they've instructed Durrani to sell again, and quickly. What I discovered, after a lot of work, is that he has a personal connection to someone high up in one of the companies buying one of the properties – the one in Brighton. Turns out this guy – he's a white guy, a lawyer called John James Ross – was also involved in buying one of the original Asuri properties, four years ago. Maybe that's how they met. On that occasion Durrani and Ross did a little deal, it seems. They paid bent surveyors to undervalue the property, ensuring Ross got the place a little cheaper. In return he slipped Durrani a bung.'

'They did that? With the Asuris' property?'

'Yes. But the amount wasn't significant – about thirty grand.'

'This is what you're going to tell Khan about?'

'Not just that, no. Thirty grand is pocket money for these types – the sort of difference that would be written off as a misunderstanding between thieves. It wouldn't get Durrani into serious trouble if the Asuris found out. They probably *assume* their people take that kind of slice. But it seems that thirty grand was just a practice run. This time, when Durrani sells the Brighton property to Ross's company, they intend to run the same scam to the tune of eight hundred grand. And that's different.' Now Mark was grinning all over his face. 'Now that really will get him into trouble.'

Andy took a breath. 'You intend to tell Khan all this?'

'You're damn right I do.'

'When?' He could see immediately what the significance was.

'My contract runs out next Friday, the fourth of June. But I'll have enough to show him by Sunday, I think. I've identified the bent surveyors, now I just need to get copies of their original documentation.'

'How?'

'I'll need to have access to the solicitors' files, or the surveyors' files, or both. I can do that on Friday and Saturday, I think. Friday and Saturday night.' He grinned. He would burgle their offices, Andy assumed, but he didn't ask. 'That's four days,' Mark said. 'I just have to keep this Durrani fucker away from my family for four days. After that there won't be a problem. Khan will kill him. The Asuris will tell him to do it. Good fucking riddance. That's why I've got you up here now. By the end of the week you won't have a target any more. I thought I ought to warn you.'

8

Paul woke in Chris's bed, his tongue cleaving to the roof of his mouth, a pounding headache pulling him down. He dragged himself into the bathroom, then stood flushing cold water over his face and head. Chris had slept in the living room, he assumed, with his instruments. It had been a good night; a lot of white wine (hence the headache, he wasn't used to white wine), a lot of Chris's music, but he remembered that it had ended on a sour note, with Chris telling him about the black eye.

Some things didn't change. His mind slipped back to how their friendship had started. Paul's first year in the new school. It was meant to be something better than the old comp – his dad was paying a lot of money for it to be better – but the first year had been no different. Paul's appearance was enough to put off the gentler kids – even at thirteen he had looked tall and hard – plus word had got round that his dad was a bouncer, which relegated him instantly to the bottom of the social heap. Consequently, for the first two terms he had no friends at all. At the top of the heap in Paul's class was a kid called Biggs, who everyone else was afraid of on account of him being the best fighter.

At the beginning of summer term Biggs started picking

71

on Chris, who Paul knew only then as 'Napier', and had barely spoken to. Chris was good-looking and popular. He could play piano – Paul had once stood shyly watching, full of admiration, whilst he played the theme from *Titanic* for a crowd of rapt teenage girls. Biggs was roughly the same size as Chris, but Chris had no aggression in him. He had spoken to Paul once in a physics class, when they'd been paired for an experiment, and Paul had seen straight away that Chris wasn't like Biggs and his mates. There hadn't been any of the scorn Paul was used to.

Biggs had a problem with Chris because Chris's girlfriend was a gorgeous, dark-haired thing that Paul hardly dared look at – Lara Durrani. She was the girl everyone wanted to be with, Biggs included. But Lara wouldn't even look at the likes of Biggs. So Biggs started to humiliate Chris, pinning him against the front wall each day before afternoon lessons began, taking his bag off him, sifting through it, removing whatever he wanted. Just about the entire class had gathered round first time it happened, the boys jumping up and down like excited little apes. The girls had looked bothered, but no one had stopped it. Paul had just sat in his place, keeping out of it. 'Don't ever get sucked into other people's fights, son.' That was what his dad had told him.

Then one day it had turned more serious because Napier tried to get his bag back. Biggs had thrown a fit, kicked the bag around, then started on Napier. That was all Paul saw before the crowd closed round them – Napier cornered, Biggs yelling at him, thumping him, threatening to cut his face with a penknife. Paul had felt physically sick watching it, disgusted. And because of that he had stood up and gone forward, ignoring his father's words.

The crowd was mixed, but mainly boys. They saw him coming and parted to let him through. Some of the girls were shouting at Biggs, telling him to leave off. Biggs had Chris's head pulled forward by the hair, like he was about to start kicking his face. Chris was sobbing and there was blood on the floor from his nose. Paul pushed through until he was right behind Biggs, then he put a hand on his shoulder. Biggs turned, surprised, and looked up at him, one hand still wrapped in Chris's hair. Paul saw the doubt in Biggs's eyes, saw him glance round the crowd and weigh it up, all in an instant. A question of pride, no doubt. His eyes were wide open, a bit crazy. He wasn't going to back off.

'That's enough,' Paul said, calmly.

You could have heard a pin drop. Behind him everything was very still. Biggs sneered, let go of Chris and turned. 'Is he your fag friend, then?' he grunted. He swung his fist up, going for Paul's face.

Paul moved sideways. The fist hit his shoulder. The other hand was coming quickly after it. He brushed it away, then jabbed into Biggs's face. One. Two. His dad had taught him about short little punches, too quick to anticipate. He hit him in the nose and the mouth. He heard something crack in the mouth, felt the teeth sharp against his knuckles. Biggs was knocked backwards, so that he was up against Chris. But he wasn't down yet. Paul brought his knee up to go for his balls. Biggs bent to avoid it, ducking his head forward, so Paul took a big swing with his right and smashed him across the side of the head, as hard as he could. Biggs hit the floor flat out.

A pause. Paul heard someone gasp behind him. He could feel the shock running through the crowd. But Biggs was moving still, scrambling away. Paul stepped towards him, raising his foot to stamp on his head. 'If you start, then you finish,' his dad had taught him. 'Always finish it quickly.' A girl's voice shouted something, trying to stop him. He caught himself, stopped, lowered his foot. Biggs had turned and was on his back. He was shaking his head, hands across his nose and mouth. The blood was frothing out between his fingers. His eyes were frightened now, submissive.

'Leave him alone,' Paul had said, nodding at Chris.

Now, eleven years later, he raised his face and stared at himself in Chris's bathroom mirror. What had it been that Chris had told him – about the black eye? Lara's brother wanted her to marry someone in Pakistan – an arranged marriage. He'd threatened her and Chris repeatedly, then last week Chris had been jumped by two guys late one night, on his way back here. A minor beating, no real damage, but Chris wasn't any more of a fighter now than he had been in his teens. He was shaken, frightened. Paul had tried to convince him it might just have been a mugging gone wrong, but Chris wasn't having that. Pasha had warned Lara it would happen, and it had.

Paul sighed. Was *this* why Phil Rathmore was paying such a ridiculous fee, he wondered? He heard Chris calling to him from the other room. He went through and saw a bleary-eyed apparition, face pallid, but dressed in what passed as work clothes, about to leave. Last night's high spirits had vanished. He looked serious. 'Lara wants us to meet up today,' he said. 'As soon as possible. All of us. I spoke to her just now. Something's happened with Pasha.'

Paul frowned. 'Like what?'

'I don't know. I need to talk to her. It sounds bad, man. You remember what I told you about him?' He touched his bruised eye, gently, then shook his head. 'I think he's done something to Lara now. I'll fucking kill him if he has. I'll fucking kill him.'

Paul waited. Chris wasn't going to kill anyone. He was

looking at the floor now, shaking, obviously trying to control himself, but Paul couldn't be sure whether it was anger or fear.

'She's too scared to meet in public,' Chris said, his voice cracking. 'It must have been bad. She said it happened on Saturday but she didn't dare tell me. She won't come here, or to a pub, or anything like that. She thinks Pasha is having us followed.'

'You think that's possible?' He tried to remember if Chris had given him any more information on Pasha, like how he would have that kind of resource available.

'I don't know what he can do. He's a fucking crook, Paul. I don't know what he can do. Christ! What are we going to do, man?' He sounded close to panic.

'Stay calm, Chris,' Paul said. 'I'm sure she'll be OK. We'll think it through. OK?' Presumably he was meant to run a kind of repeat performance of their childhood. Confront Pasha, give him a talking to. And after all, that was what he was being paid to do. He kept his face down thinking about it, tried to keep the guilt out of his eyes.

In the end they agreed on Paul's new place, the flat Chris's dad was paying for. Lara arrived just after eleven. She came with the friend whose house she'd been staying at.

Lara and Chris went straight into a tight, long hug at the door. Lara had her head buried in his shoulder so Paul couldn't see her face. He waited awkwardly behind them, until the friend came around them, looking embarrassed. She introduced herself and shook his hand politely. 'Jules Clarke,' she said. A very precise, upper class voice. 'I've heard a bit about you.'

'Nothing bad, I hope?' Paul said.

'Mainly from Chris. You and he were best friends at school, right?'

'Right. I suppose so. Yes.'

'And you're just back from the army?'

He took his eyes from Chris and Lara and looked at her. She was tall for a woman – just over six foot – slim and very pretty. Same age as him, roughly. She had short blonde hair, spiky and messed up like she'd just got out of bed and hadn't done anything with it, though he supposed that was an expensive illusion.

'Well, about a year ago,' he said.

She nodded, clearly unsure what to say about it. 'Was it tough?' she asked, finally.

'The army?'

'Yes. I always imagine it must be terribly hard . . .'

'No,' he said. 'It's an easy life. Boring, really.'

'That right? You didn't have to . . .' She had to think about it, censor herself, maybe. 'Go anywhere awful?' *You didn't have to kill anyone*, was what she had wanted to say.

'I don't think so,' he said. 'Uncomfortable, perhaps. Hot. Cramped. But you get used to it.'

'Like being on an aeroplane, right?' She pointed at his head.

He frowned.

'Uncomfortable. When you're that tall, I mean. You must get used to it pretty early on.'

He laughed politely. 'You're tall yourself,' he said. She smiled, but she was staring at him too intensely, scrutinising him. Finally, behind her, Lara split from Chris. There were tears on her face.

'I'm so sorry,' she said, moving immediately towards Paul. 'I'm so rude.' She came straight at him and hugged

76

him. 'I haven't seen you for so long, Paul,' she said, face against his chest. 'I've thought about you. Missed you.'

He could smell her hair, her perfume. He hugged her, aware that his heart had done something weird as she had come towards him. Then she stepped back. He saw her face again, wet with tears. 'You OK, Lara? Chris has told me a bit about what's happening . . .'

She wiped her eyes on her sleeve. 'I'm OK,' she said. 'Let's all go and sit down. I'm so glad you're here, Paul.' Her voice had changed. She had the same posh accent as her friend now. No more flat Manchester vowels for her.

They sat down on the neat white sofas in the living room. Lara was wearing a red T-shirt he recognised, a very faded old thing that advertised a band Chris had been in when they were at school. The Heat. They'd played one disastrous, deserted gig in a community centre in south Manchester. He'd been there watching, with Lara and about ten other people, Lara and he wearing this T-shirt. His was long gone, of course, but she was still wearing hers. She had a plain yellow scarf on above it, wrapped tightly around her neck despite the weather. Tight black jeans, flat brown leather shoes, a large cloth handbag. She looked older, he realised, but not in a bad way. There were lines at the corners of her eyes now, the cheekbones and jaw more prominent. But if anything she'd filled out a little. She was an adult now, and that was mildly disconcerting. The hair was the same lustrous, rich dark mass that he remembered.

He watched her settle next to the little metal coffee table, Jules beside her, then she put a hand out for Chris to hold. He was on the chair next to hers. She wasn't crying now, but her eyes were frightened. The same dark brown, beautiful eyes. Had he really told her what he felt for her, once? He remembered it with an internal cringe. They were sixteen by then, and very close. Often he had seen more of her than Chris did. Until this moment he'd forgotten exactly what it had been like. When he'd told her what he really felt she had laughed, embarrassed, then kissed him gently on the cheek. 'You're so sweet, Paul,' was what she'd said.

He sat opposite her now and tried to look normal. But he was feeling unexpected things, his pulse quicker. He swallowed hard and tried to focus on what was being said. 'Paul used to steal DVDs for me,' she was saying, explaining their childhood to Jules. Paul cleared his throat and pulled a wry face.

'Seriously?' Jules asked.

He shrugged. 'I was younger,' he offered, like an apology.

'I didn't know he'd nicked them,' Lara added. 'Not then. Chris was always too busy with music. Same then as now.' Little glance at Chris. 'But Paul and I liked the same movies. The same romantic shit. You wouldn't believe it looking at him, right? He had an unlimited supply of them. Anything I wanted to watch, it was in his "collection".' She laughed about it. 'I spent a lot of time at his place. We watched all sorts of old stuff – eighties stuff. His mum was always working so we had the house to ourselves. Just me and Paul. You remember, Paul?'

'I remember like it was yesterday.'

'We were neighbours. I was in Rusholme, Paul was in Chorlton. A ten minute walk. Chris was miles away.' She waved her hand at him. 'I spent more time with Paul than Chris,' she said. 'You remember, Paul? That was how we became such good friends. I could tell you anything, trust you with everything.' She looked at him and smiled beautifully, but her eyes were searching his face, looking for some kind of confirmation that it could still be like that, perhaps.

She seemed more complicated than when younger, some of her composure gone. She was still like something you would see in a film, though. Perfectly symmetrical features. An enchantment about her.

'We met through Chris,' Paul said. 'They were an item.'

Jules was staring at him again now, an odd smile on her lips. Her eyes moved to Chris and the smile vanished. Chris was sitting staring at them, waiting anxiously for Lara to tell him what had happened to her.

9

Andy had taken a hotel in Wakefield Tuesday evening, then phoned Snowden first thing Wednesday with the information about Mark's plans for Durrani. That had put the cat amongst the pigeons. If Mark, aka Simon Parker, intended to report Durrani's scam to Raheesh Khan before the first of June – the finalisation date for the sale of the Asuri properties – then their operation on Durrani was buggered. It would be rendered redundant even if they managed – as Stanesby had instructed – to somehow get the sale date delayed by scaring off the solicitors handling the sales for Durrani. It would be redundant because as Mark had pointed out, Durrani would probably be dead.

Snowden had taken instructions direct from Stanesby and the order had come back to stall Mark until they could decide what to do. So Andy had called Mark around midday, but Mark wouldn't talk on the phone, so there had to be another evening meeting in another secluded area – this time somewhere near Saddleworth Moor. In the end it was after one on Thursday morning before Andy had got home, exhausted and irritated.

The kids were oblivious to his work patterns. Four hours later he was up at the usual ungodly hour with Magnus. He got him ready and off to school, all before Helen was even up with Sophie, which he supposed meant she'd had a bad night, though he'd heard nothing, hadn't even heard her leaving his bed, he'd been so wrecked.

At nine, when he got back from the school run, there was still no sign of them emerging from Sophie's room, so he made himself another coffee and took it out to the conservatory. They had a white metal table and chairs there. He settled down with his laptop to read an interim report on Christopher Napier.

Over the last forty-eight hours Hemmings had thrown some resources at Napier, but not much had been learned. He was the twenty-four-year-old son of a political researcher called Diane Napier. She lived in Cheshire. There was no father listed on his birth registration. He'd attended a minor public school in the Manchester area and was in a rock or pop band that was either on the cusp of some success, or going nowhere, depending which website you consulted. He'd probably met Lara Durrani at school.

By Wednesday morning they had a mobile team on Napier, who was in Camden with a man called Paul Curtis. There was digest information and surveillance footage covering their movements throughout Wednesday, including meetings with Durrani's sister and a woman called Julie Clarke. No sign of a threat from Pasha Durrani, though. Curtis was ex-army, huge, and looked like a bodyguard, but he'd been to the same school as Lara Durrani and Napier. He had juvenile convictions for theft and assault. The only really curious piece of information unearthed was that the flat he was in was owned by a prominent Tory peer – Lord Philip Rathmore – who had just been given some role in the new coalition government. There was a coincidence there that stuck in Andy's brain immediately, though he had no idea how to interpret it, because Rathmore was also the owner of the eight-million spread in North Yorkshire that Pasha Durrani was in the process of buying, albeit through a company that looked like it had nothing to do with Durrani. The coincidence might mean something, it might not. Andy slotted it away in his head as something to come back to. The report ended with a request for further instructions. The resources Hemmings had allocated couldn't be spread too thin – so it was a question of prioritising their efforts. Who did Andy want to know more about – Chris Napier, Paul Curtis, Lara Durrani or Julie Clarke?

A voice spoke from behind him, interrupting his thoughts: 'Has Magnus already gone?' Andy turned to see Helen standing in the conservatory doorway, Sophie in her arms, both still in nightwear. He closed the laptop and turned his chair.

'Half an hour ago,' he said. 'We didn't want to bother you.' Helen looked sleepy, pale. 'You have a difficult night, love?'

She rolled her eyes. Sophie was wearing pyjama bottoms, no top, and was pressed against her shoulder, still dozing. 'We had to come down and watch TV at two thirty,' Helen said. 'She couldn't sleep at all. We were up for two hours. Sorry I slept in.'

'That's OK. Sleep whilst you can.' She was wearing a slip only, showing her legs, which were unshaved. He moved his eyes quickly over her, not wanting her to see him looking. She would be self-conscious about her legs. Before Sophie she had showered every day, shaved every other day. She didn't have especially prominent body hair, but the growth on her legs was pretty long now. Noticeable, certainly. Her hair looked greasy too. Her beautiful, dark red hair that he had once found such a turn-on. Along with the myriad of freckles. They were still there, at least. He smiled at her, trying to keep all these thoughts far from his eyes. It was peculiar, he considered, how much female beauty and sexuality depended upon the systematic illusion that women were hairless. Could he ever get to see her as something sexually attractive *exactly as she was*?

'What you thinking?' she asked, suspiciously.

'You look good,' he said, quickly. 'That's all I was thinking.'

'Yeah, right. Like someone who hasn't slept properly for three years and has had two kids camping inside her body for eighteen months.'

Like someone who hasn't bothered to shave, he thought, but immediately felt terrible for thinking it. 'You still look beautiful to me,' he said, then added, 'I still love you.' That much, at least, was true.

She smiled at that. 'You off today?'

'I'm meant to be. I was—' On cue, his mobile started to beep. He took it out and read the text. It was from Snowden. He wanted him in for an urgent meeting with Stanesby. Immediately. 'Not any more,' he muttered.

He decided to drive there. The car was running on the reserve tank, so he pulled into the petrol station on Alexandra Avenue, about one hundred yards from the house. He filled the tank and then walked to the shop to pay. There was a short queue. He waited, thinking that the roads looked relatively clear so he could probably get in to town a bit earlier, in time to speak to Luntley and find out what Durrani had been up to overnight.

The door opened and someone joined the queue behind him. He got his wallet out in preparation, then had a sensation that the person behind him was too close. He turned to look, frowning.

Pasha Durrani.

He was standing right next to him, dressed in a business suit and pressed shirt, no tie. Durrani's face was about a foot from his. He was staring straight at him.

Andy jumped before he could stop himself. His heart skipped, then he felt the flush of adrenalin entering his blood. He took a breath, his free hand clenching automatically. His heart started to pound, his brain racing to take in the detail.

'Sorry,' Durrani said. He stepped back a pace. He was looking at Andy with an unreadable expression. It was *definitely* him. No doubt about it.

Andy let a breath out. No threat. Durrani wasn't moving on him. No immediate attack. He tried to relax his facial muscles. He saw Durrani look down at his clenched fist, then back up to his eyes. But there was no reaction, not even a frown.

Behind Andy the queue moved and the cashier said something to him. But Andy couldn't turn, couldn't get his eyes off Durrani. It felt like minutes, stuck like that, staring at him. It could only have been a few seconds though. 'You're up,' Durrani said, nodding past his shoulder towards the till.

Andy forced himself to turn and pay. His hands were shaking as he got his credit card out. He could see the cashier looking at him sideways, noticing his nerves. Fucking useless, he thought. Fucking useless. He had to get control of himself, be professional about it. Who did Durrani know in the area? There had to be someone, some reason he was here.

He took long, slow breaths, as quietly as possible, forced

his legs and arms to relax. Then glanced back casually. Durrani was still there, still looking at him. Their eyes met again. No expression at all, no movement.

Andy turned back and finished paying, then moved away, passing Durrani without looking again. As he reached the door he heard Durrani give the cashier a pump number. He stepped out onto the forecourt, the adrenalin still priming his senses.

He saw Durrani's Jag right behind his Audi. He walked to his car, got in and pulled a map from the glove compartment. He opened it and put his eyes down, concentrating with his peripheral vision. He saw Durrani come out and walk right past his window. Then get in his car, start it, pull out and drive past him. He looked up as Durrani turned onto Alexandra Avenue and accelerated away. His route would take him to the turn off for Andy's road.

Andy pulled out after him and dialled Luntley's number on the hands-free. His heart was still thumping away, his breath short and fast. Luntley answered at once.

'Have we got cover on Durrani?' Andy asked. His voice was stressed.

'No mobile cover,' Luntley said, immediately. 'There was a problem with one of DI Pearce's teams so Hemmings pulled the schedule for Durrani and moved our B team to Napier. There's some technical issues too.'

'Fuck.'

Up ahead Durrani drove straight past Andy's street.

'Is there a problem, boss?' Luntley asked.

Andy took the next left and pulled the car into the kerb.

'What technical issues?' he asked.

'The trackers are down.' They had several trackers placed

in Durrani's various cars, allowing them to plot the route of the vehicles via GPS.

'All of them?' Andy asked.

'Two of them.'

'Do we have the one in his Jag?'

'No.'

'Something's happening. I just eyeballed him. He came into a petrol station right behind me.'

Luntley was silent.

'He was in the Jag,' Andy said. 'The Jag without the fucking tracker. Call that a coincidence?'

'What do you think, boss? You think he knows?'

Andy tried frantically to think it over, running through the detail in his head. Could it really be that Durrani had just come in to get petrol, a pure coincidence? 'I don't know,' he said. 'I don't know. Ring me as soon as the trackers are back on line.'

He drove back home and parked a little away from the house, but so he could see it. He didn't want to go in and worry Helen. He imagined the whole incident again, focusing on Durrani's responses. They had been odd, he decided. No reactions at all, staring at him longer than was natural. But was that because of the way he had reacted? He had jumped with shock, locked eyes. Durrani would react to that kind of thing. It might all be nothing. Or it might mean they were blown. But even if they were blown, how would Durrani find out his address? That could only come from an inside leak. He started brooding on that, putting it together with the information that Mark had given him about Durrani being aware of his attentions. There was a lot to worry about suddenly.

Snowden called him ten minutes later and he recounted what had happened. Snowden was waiting for Stanesby to show up. 'I can't get in to the office until I know where Durrani is,' Andy told him. Snowden didn't argue.

He waited for another hour outside the house before Luntley called him. They'd fixed the tracker reception. Durrani's Jag was on the way up the M1, heading north. Andy was only slightly relieved.

'We can get a team on him,' Luntley said. 'You want that?'

'No. Pull back. Assume he knows. Pull everyone off him until we can assess it properly.'

10

Pasha came off the M1 just north of Nottingham and followed the satnav to a deserted country lane about five miles from the motorway. He pulled onto the verge at a spot he'd agreed with Caserne, cut the engine and waited for him to arrive.

For a few minutes he stared out of the window without seeing anything, then he leaned his head in his hands, rested his arms on the steering wheel and tried to relax.

He was losing control of his life. Too many balls in the air, all of them threatening to fall at once. Everything he did now he did on autopilot, following through the logic of each intricate piece of the desperate jigsaw that was his life. There was no time to consider responses, no time to think things through. No point either. He had committed himself to this a long time ago. He was way beyond the stage where he could call a halt. What he had started eight years ago was like a juggernaut, coming right at him.

Every night now he woke up in a panic, dreaming he was drowning, arms thrashing at the sheets, gasping for breath, layered in sweat. It didn't get much better when he found the clock and fixed himself in time and place, in his bed, alone, dreaming about things that were actually happening, things he was actually doing. He couldn't believe what he had become.

He pressed the window button, lowered it and spat into the bushes alongside the car. He felt dirty, his mouth smeared with something bitter. For months now he'd had a phantom smell in his nostrils. It wasn't there all the time, but he'd learned what could trigger it. He had it now because the air coming through the window was suddenly colder. That was all it took. He sniffed cautiously and recoiled. Human shit. What was going on with him? He scrutinised the base of the hedge and sniffed again. He couldn't see anything, but the smell was still there. He wound the window up. Behind him, in the rear-view mirror, he could see Caserne's car pulling onto the road and coming towards him.

Caserne was the sort of person he relied upon now, a psychotic butcher who had no compunction about slitting people's throats, provided he believed that was what Allah required. *His* version of Allah. He lived in a world of alien moral certainties. Caserne was the name he used in the UK – Thierry Caserne – but there was something more Arabic on his passport that Pasha could never remember. He was French Algerian. Pasha had no idea what twisted trajectory had led him to believe his role in life was to kill people for the sake of jihad, or what had brought him to the UK and the grotty little terrace he occupied in North Kensington above the butcher's shop he worked in. He didn't want to know. These days the world was full of suicide bombers and throat-slitters, all castes and creeds. Usually they were younger than Caserne – Pasha put him near to forty – but they all had that divine light in their eyes.

He'd dabbled with it himself as a teenager, so he knew how it worked. When he dealt with Caserne he tried to keep things very simple, very clear. They were doing God's business, the victim was white, the money was good. That's what it came down to. Caserne had more than once referred to time spent in a Moroccan prison, but Pasha knew he was a clean sheet if you ran his name through the various UK police systems, which was mainly why he had been introduced to him. Why he put up with him.

He watched Caserne's car, an innocuous blue Mazda, slide in behind his own. 'God help me,' he whispered. 'God fucking help me.' His hands were shaking, his heart too fast. That was because he'd allowed himself to reflect a little. This morning, at four in the morning, when he couldn't sleep and there was nothing else to do, he had ended up being sick as he brooded on the mess he was in – he had actually run to the toilet and vomited.

He released the door locks and let Caserne climb into the passenger seat. He was wearing green combat trousers with too many pockets, jump boots and a quilted black body-warmer over a white T-shirt, his arms bare. On the road a car passed them at speed. Too fast to have noticed anything. Pasha looked over at Caserne and licked his lips. His mouth was dry, his palms sweaty.

'Something wrong with you, brother?'

It was Caserne asking him the question, in that soft, irritating French accent. Pasha glanced at him, saw the brown eyes looking at him with concern. Was there actually an empathy there? It was unbelievable. Pasha had seen what he could do. When people were like that in the movies there was always something that gave it away, some mad look, some birthmark, or involuntary twitch, a way they had of speaking. But close up Caserne was just like anyone else. You had to talk to him before you realised there was a piece missing.

'Yeah. There's something wrong,' he said. 'Come with me.'

He stepped out and went to the boot. The air was chill, but he hardly noticed. He opened it and took out the angled mirror he'd got from Khan's security guy, Salim Feroz. Caserne was standing beside him. He bent over and placed it under the car, just by the right rear wheel. 'See that,' he said. Caserne looked, frowned.

'I can't see anything.'

'The grey box, about the size of a match box, just between the wheel arch casing and the—'

'Yeah. I see it now.' He straightened up, shrugged. 'What is it?'

'It's a tracker. Take a good look at it and remember what they look like. That particular model comes from your homeland . . .'

Caserne stepped back and raised his hands in protest. 'My home is with Allah, praise be unto him.'

Pasha nodded. It was comical, the rubbish they came out with. 'Whatever,' he said. 'It's an expensive piece of French hardware that transmits the position of this car to people we don't want to know.'

Caserne smiled. 'But we know it's there. You want me to move it?'

'You can't. They are wired to let them know when you pull them off.' Here he was again, following through, on autopilot. He'd spooked the cop – Christ, would he have even dreamed of doing something like that a few years ago – just walking right up behind him in the filling station, staring right at him – he'd done it exactly as they'd told him to.

'So what do we do?' Caserne asked.

They had told him that the encounter at the petrol station would be enough to get SO15 to pull the mobile teams they had following him. He prayed they were right. If so, that just left the tracker. 'We go in your car,' he said.

11

John James Ross was fifty-eight, average height, with a broad upper body, not much paunch and short hair that was mostly white. Today he wore a dark suit, jacket off and hung in the back of his Range Rover, black brogues shined to a mirror finish, a crisp pale-blue and white striped shirt and a navy blue tie. This was the way he always dressed when meeting Pasha Durrani, or transacting any kind of business – he wanted to look like a stockbroker, someone wealthy, but not off-puttingly so.

He had been born in Edinburgh, into a family with some considerable wealth – and even a title, of sorts, some way back in their history – and had never known real financial hardship. That didn't stop him worrying about these things though. He had a wife, Victoria, and two daughters, Becky and Sally, who were now in their teens and off to boarding school. He spent a lot of his time preoccupied with an irrational obsession that he would one day lose everything he had and the girls would have to fend for themselves.

He had thought a lot about that recently. He thought about it now as the blue Mazda came into view. He was sitting sipping from a flask of coffee in his Range Rover in a lay-by in Epping Forest, surrounded by trees – already dense with summer growth, though he hadn't noticed that. It was midday, bright daylight, everything visible, nothing to fear.

He kept telling himself that. The Range Rover window was down and he tipped the dregs of his coffee out as the Mazda slowed to a stop in the lay-by opposite. His hands were shaking so he had difficulty fitting the cup back onto the thermos.

He had no specific reason to be afraid. He had met Pasha Durrani at least four times in this very place, and nothing had happened before. But he had been this nervous each time.

He opened his car door and stepped out onto a surface of mud and decaying leaf litter, placing his feet gingerly to keep the dirt off his shoes. He watched as Durrani manoeuvred the Mazda tight against a tree, allowing space for other vehicles to pass. There was someone in the passenger seat, he noticed. That was different. It added another ten beats to his already speeding pulse.

Partly, his predicament was due to Durrani himself. His relations with him hadn't started with him sweating and nervous every time he met him. He could still clearly recall the first time. That had been at a vintage car auction in Kent, four years ago. He'd been after a rare type of Porsche, of which only a few hundred had been made in the seventies. Not a particularly expensive car – the reserve was set at thirty-five grand – but he was buying with an eye to the future. Cars of that type of vintage – which would be collectors' items in the future, which would appreciate well – that was his particular niche. It was what he spent most of his free time doing.

Before meeting Durrani this activity had seemed reckless to him, a vice that had kept him awake at night sometimes. He had never been able to fully disclose to his wife the extent of his spending, and indeed had no doubt that were she ever to discover that he was presently the owner of twenty-five cars of varying vintages, all stored on a property in East London which he had bought specially for the purpose, and without telling her, he was quite sure she would be astounded. She wouldn't divorce him, but it would be acutely embarrassing. Like being caught masturbating, God forbid. It wouldn't help to explain that the cars were collectively worth slightly more than he had paid, because it was the secretive, compulsive nature of his buying and selling that was the essence of its attraction for him, and it would be that that would confound and worry her.

At the auction Durrani had started talking to him. That was how it had started – with Durrani initiating it. Durrani was a collector himself, or so he had claimed. Ross doubted that was true now, but he had believed it at the time. Why not? Durrani had been an energetic young man, knowledgeable, confident, clearly wealthy, well-dressed and pleasant to talk to. They had talked through the catalogue together and Durrani had offered to source another example of the Porsche, after Ross had indicated disappointment that the catalogue example had been withdrawn. They had exchanged business cards, then three weeks later Durrani had rung him with information on a similar model that had duly been obtained at a significantly reduced price. That had been the first step.

Ross had suspected the car was stolen as soon as Durrani gave him the price. He had even stalled and thought about it for a few days. There was nothing he could do with a stolen car, in terms of immediate resale. Perhaps it would be easier to resell twenty or so years down the line. Perhaps not. But he had agreed the purchase nevertheless. Why? At the time there had been an elaborate justification mechanism. He had encouraged himself to see the purchase as part of the thing that was going on with his car buying habit

– something set aside and separate from his ordinary life with Victoria, the children, the company. That side of his life – the secret side – was like a gambling addiction. And he assumed Durrani himself was unaware that the car was stolen, something else he now doubted. What he was now sure had happened was that Durrani had deliberately selected and targeted him.

There had been two more cars after that – both probably stolen at some point in the past – then the offer of real business, for the company. Durrani was selling a very nice piece of real estate. He could offer preferential terms. In the end they had completed that sale, and together ran a little scam on the side – something inconsequential Durrani had dreamed up, *just to see if they could do it.* They had become quite friendly by then. The scheme had been hatched on a golfing trip to Gleneagles, amidst much boyish laughter and alcohol. At his age, of course, Ross knew he ought to have known better. That was four years ago.

Now they were doing it again. Only this time the amounts to be 'stolen', if that was the right word, were more significant. And Durrani and he were no longer friends. Before Durrani had showed up with this new scheme he had barely spoken to him for over two years.

But he couldn't say no. Because Durrani knew things about him. Damaging things. The cars, the little property scam. Durrani had never threatened him, never said anything to overtly place pressure, but Ross had felt the pressure. It was what he felt now as Durrani got out and crossed the road to him, all smiles and false bonhomie. 'John! How are you, my friend? It's good to see you again.' He was dressed in a smart blue suit with a white shirt open at the collar, no tie. Shaved and smelling of aftershave.

Ross nodded at him, eyes looking past him at the other

person getting out of the Mazda. 'Who's that?' he asked, then shook Durrani's proffered hand. He wanted to ask about the scrappy car too, but didn't.

'Staff,' Durrani said, dismissing the man as inconsequential. The man was middle-aged, heavy, and dressed in a slightly soiled, quilted, sleeveless top. He looked like an East End market trader.

'Let's sit in your car and chat,' Durrani said.

Ross opened the front passenger door for him, but Durrani helped himself to the rear door. Ross moved round to the other side and saw the other man take something out of the boot of the Mazda, a long metal pole with something on the end. Ross got in the rear of the Range Rover, next to Durrani. 'What's your man doing out there?' he asked, frowning.

Durrani settled his eyes on him and spoke slowly. 'He's going to check under your car for tracking devices. Then we'll let him do the inside with a scanner.'

'Tracking devices? I haven't got one fitted . . .'

'You know what they are though?'

'Of course. You can fit them in case the car gets stolen. To track it.' He was still frowning, hoping his expression demanded an explanation.

'Or the police can fit them,' Durrani said, smiling. 'Without you knowing.'

'You think that might have happened?' He began to worry about it immediately.

'Who knows?'

'You have information to that effect? You must have, or why are you getting him to do that? Why now? You've never done that before.'

Durrani smiled again, eyes very firmly holding his. 'Do you know why I'm here, John?' he asked.

Ross frowned even deeper. Something in Durrani's tone was off, different. He heard a little alarm bell in his head, but couldn't place the source of the warning. 'To finalise things with—'

'Don't fuck around. What are we going to finalise?' Durrani was staring fixedly at him, eyes hard.

'The property sale. In ten days or so we have to—'

'You know that's not going to happen.'

He was momentarily distracted. The other man was scraping around beneath his car with the pole. 'What *is* that man doing?' His voice had gone up a bit.

'You heard me.'

He brought his eyes back to Durrani, then had an uncomfortable feeling of being boxed in. He had to resist the urge to open his door, to let in some air, to run, even. Durrani had never spoken to him like that before. 'You're nervous about something,' Ross said, realising it only as he said the words. 'What is it?'

'You tell me.'

'I have no idea. You said just now – you implied just now – that there was a problem with the sale? Is that it?'

'You fucking bet it is.'

He could feel the hostility now. All the pretence at friendship was gone. That worried him, but only because of the man outside. Durrani was younger and fitter than he was, but he was still sure he could handle him. Despite the bravado, Durrani had the air of a man who had never been in a fight, either on the sports field or off. And he was small, relatively speaking. But two against one – that wouldn't work. Suddenly the front passenger door opened and the other man climbed in. 'Clean,' he said. 'I can't see anything, boss.' He had an odd accent, something foreign.

'Give me the detector,' Durrani said. Ross watched,

trying to work out what the real threat might be. He definitely felt threatened, but nobody was blocking his door or holding him. He could turn and get out and run at any time. So why was his scalp prickling? Why was his heart so loud, the sweat running down his neck?

The scruffy man passed Durrani a small box with an aerial and some buttons and lights. It was like something out of a silly spy movie. Durrani messed around with it then looked at it intently.

'What are you doing?' Ross asked him.

'Checking if you're bugged.'

'For Christ's sake. Why would I be bugged?'

Durrani ignored him, attention on the device. 'Phones off,' he said after a moment. He took a mobile out and switched it off with one hand. In the front seat the greasy man did the same. 'Yours too,' Durrani said, looking at him. 'It won't work otherwise.'

Ross sighed, feeling irritation, but not enough to get past the inexplicable anxiety. He took his phone out. Durrani took it off him. Not roughly. He just reached across, took it and passed it to the man in the front seat, who then switched it off. 'You won't be needing that,' Durrani said quietly, head down on the electronic device. 'Not for a bit.' After a few seconds he pressed a switch then put it down on the seat beside him. 'Maybe you're not bugged,' he said. 'But do you know why our solicitors have backed out?'

Ross opened his mouth to ask a question, then he realised what he had been told, closed it, thought about it. So *that* was what was going on. 'There's a problem with the solicitors?' he asked.

'You could say that. They've quit. Told me they won't do it . . .'

'Why?'

Durrani stared at him. The man in the front seat was turned round and staring at him too.

'You tell me,' Durrani said. 'They say they will have to submit suspicious transaction reports to the Metropolitan Police. So what do you think they know? And how?'

'I haven't a clue. This is the first I knew of this—'

'You sure about that?'

'Of course . . .'

'You sure you didn't have a little word with them, say something about me?'

'Like what?'

'I don't know. But I'm going to find out.'

'I don't know what you're talking about. What do you mean – you're going to find out?'

'You're going to tell me. Because I'm going to make you tell me.' Durrani said it calmly, then looked at his fingernails.

'Have you gone completely mad?'

Durrani laughed. 'No. I don't think so.' He nodded at the man in the front. 'Get him out,' he said.

The man opened his door, got out, started walking around the car.

'Let's go for a little walk in the woods,' Durrani said.

Ross could feel his heart going into overdrive now. 'Is this some kind of joke?' he asked, voice high-pitched. He was thinking about his daughters. What would he tell them if it came to some kind of fight with this man, if the police found out, if everything he had done was discovered? Beside him his door opened and the other man was standing right beside him. He saw there was a short, filleting knife in his hand. Not pointed at him, just held loosely. The man reached in and placed a hand on his arm. Suddenly the extent of the problem came home to him. He had misread the entire situation. He started to tremble.

'No,' Durrani said. 'No joke. No joke at all.'

12

Paul had spent most of the last twenty-four hours looking
into Pasha Durrani – and what he had discovered had not
been welcome – but he'd passed little of it back to Lara and
Chris.

Paul had an 'uncle' in Manchester called James Chapman
– uncle Jimmy. He wasn't a real relative, but had been
around as long as Paul could recall, always kind to him,
always ready to help, something which had been especially
important in the months after his dad had been shot. Paul
had assumed back then that Jimmy was a friend of his
father, but later discovered from his mother that Chapman
was a notorious Manchester drugs importer, a man who had
employed his father as protection for many years. Paul
guessed his mum loathed Chapman, but the antipathy
hadn't got in the way of practicalities. Far from it. Paul had
spent his teens thinking of Jimmy as a kind of surrogate
father, mainly because if they ever needed money Jimmy
was the provider, and usually, when that happened, he
would come round to the house, ask after Paul and give
him some kind of paternal lecture on keeping out of
trouble. It was because of Jimmy that Paul had been able to
continue at The Academy after his father had died.

So now it was James Chapman he turned to first for information on Pasha Durrani. These days Chapman owned

night clubs and casinos in Spain and Holland. He spent most of the year at a place in southern Spain, visiting the UK and Holland only if he had to. Paul spoke to him by mobile and was surprised to learn that Chapman hadn't needed time to look into Pasha Durrani. He knew him already.

'Not someone you should be mixing with, son,' he'd said. 'What's the problem?'

'No problem. Just a job.' Paul explained that he had known Pasha's sister at school.

'Things are different now,' Chapman said. 'He's a big boy now. Tell us more about the job.'

'Someone I'm meant to be watching has a problem with him.'

'Then they should be very careful.'

'What's he into?'

'He does work for Raheesh Khan. You know Raheesh?'

'I've heard of him.' He hadn't.

'Raheesh is a powerful man. Employed your dad once. I wouldn't cross him. Not ever.'

'What does Pasha Durrani do for him?'

'I don't know the detail. The rumour is they're family, somehow. So be careful. It goes deep with that lot. It's never just business. They're not like us. No matter what you do for them they've still got their heads in the extremist filth they came from. Wouldn't surprise me if Khan was funding al-Qaeda. Keep off it, son. That's my advice.'

It was racist, of course. James Chapman was nothing if not typical of his class and type, with experiences and views Paul was far from sharing. But Paul still had to take the information seriously. So he checked with two contacts picked up through jobs in Afghanistan, both now living in London, one with connections in the Met. It took them longer to get back to him, but when they did the information had been the same. Pasha Durrani was connected. Keep clear.

Paul tried to marry the image of the Pasha Durrani he'd known vaguely as a child with the present more threatening figure. That wasn't easy. Pasha was three years older than Lara, and had gone to a different school, so contact had been limited, but Paul couldn't recall him being in any Asian gangs or involved in violence or crime.

That things were now different was both worrying and reassuring. Paul had a good idea how major criminals worked. Pasha Durrani wasn't going to do anything too risky or conspicuous. He wanted his sister to marry someone – Lara had told him all about that – wanted that badly enough to have left a ring of bruises round her neck when he'd lost patience with her refusals. But that had been in his own home, between family. He would think long and hard about making things more public or dramatic. Paul wanted time to consider how best to react to Pasha, but meanwhile his plan was to stick close to Chris, just in case he was missing a piece of the jigsaw. If Pasha was going to really hurt someone, it wasn't going to be his own sister.

For tonight that meant covering Chris at a Turn Again gig in Finsbury Park. The venue was a pub named after and not far from what had once been The Rainbow – a legendary venue throughout the sixties and seventies. The pub had a big, low-ceilinged room built at the back; the bands played on a stage at the far end and the audience wandered in and out from the huge bar area, with drinks and food, and whatever took their fancy. There was no seating and the lighting was basic – a rack of spots so close to the stage Paul thought they might burn Chris's face. There were rooms off to the side of the stage, next to the toilets used by the patrons, where you could set up. The pub charged a twenty quid entrance fee and gave 40 per cent of the gate to the band. Chris had warned him that the place would get packed.

The pub provided bouncers on the main doors, but nothing in the hall itself. That had worried Lara more than Chris. Once she had departed with Jules, it had taken Paul less than twenty minutes on Wednesday to convince Chris that he would be safe to do this gig, that Paul would be right there should Lara's brother decide to walk in, which, he had insisted, was not going to happen.

But the truth was that he didn't know that for sure. So when ten o'clock came and the band wandered onto the stage to kick off he found himself standing anxiously at one side of the stage, scanning the rows of faces in the semi-darkness past the spots. He didn't think Pasha would show up in person, but it was an all too easy matter to pay some loser to throw something or jump up and have a go.

Chris started the set with the title song from the newly cut disc. By then there was only a little space left at the back of the hall and the crowd was dense at the front, pressed up against the stage. Chris stepped back and started a series of long sustained guitar chords, head down and on the instrument, but the bassist was still chatting to someone at the front. Chris had to look over to him and shout something before he finally stood back and started playing. Then the place woke up. At the front they were dancing immediately, at the back a loud cheer broke out.

The song was typical of what Chris wrote, an uneasy combination of heavy, poetic lyrics and sinuous, beautiful melodies, some catchy, some more challenging, all of them sung with a haunting, unique voice which was totally original, a cross between a throaty black soul growl and a higher, more melodic, modern Manchester thing. Behind it all, a good solid dance beat. Paul knew how his friend sounded from the recordings he'd heard, but they didn't do justice to the live experience. In the flesh, Paul had heard nothing quite like it. For the first four songs he forgot the mass of faces and arms and just stood watching Chris.

The volume, as usual, was loud enough to make the bass strike your chest like a blow. Paul's initial position had placed him right next to the rack for the bass, so he had to move back quickly. He ended up slightly behind the band and halfway through the door leading off to the changing rooms and toilets. From there it was difficult to see the hall clearly past the glare from the spots, so he decided to squeeze down the sides until he was in a better position. He stepped backwards and almost tripped over someone. Turning, he was surprised to see Jules, Lara's friend, standing right behind him. He mouthed an apology, but she moved off, beckoning him to follow. They ended up in the narrow corridor that led down the side of the hall, with the wall between the band and themselves. That meant he could hear her better, but he could see nothing.

'Are you on guard?' she asked him, still having to shout above the music.

He glanced back anxiously, then remembered his fears – Chris's fears – were probably foolish. He took a breath. He could give it a moment. 'Yes. Is Lara here?'

Julie shook her head. She was holding an unlit cigarette. 'She won't come out. Too scared.'

'She's been to work?'

Another shake of the head. 'She thinks Pasha will kidnap her.' She frowned, looking angry. 'He told her he could do that. I can't get her to do anything but sit around worrying. I went to her place in Clapham this afternoon, picked up some stuff. But maybe you need to speak to her.'

Whilst he thought about that Julie started to say something else, but her voice was too low to pick it up. He leaned towards her, shaking his head and pointing at his ear. He caught a trace of some scent coming off her, then his eyes flicked over her as he moved. She was wearing a short black leather jacket and a skirt that stopped just above her knees. She had long, finely toned legs. She looked like a fan, like any of the others out there. But beautiful. She had turned her nose up at Chris's music when they'd been talking about it yesterday, like it was an in-joke between the three of them that she hated it.

'Why are you here?' he shouted. 'I thought you hated this stuff?'

She put her lips right against his ear and hissed into it, gently enough to be intimate, but loud enough to hear. 'I do. I'm here because I'm worried. I came to see you.' Her hand held his arm as she spoke.

He moved his head back and looked at her. His ear was tingling, slightly damp from her breath. She was standing very close to him, but that was because she had to, because there was no chance of hearing if she didn't. There was no good reason why she should be holding his arm though. He didn't know what to say. Behind them the band started another number. 'I have to get back in there,' he shouted.

She held up her cigarette. 'You smoke?'

He shook his head. He hadn't smoked in three years.

'I'll go out the side door and smoke,' she said. 'Come out when you can. I need to speak to you properly.' The words were spoken like an instruction. She turned and walked away, heading for the door by the toilets. He was about to shout after her, but right then Chris stopped singing, mid-lyric. Paul heard a falter in the beat. The bass and the drums kept going, but Chris was silent – no voice, no guitar. Paul stepped back through the doorway and saw Chris had stepped back from the lights and mike, and was staring out towards where Paul had been standing, desperately looking for him. There was a look of panic on his face.

Paul stepped quickly up to the edge of the stage. Chris saw him and took the guitar off. Paul could see the drummer frowning. He'd met both the other band members earlier. They hadn't seemed much like Chris. More like what you'd expect from a band. The bassist was stoned. They had both been friendly enough, but the drummer was scowling at him now, as if he were responsible for pulling Chris away mid-song.

'They're here,' Chris yelled at him, once he was close enough.

Paul cupped his ear and shouted back: 'Who?' He was right by the bass rack again, barely able to hear a thing.

Chris dragged his arm and took him away from the stage, into the doorway he had just come from. There was a half-hearted boo from some of the crowd, the drum and bass beat went on.

'The guys who jumped me,' Chris said. His eyes looked frightened. 'They're out there. They made a sign, pointed at me . . .'

'OK. Stay calm.' Paul put a hand on his arm. 'I'll go and speak to them, chuck them out. OK?'

Chris nodded furiously. 'OK. OK.' There was sweat all over his face and chest.

'Don't worry about it,' Paul said. 'Get back up there. It's sorted. OK?'

Chris's eyes looked doubtful. 'OK,' he said again. From behind him Paul could hear the drummer shouting something at him, off mike.

'Where in the crowd?' Paul asked. 'Whereabouts were they?'

'The back. They came forward, pointed, then went back. I think they were heading out.'

'All right.' He gave Chris an encouraging push back towards the stage then followed him, heading right into the front row. The bodies parted. He had his hands up to his eyes, shading them from the fierce glare, looking past it. He stood still for a moment, people pushing up against him, the drum beat assaulting his ears.

Once his eyes adjusted, he scanned the crowd around him, taking his time. He squeezed to the side wall and started to work his way towards the back. To his left he saw the doors onto the corridor leading down the side of the hall. They were wide open.

He walked quickly over. This was the way to the toilets, to the rear exit and to the dressing rooms – the area where he had only just been talking to Jules. There was a handful of people headed for the toilets. At the far end, opposite the stage entrance where he had just spoken to Chris, the rear doors into the alleyway outside were open. Jules had presumably gone out there for her fag. He ran up – not sprinting, but fast, slightly worried that the two guys might have doubled back and used this route to the stage. But when he got back up there and the music rushed at him again, all he could see was Chris and the band, still going in the lights. He turned to the open outside exit – a fire exit, in fact – then stepped over to it.

The air was cool on his face, but thick with the smell of rotting garbage. The alley ran between the hall and the adjoining building. The walls were high, red brick scrawled with graffiti and torn posters for bands who'd played in the pub. He could hear voices, tense. About halfway along the alley he could see a huddle of figures. He started to run towards them instinctively, before he was even sure who it was.

They separated out as he approached. Jules, back against the wall, voice high and strained, and two men in front of her, blocking her in. One with a hand on the wall beside her head, the other very close to her, hands in front so Paul couldn't see them. They both turned as they heard his feet, then spoke quickly to each other. He picked up speed. He had to cover about fifty feet to get to them. Jules shouted out to him, a shout for help and a warning, her voice frightened. He shouted back, as loud as he could. Then suddenly the two guys broke and were running, away from him, off towards the street. He passed Jules, going at full sprint now, noticing only in his peripheral vision her rigid face, the way she was holding her bag to her chest. He was gaining on the last one, who kept looking back. A young Asian, maybe only twenty years old, much slighter than him. If he could catch him there wouldn't be a problem.

Then they were out into the street and really running. He pulled up and caught his breath, watching them flee. They split up at once, as if by pre-arrangement, but didn't slacken their pace once they knew he'd stopped. He watched them until they were out of sight, then ran back to Jules.

She was standing by the wall crying. He put a hand on her shoulder, told her they were gone, then breathlessly asked her what had happened. He was assuming it was an attempted robbery, but he was wrong.

'They wanted Lara,' she said. 'They followed me here from her flat. They wanted to know where she was. They went through my bag. They were looking for my address, my keys . . .'

'Is that where Lara is now?'

She nodded. 'She's at my place.'

'Did they get your address? Did they get anything that would tell them where she was?'

'No. I grabbed it off them.'

'You did well.' He stood beside her and put an arm awkwardly round her, trying to seem reassuring. 'They're gone,' he said. 'Nothing to worry about now.' She was shaking like a leaf. 'Did they say anything else?' he asked, as gently as he could.

'One had a knife,' she said. 'He held it to my chest. I was so frightened. He said he was going to kill me if I didn't tell them where she was.'

13

At eleven Andy stood under the trees at the end of his back garden and spoke to Luntley on his mobile. Helen and the kids were already in bed. Luntley had just taken the shift change at Acton and had been unavailable since he'd knocked off earlier in the day, so didn't have a clue what had gone on since Durrani had eyeballed Andy in the service station. Andy explained it all to him: 'I was in meetings all day,' he said, speaking very quietly. He stooped under the lower branches of a plum tree and peered through the bushes by the five foot fence that bordered the property. 'Stanesby decided we should get the cover back up,' he said. 'Get the probes on line again, get a team back on Durrani and a team on Napier, but it took so fucking long to reach the decision we were too late. Durrani had vanished.'

'What about the tracker in his Jag?'

'That's working, but the Jag was found abandoned in a lay-by off the M1, near Nottingham. He's loose and free. Has been nearly all day. He could have been doing anything. He could have been right here, in fact. That's my worry. That it was no coincidence.' He parted the bushes and looked down the dimly lit service alley which ran down the back of houses. There was no movement, no one there.

'How would that work, boss?' Luntley asked. 'I don't get it.'

'Nor do I. If it wasn't a coincidence then he got my details from inside, from one of our team, or someone higher up.'

'Or someone with access to the computer systems. That could be a couple of thousand people, including civilian staff. Doesn't mean the team's dirty.'

'That's what Stanesby kept saying. They're looking into it, they say. Meanwhile I'm here and there's no chance of me sleeping tonight. Not until we find Durrani.' He walked back towards the house and stood in the shadows there, looking out whilst he briefed Luntley on what teams were available, which resources to prioritise, what the chain of command would be for the night. 'I was promised three teams,' he said. 'One on Napier, in case Durrani goes for him, one on Durrani's Richmond address, and a reserve. Then there's you, co-ordinating it, and two from Dev Johal's teams to assist you. They should already be on. If they didn't show then let me know. Call me any time. I probably won't sleep. I want to know as soon as we find him. Got it?'

He went back in and locked the doors, double-checking every lock. They had an alarm system which they never used because it had gone off too many times for no reason, scaring the kids, but he set it now so that all the downstairs rooms were covered. On the way up the stairs he scanned the street through the curtains. No sign of the local uniforms yet. Snowden had promised to arrange a presence in the street, but Andy expected that nothing would come of it. The local division would have their hands full with volume crime – the drunks, the fights, the burglaries. They wouldn't want to waste resources on the unfounded suspicions of another command.

So he crept into bed next to Helen and lay there, staring

at the ceiling, consciousness fixed on any and every little noise he could hear around the house.

An hour later he was put out of his misery. His mobile started to vibrate on the bedside table. He got up and crept into the bathroom next to their room to take the call.

'We've found him,' Luntley said.

Andy sighed. 'Thank God for that.'

'That's the good news.'

'Where is he?'

'That's the bad news. He's at Napier's flat in Camden. He arrived about ten minutes ago and let himself in via the communal entrance. He buzzed someone in one of the other flats and spun a line. They let him in.'

Andy swore. 'Is he alone?'

'Yes.'

'Which team is covering the flat? Remind me.'

'No team. It's Dan Barrett. He's alone, in a car . . .'

'Is Napier still in Finsbury Park?'

'Yes. But the B team had him and they're done for the night. Dan is all that's left.'

The resources weren't enough. Not enough to plug all the holes.

'Dan wants instructions,' Luntley said.

Andy started to think about it, his brain clearing quickly now he knew Durrani was nowhere near Helen and the kids. 'We need to get a team in to stay with Durrani,' he said. 'I'll call Snowden about it . . .'

'Dan wants to know what to do if Napier comes back, boss. That's what he's worried about.'

'Something is going to happen, clearly.'

'Or he wouldn't be there. Right. He's waiting for Napier, obviously.'

'Where exactly is he?'

'Dan thinks he's in the communal part, the stairwell area. He hasn't seen him use the lifts or stairs.'

Andy thought some more. 'OK. Dan will have to cover it,' he said. 'Tell him to stay fresh. He'll have to watch it as best he can. If Durrani is just going to put the kid against the wall and threaten him then we can keep out of it. If it goes further then Dan will have to intervene. But he should try to do that without identifying himself.' He paused. 'You got that?'

'Yes. But what if the target doesn't do any talking? What if he just jumps out and drops Napier?'

Andy twisted his face into a grimace. It was possible. 'I don't think so,' he said. *Christ*. Could he take this decision? 'I don't think he'll do that. But I'll take my orders from Snowden and get back to you.'

14

Friday, 28th May, 2010

It was nearly two by the time Chris got back to Camden, by which time he was utterly exhausted. It was the same after every gig. He put everything into it, ended up in a clumsy daze. The buzz and frenzy of standing up there, the crowd all dancing and singing along, led to a kind of manic euphoria. When that passed he often felt low and lonely, no matter how much company he had. The drink didn't help. There hadn't been too much of that tonight, but all the same the high was long past as the cab left him standing in the street outside his apartment block.

The doorway was operated by punching in a code, which he was prone to forget frequently as it was changed every two months. He stood for a moment with his finger paused over the keypad, guitar in his other hand, the rucksack with his music and gear heavy on his back, trying to recall the latest set of numbers.

He pressed the buttons on the doorpad. Nothing happened. 'Fuck,' he said, aloud. He stepped back and tried to think. Four numbers. He tried a new sequence – 5079. The system buzzed and the door clicked open. He smiled, pushed it further ajar, and stepped in.

The light switch was to his left. He reached for it, but

right at that point his phone started to ring. He tried to get it out of his jacket pocket, but fumbled around in the dark, then had to put the guitar and rucksack down and open his jacket. He got it out in time for the last ring to reverberate too loud around the dark hallway. Too late. He hoped it hadn't woken the couple who lived in the ground floor flat. Then he remembered they were away for a couple of weeks, on holiday. He looked down at the screen and saw it had been Paul trying him. He would call him when he got upstairs, he decided. Paul had completely disappeared about halfway through the gig. There had been some texts from him, but Chris hadn't managed to read them yet. His hand was almost touching the light switch when he heard the movement towards him.

He spun quickly. Someone was coming at him from the shadows behind, moving very fast. He had time to see something swinging towards him, then the world lit up. A bright blaze of white and orange.

There was a gap. Nothing happening, just thick, silent darkness. Then a sensation of something spinning away from him. Then – crash! - noise in his ears. He saw it all happening again. A man swinging something at his head, the crack as it struck his left temple, the shatter of glass. He realised he was already on the floor, holding his head, shouting something. There was wetness all down one side of his face, in his eyes, someone holding the front of his jacket. 'Shit! What have you done? Shit!' The words were coming out of his mouth but he felt detached from them, like it was someone else speaking. He couldn't see properly. He struggled to get his feet to work, to scramble backwards, out of the way, but couldn't get anything to move. What had happened?

'You listen to me, you little white fucker . . .'

His vision cleared. His hands moved. He wiped his eyes. He was breathing in big, shocked gasps.

'*You listen well. Because this is your last fucking chance. Can you feel that?*'

The man's face was right in front of his. Chris was on the floor, on his back, the man was bending over him, his breath all over him.

'*Can you feel that?*'

He realised with horror that it was Lara's brother. Here, in the flesh. Finally, he recognised him. He tried to say his name – Pasha – but his mouth wouldn't move.

'*That's a broken bottle pressed against your neck you little cunt. I could kill you now.*'

He couldn't feel a thing. He started to shake uncontrollably.

'*You keep off my sister. You never see her again. Not even once. Got that? Because if . . .*'

A noise from the side – from the direction of the street? Suddenly Pasha was standing. Chris heard the thing that had been in his hand drop. Someone was pounding furiously on the glass door to the street, almost breaking it in. Pasha yanked it open and Chris had a glimpse of a short, muscular man, black, yelling something. Then Pasha was pushing past him and running. The man turned as if to chase, but stopped. Chris managed to get himself turned over. His legs were working. He wiped the stuff out of his eyes again and saw that it was bright red. Blood. He could feel it pulsing steadily out of his scalp. 'Shit,' he said. 'Shit.'

Then the man was leaning down beside him, telling him to sit back, to take it easy. 'I'll get an ambulance,' he said. 'Just stay still.'

15

Andy got the call at ten to three. Unable to sleep, he'd been sitting downstairs drinking tea in the darkened house, waiting. When the phone buzzed he expected it would be Luntley. Instead, Snowden's number flashed up.

Snowden told him Durrani had attacked Chris Napier with a bottle. Napier was in A&E at St Mary's, taken there by DC Dan Barrett. Durrani was on his way back to Richmond with a team following him. He wasn't behaving as if he knew he was being watched, so maybe they were still in business. *A close shave*, Snowden said.

The understatement of the year, Andy thought.

After the call, Andy cut the connection and sat in silence, thinking hard. Above him, from one of the bedrooms, he heard one of the kids cry in their sleep. He couldn't be sure which. As they had got older their cries had got more and more similar. He waited to see if Helen woke up. When she didn't he tiptoed back up to their room and slid into bed beside her. She mumbled something and he put a hand onto her side. She felt red hot. 'Everything's OK,' he whispered. 'Just sleep.'

It was another hour before he drifted off, though, and even then he kept waking up, imagining he could hear things downstairs. It was nearly five before he really started to sleep properly.

An hour later he was suddenly awake, the mobile buzzing again. He fumbled clumsily in the darkness, found it and held it to his ear. 'John James Ross,' Luntley said.

Andy looked around him. He was in his bed alone. Helen must have gone into the other room, with Sophie. He had heard nothing. He sat up, rubbed his eyes and peered at the time on the alarm clock. 'It's six o'clock,' he said, confused.

'Sorry,' Luntley said. 'But Essex police have found Ross. You remember who Ross is?'

'Ross? John James Ross? The guy Durrani is doing the scam with?'

'That's him. He's been murdered.'

The post mortem was being done at East Ham morgue, for reasons unknown to Andy. It was scheduled for eight thirty. He managed to get a number for the DI in effective control of the Essex enquiry, rang him, spoke to a DC and arranged to meet at the morgue at ten.

Luntley had been notified of Ross's death because they had a flag against Ross's name on the PNC. For security reasons the flag didn't identify the interested unit, and only required notification of any information to an anonymous office in New Scotland Yard. The Essex force had complied and made contact.

For once the kids slept late. Andy left at nine, without seeing either Helen or Magnus and Sophie. He was relieved to see a marked car not fifty feet from the house, two uniformed officers inside, both awake. He thought they might be sufficient deterrent, given they now had a team on Durrani anyway, and Helen had told him last night she was going to be in all morning, but he still felt nervous leaving her. He planned to be back long before lunch.

The morgue was in a sixties building that looked like a

school, from the outside, on East Ham High Street. Andy parked illegally on the High Street and ran in. A DC from Essex Major Investigations met him in an empty public waiting room and then disappeared down a corridor to notify his DI. It was after ten now and the autopsy was still going on. After a few minutes a thin man appeared, average height, with thinning light brown hair, and glasses, in hospital whites and latex gloves, slipping a mask from his face as he came towards Andy. 'DI Carl Aderhold,' he said, holding his hand out.

'Andy Macall.' He shook the gloved hand reluctantly. The man had just emerged from the autopsy room. Andy hoped he hadn't been touching anything.

'What unit are you from?' Aderhold asked.

'SO15.'

'I see.' He nodded, thinking about that. What did his corpse have to do with terrorism, he was wondering? 'Is there something we should know about?' he asked.

'I have no idea,' Andy lied. 'There's a flag on the PNC, so I'm here. They don't tell me what it's about.'

Aderhold smiled slightly, aware that he was being fed a line. 'What do you want to know?'

'Can you tell me cause of death?' Andy asked.

Aderhold sat down on one of the chairs. He had tired eyes, Andy noted. Presumably he'd been up all night.

'It's all speculation really,' Aderhold started. 'Ross was found dead across the rear seats of his Range Rover, which was parked up in a fairly isolated spot within Epping Forest, near Loughton. He was found around ten last night and had probably been dead several hours. There was a trail of blood leading from the car into the woods. He had a single deep wound to the right thigh. My SIO thinks he was mugged.' He scratched his head and pulled a face, as if the words he'd spoken were barely believable. 'He thinks it went like this.

Two or more men found Ross walking in the woods. They jumped him, bound his hands and wrists, went through his pockets and found various cards. They then tortured him to obtain the PIN for his ATM card.'

Andy frowned. 'Torture? Like what?'

Aderhold shook his head. 'They very carefully . . .' He stretched his right leg out. 'They very precisely cut an area of his trousers away. Here.' He moved the hospital gown aside and indicated a square area on his upper thigh. 'Then they used their extensive anatomical knowledge to make a precise incision in the thigh, severing the femoral artery.' He looked up at Andy and raised his eyebrows. 'Then they applied a tourniquet and requested the PIN. Simple. No PIN they remove the tourniquet.'

Andy's turn to shake his head. 'That's all very exact,' he said. 'You know all this already?'

'That's what my SIO *thinks* happened. What we *know* is that the material was cut from the trouser leg and the muscle opened with a very sharp implement. Not slashed. A very precise cut. The cut severed the femoral artery and there *was* a tourniquet applied. His hands and feet were very tightly bound. All this happened in the forest, about twenty-five feet from the car he had come in. He probably limped back to the car himself, having been cut free, somehow, bleeding heavily – as opposed to being dragged there. That's what we *know*.'

'Not slashed? He was stabbed, then? Is that what you mean?'

'It's Prof. Greville in there,' Aderhold said. 'He's usually reliable. He says this is a precise *incision* to sever the femoral artery, by someone who knew it was there.'

'A doctor? A surgeon?'

'Hardly. You can learn anatomy from the net these days.'

'And this is the cause of death?'

'Yes. He bled to death. Without the tourniquet it takes about twenty minutes to lose sufficient blood to pass out. Most of the bleeding was done in the forest.'

'No emergency call?'

'No. No mobile recovered. He has one, so we assume they took it. We're trying to trace it.'

'And no tourniquet. Once they were gone he could have put another one on, in the car.'

'I suppose he was either too weak by then or they sat with him, until he bled to death.'

'All for an ATM PIN?'

'It's not my theory, as I say.'

'What do *you* think happened?'

'It looks organised to me, professional. They tortured him, for sure. They cut his leg open and threatened to let him bleed to death. But I doubt they were after a PIN.'

Andy looked quickly away from him. *Christ*, he thought. Suddenly he knew exactly why it had happened. Aderhold was still talking, speculating about drugs crime, but Andy wasn't listening now. 'I have to make a call,' he said.

As they stepped out of the room a uniform PC was bringing a red-faced woman through the public doors. The woman was walking normally, speaking: 'There will be some kind of mistake,' she was saying. 'My husband was not the kind to go for walks in the woods. It cannot be him.' Her voice was high, imperious, public school, but trembling beneath the false courage. Andy stopped and turned to Aderhold. 'Who did the ID?' he whispered. Clearly it hadn't been the wife. That would be why she was here now, to confirm it. 'Are you sure it's John James Ross?'

'We used a business partner. It's definitely him. The wife is here to confirm.' He moved away from Andy towards

Ross's wife. Andy watched him greet her, then point to the room they had just come from. They walked past him in silence, the woman shaking visibly. Her world was about to collapse around her. Andy tried to recall what he knew about Ross. Did he have two young daughters?

He waited until they had gone in and closed the door before calling Snowden on his mobile. 'Has someone called Durrani's solicitors?' he whispered. 'Has that already been done?'

'Yes. Where are you? What's up?'

'When?'

There was a pause. 'Tuesday afternoon. Right after our meeting. Pearce's team handled it.'

'Who did they say they were? What was the cover?'

Snowden sighed. 'Ross. One of the buyers. They said they were from his company. This was before you told us Ross was the guy Durrani was doing the scam with . . .'

'Christ almighty. I knew it.'

'What's the problem? Where are you?'

'They haven't told you? I'm at East Ham morgue. Ross is fucking dead. Durrani killed him.'

Silence.

'We did this,' Andy said. 'We killed this man.' He began to pace up and down.

'Can anyone hear you, Andy?' Snowden asked calmly. 'Shut the fuck up if they can.'

Andy walked through the entrance doors into East Ham High Street. The traffic was loud. 'We should have thought it through,' he shouted into the phone. 'This was a fuck up. A total fuck up. Durrani thinks Ross stitched him up – told the solicitors about their little scam. So he fucking killed him. It's our fault. We have to come clean on this. The enquiry are saying it was a mugging. We have to come clean and get them onto Durrani.'

16

'And where is he now?'

Phil Rathmore asked the question from the other side of the room. They were somewhere within the Ministry of Justice building on Petty France, in an empty second floor room that Paul had been escorted to, super-politely, by a civil servant.

Rathmore was dressed much as he had been when Paul had last met him, five days ago, but the air of wealthy languor was gone. He looked decidedly stressed and anxious now.

The room was large enough to be a meeting room, but there was no table at all, just a selection of chairs stacked against the walls and a layer of undisturbed dust over most surfaces. Paul guessed it was being used as a storeroom, and that it was as far out of the way as Rathmore could arrange.

When Paul had finally got him on the mobile Rathmore had made it clear he was unhappy to even speak to him, until Paul had given him the gist of what had happened. Now he was pacing the space available, obviously disturbed by Paul's presence there, too close to interests that could damage him. 'They're both at the place you got for me,' Paul said. He stood at the other end of the room, legs apart, roughly in the 'at ease' position. He fixed his eyes on

Rathmore and kept still. It was just like waiting for a dressing down from an officer.

'Both?'

'Chris and Lara. She came first thing this morning.'

'Lara.' Rathmore said the word with obvious distaste. Not the reaction Paul would have expected. Chris had always given him the impression his father had liked Lara. Rathmore looked at his watch, perhaps the fifth time he had done so. 'I remember her only vaguely,' he said. 'She's a Pakistani. I remember that.'

Paul had just finished telling him almost everything he knew about Pasha Durrani, and everything that had happened in the last twenty hours, culminating in him bringing Chris back from hospital in a cab and Lara's arrival a little later. Rathmore had paced around, head down, saying little whilst Paul spoke. There had been a few questions here and there, but no real surprise. Paul had the distinct feeling that he was telling Rathmore a lot that he already knew.

'And he's not seriously hurt?' Rathmore asked again.

'He has a sore head and ten stitches to a gash in his scalp. He's shocked and disturbed. But his skull isn't broken and the wound will heal OK. They didn't keep him in.'

'Thank God for that.'

As the band had been finishing the set Paul had left the venue to take Jules to King's Cross. He'd come immediately back to Finsbury Park, only to find the band already departed from the venue, in search, he was told, of some other place to 'wind down'. He assumed Chris had not got his text messages asking him to wait. That had made him feel guilty even then – given he was supposed to be minding Chris – though not half as much as he was later to feel. From Finsbury Park he had tried unsuccessfully to raise Chris via his mobile, then finally found a cab to get him to

Camden, just in time to find a neighbour cleaning copious quantities of blood from the hallway of Chris's block, at nearly three in the morning. Chris, he had been told, was at St Mary's.

By the time he had got there the man who had brought Chris, in his own car, was gone, and a nurse was applying a dressing to Chris's head. The police had been called, but hadn't showed. Just as well, as Chris was adamant that he couldn't speak to them – not until he'd first spoken to Lara. He'd had an X-ray, but no scan, no blood transfusion. The man who had brought him had used effective first aid, apparently. Chris was feeling sickly and wobbly, but an hour later he was duly discharged into Paul's care with advice about concussion symptoms and a check-up with his own doctor. There was no question of giving him a night in hospital. Not these days.

They had got back to Paul's around four, Chris sleeping in the cab, then in Paul's bed, whilst Paul wandered around, waiting until seven before calling Rathmore.

'And the police came to see him this morning?' Rathmore asked. 'Tell me again what was said.'

A policeman had finally showed up at just after nine, before Lara's arrival.

'Chris wouldn't tell him anything,' Paul said. 'Lara wouldn't want it – wouldn't want her brother arrested. I think that's why he refused.' Chris had insisted that he would not make a complaint. Paul had silently watched the little verbal tussle that followed – the uniformed PC insisting it would be in Chris's best interests to give a statement, Chris insisting there was nothing to say. Paul thought he did well to stick to his guns, though had felt uneasy about it. He knew very well the problem, of course: Lara and Chris had already had long conversations about whether to involve the police, some of which had resulted in arguments. Lara was dead set against, Chris less so. But Chris's determination had made Paul suspect that there must be some direct threat to Lara that he wasn't aware of.

'I wasn't mentioned?' Rathmore asked. He cleared his throat, unhappy to voice the question.

Was this *the* burning question for him, Paul wondered. Was this his real concern, the real reason he had contracted Paul to watch Chris? A rumour starting about his past, spelling the end of his political career.

'No,' Paul replied. 'You weren't mentioned. Why would you be?'

'Because I'm his father.'

Paul shrugged that off. 'My main worry,' he said, 'is that Durrani is the type of person who might not stop with a warning. Did you know about him when you first spoke to me?' It was the first time he had asked the question directly.

Rathmore shook his head without looking at him. 'Of course not.'

'Did you know there was a specific threat to Chris?'

'I would have told you if I'd known.'

Something about the tone of his response made Paul almost sure he was lying.

'And what's to be done now?' Rathmore asked.

Paul shrugged. 'I think you need to try to find out more about Durrani. Chris and Lara won't involve the police . . .' He paused, to see again if Rathmore wanted to react to that. He didn't. Paul would have expected some kind of insistence on police involvement, but clearly that was too frightening a prospect. Paul had looked Rathmore up on the net. He was a junior minister, with some kind of responsibility for police policy in the House of Lords. He stood to lose a lot if the story of Chris's existence got to some tabloid journalist. 'But I'm sure the police must know about Durrani,' Paul continued. 'Maybe you can get them to put some pressure on him.'

'Out of the question. I can ask about him, maybe, but I can't abuse the position I'm in. The better way forward is for you to get Chris to leave her.'

'Sorry?' Paul frowned. Had he really heard that? 'Get Chris to leave Lara, you mean?'

'Yes. That solves Chris's problem. That's the easiest way. The only way.'

Paul was astonished. 'It doesn't solve anything,' he said. 'Chris and Lara are close. Very close. Chris isn't going to leave her because of this.' He laughed at the idea. 'It doesn't work like that.'

'Doesn't it? I know he was keen on this girl when he was younger, but he's older now. He has to be reasonable. You have to bring some pressure to bear, I think. You've been around. You know how it is. Think of a way.' He walked closer to Paul, eyes on him now. 'I can arrange a bonus if you can pull it off.' He smiled suddenly.

Paul held his tongue with difficulty. He felt the blood flush his skin. Not embarrassment – though the suggestion was certainly embarrassing – but anger. He was feeling what Chris would have felt, had this man stood here and suggested that to his face.

'A handsome bonus,' Rathmore said, not noticing anything. 'Say one month's pay. Was that seven thousand? I'll pay that if you can do it.'

Paul shook his head. He wanted to say something, but didn't trust himself not to shout if he opened his mouth.

Rathmore noticed the emotion now. He looked away. 'I'm so glad you're in on this, Paul,' he said, smoothly. 'You're my only link to my son. If I had him here, now, standing where you are, then I'd give him a little paternal talk. I'd explain to him.' He began to pace again, presumably thinking about what he might say.

'That wouldn't work,' Paul said.

'No. I'm aware of that. That's why I brought you in . . .'

'Nothing like that will work.'

'But there's nothing else to be done, is there? They won't involve the police. So what are the options? There aren't any. He has to leave her.'

There was a knock at the door. Rathmore stopped speaking, looking at it. It opened and the same civil servant stepped in. 'They're waiting for you, minister,' he said quietly.

Rathmore looked at his watch again. 'Damn. Yes. Tell them I'll only be a few moments, William.' He waited for the door to close on the man then marched over to Paul. 'Get them to stop seeing each other for a while,' he said. 'A cooling-off period. To think about things. If you can do that I'll reward you . . .'

'I don't want a reward.'

'Well, do it for Chris then.' He almost snapped the words out. 'It's the only thing that can be done.'

'Have you got somewhere they can go to?'

Rathmore frowned. 'How do you mean?'

'I'm not happy with them in my place. I think Durrani might already know about it. It's too close to Chris's flat. But I need to think about what to do. I need some time. Have you got anywhere outside London where they can go for a while?'

'What's the point? What could you possibly do?'

'I don't know. But I'm not going to try to split them up.'

Rathmore took a deep breath, staring at him. Paul could see anger behind the eyes, but the face was trying to give nothing away, to hide it.

'When we were kids you had a place up north,' Paul said. 'Rathmore Hall. Maybe if—'

'That's sold. A long time ago.'

Paul nodded. 'OK. Well maybe I'll have to—'

'Let me think about it. I'm sure I'll come up with something.' He looked at his watch again. 'But meanwhile I have to be somewhere else. You've done well, Paul. You've done well so far.'

'I haven't done anything . . .'

'He isn't dead or seriously injured. I'm sure that's in some way down to your involvement. But you must think about what I've suggested. Not for the money, of course. But to solve this thing. It would be best for both of them, I think, if they weren't involved with each other. It's a cultural thing – all this trouble – it's a classic clash of cultures. Relationships across the racial divide don't usually work. This Lara might look like us, but she's not. You know that. An arranged marriage might seem mad to us, but that's the culture this girl comes from. She will return to it eventually – leave Chris high and dry. You have to convince him of that.'

Paul raised his eyebrows. He was almost sure this wasn't the sort of opinion Rathmore would have voiced during the recent general election campaign.

'It isn't going to go away,' Rathmore continued. 'It's part of what she is. Chris has to realise that. You have to get him to see that. You know about these people. You've lived with them. If you speak to him then he will take it from you. That's why you're there. To guide him.'

Paul shook his head again. 'I'm not going to do any of that,' he said. 'That's not the way to solve this.' He had to quit, he realised. He had to tell Rathmore he couldn't do

129

the job. Beneath the veneer Rathmore had racial views on a par with Jimmy Chapman's.

'I'll think about what you've said,' Rathmore said. 'But you have to think about what I've said. It makes sense. We can speak later today, by phone.' *By then you'll agree with me* – that was the implied conclusion. Rathmore was at the door already. He turned only momentarily. 'But meanwhile, you will remember the sensitivity,' he said. His guard dropped, and for a split second he looked like he might be really panicking inside. 'For God's sake don't let any of this get out. Not to anyone. I'm relying on you, Paul. I'm trusting you on that.'

17

Andy was back at Acton by eleven fifteen, focused on the feeds from Durrani's Richmond house. But nothing was happening. Durrani was in bed, sleeping the sleep of the innocent, completely unmoved by what he had done during the preceding twenty-four hours. Which Andy was certain included murdering Ross. The command team didn't agree, however. At eleven thirty Stanesby and Snowden showed up, wanting an urgent meet about it.

Stanesby brought someone with him – a man Andy had never met before. He looked mid-fifties, walked bolt upright and introduced himself with a curt shake of the hand as 'Jeff Fletch, from Thames House'. Andy looked blankly at him. Thames House? Did he mean the Security Service HQ?

'Jeff's our main Security Service liaison point,' Stanesby said, seeing that Andy hadn't got it.

MI5. What were they doing here?

He suffered the short walk to the tiny conference facility, a dingy little room with a circular table that would seat four, at a push. Four of them walked to the room – Andy, Stanesby, Snowden and Fletch – but when Andy got in and sat down he noticed that Snowden hadn't followed them in.

'Let's make this quick,' Stanesby said, immediately.

'The boss . . .' Andy said, pointing to the door, and meaning Snowden.

'He was showing us the way here,' Stanesby said. 'He's not invited. Just us three for this.'

'But we'll need him to . . .' He stopped himself.

They all sat down. Stanesby looked at Fletch, as if waiting for a cue, but Fletch didn't react. Stanesby had placed himself opposite Andy, but Fletch was sitting right next to him.

'We need to urgently co-ordinate our actions on this,' Stanesby said. 'So tell us what has been arranged so far with Johnson.'

'Johnson?'

'Mark Johnson. Your friend. You were to stop him giving damaging information to Raheesh Khan.'

Andy shifted uneasily in his seat. Stanesby had used Mark's actual name, not the Simon Parker codename. And why was he even mentioning that now? Twelve hours ago Durrani had killed someone. *That* was what they needed to urgently discuss.

'Did you hear me?' Stanesby asked, when he didn't respond at once.

'Yes . . .' He was frowning and staring at them, trying to work it out. 'But aren't we here to talk about the murder? To co-ordinate our response to *that*?'

Stanesby sat back, head against the wall behind him, and looked irritated. He had civvies on today. A grey suit. He took a pen from an inside pocket and twirled it a little. 'We'll come to that,' he said. 'First things first though. What did Johnson say? Did you get his agreement?'

Still frowning, still feeling confused, Andy shook his head. First things first? Clearly he was missing something. 'I stalled him,' he said. 'That was what I was asked to do. But he intends to go to Khan as planned. Obviously. That was what he was contracted to do by Khan. It's his liveli-hood. He has to . . .'

He stopped. Stanesby was shaking his head, looking at Fletch, but Fletch was now looking at a notebook he'd opened in front of him. He had on a pair of thin-framed reading glasses. There had to be a reason they were dis-cussing this in front of him. But what?

'I'm sorry,' Andy said. 'But don't the events of last night eclipse all this? Durrani has killed someone. At the moment the team investigating that death are ignorant of crucial information that we have . . .'

'We don't know that, of course.' It was Fletch who spoke, the first thing he had said since introducing himself. Andy shifted his chair sideways and looked at him. Stanesby had been about to say something, but had closed his mouth immediately. Suddenly the order of rank was clear. 'You're guessing,' Fletch continued. He spoke very slowly and pre-cisely. He wasn't looking at Andy, just at the notebook in front of him. 'You're guessing that Durrani had something to do with this murder. Assuming, even. But you don't know. No one does.'

Andy looked at Stanesby, unsure how to reply.

'It was Mr Fletch who authorised that you should be Mark Johnson's controller,' Stanesby said, as if that ex-plained everything.

'Yes,' Fletch said. 'We very much wanted the information Mr Johnson could provide.' He looked at Andy over the top of the glasses. 'And since there was a danger he wouldn't continue to give it if we stuck to the rules, we decided to relax them and allow you to handle him. And it's working very nicely, no? He's unearthed some first-rate material on Durrani. Everything is going exactly to plan.'

Andy shook his head. Exactly to plan? *Except for a murder.* 'I don't really get what—'

'Except,' Fletch said, raising his voice slightly to silence him, 'except for this intention to provide a report on Durrani's fraudulent activities directly to Raheesh Khan.'

That again. Andy opened his mouth to argue, closed it again.

'No good at all.' Fletch shook his head, as if he were a prep school master and Andy had let him down by dropping a catch. 'No good at all. The whole point of this operation is to get leverage on Durrani. The report Mark Johnson is preparing will do that. But the leverage won't be much use to us if Khan kills Durrani. Which he would, I think, if he were to discover Durrani was so very untrustworthy.'

The whole point of the operation is to get leverage. Was that what he had said?

'This is why I had to stall things two days ago,' Stanesby said. 'You understand now?'

Andy shook his head. 'We're not trying to arrest Durrani? Prosecute him?'

'No,' Stanesby said. 'Quite the contrary.'

'Your friend hasn't given any preliminary reports to Khan yet, has he?' Fletch asked, taking his glasses off.

'Probably,' Andy said. 'He's probably hinted. I'm not sure. Khan must have had suspicions anyway, of course . . .'

'Oh dear,' Fletch said, smiling. 'That's really not very good, is it?'

'I'm sorry,' Andy said, bristling. 'But I hadn't realised the point of our operation was to provide leverage on Durrani. No one told me that.' And what did it matter now? They might be able to stop Mark scuppering their plan, but they couldn't withhold information from the murder enquiry.

'That's why we're spending all this time watching him?' he asked.

'Naturally. And it's all very useful. You should be assured of that. As much information as we can get about him – that's the goal.'

'So you can turn him?' Andy asked, stating the obvious by now. 'So we can get Pasha Durrani to work for *us*?' He sounded incredulous, but neither Stanesby nor Fletch batted an eyelid.

'Yes. Precisely,' Fletch said. 'So we can get him to work for us. Durrani's the prize. If we could get him on board that would be a priceless advance on the really big hitters. That's right, Commander Stanesby?'

'Without a doubt,' Stanesby said.

'But he's not much use dead,' Fletch continued. 'So you must help us here, Mr Macall. I think your friend Mr Johnson needs to be persuaded in whatever way is necessary. He has to provide this report to yourself – and thence to us – and not to Khan. Then we can use it. Giving it to Khan is out of the question. You think you'll be able to achieve that? I can authorise very large sums of reward money, if that would assist.'

'But Durrani will be investigated for murder now. It won't matter what Mark does—'

'As I said, you're making assumptions about this murder. Best just let the Essex police get on with it, I think. Best not to interfere.'

'They think it was a mugging. They have no leads which point at Durrani—'

'Maybe he didn't do it.'

'So who did?'

Fletch shrugged. 'Not my job to find out. The main point I take out of it all is that Durrani will not now be able to run his scam on the Asuris, because his partner in that enterprise – Mr Ross, the man who was due to slip him the bung – is dead. So it would be doubly unfortunate if your friend Mark were to notify Raheesh Khan about Durrani's plan. That's the main point.'

'But a man is—'

'Did you hear me, Mr Macall? *That's* the main point. Before we continue can we be sure you understand that?'

He stared at Andy, face straight. Andy stared back, too confused to say anything. After a little, Fletch smiled at him, a fleeting, patronising thing. 'So let's get back to business,' he said. 'Your friend now knows who the fraudulent survey company is. Am I right?'

'Yes.'

'And he intends to get proof that they deliberately under-valued the Brighton property, with the connivance of both buyer – Ross – and the seller – Durrani – for a fee.'

'Yes.'

'He will commit burglaries to achieve this? Or buy the information?'

'I have no idea.'

'That's best. But we should assume your friend will be out of pocket. So will you need money to persuade him to give this information to us and not to Khan?'

Andy took a breath, got his mind to consider the question. 'No. Mark isn't worried about cash. He's worried Durrani will harm his family . . .'

'But that will change if *we* have this information. There won't be any sense in attacking Mr Johnson then. It will be *us* Durrani will have to worry about. In case *we* give the information to the Asuris. And that threat is what we will use to reel him in. You understand?'

'Yes. Perfectly.'

'Good.' Fletch started to stand. Andy couldn't believe it. As far as he could read it, they were instructing him not to co-operate with Essex police. In fact, they didn't seem preoccupied with Ross's death at all.

'Contact me directly from now,' Fletch said. He handed Andy a card. 'That has my details. If I can assist in any way you must call me. And let me know as soon as you've spoken to Johnson, please. You and I will work together on this now.'

18

Lara knew what she had to tell Paul, but it was still difficult to start. She looked at Chris, sitting beside her. He looked terrible, face very pale and drawn, though Paul kept telling her he was OK. She had to keep reminding herself of that, because every time she looked at him she felt a surge of panic in her throat.

They were in Paul's place, in Camden, on the white sofa there, Chris sitting beside her but leaning further back, resting his head. He was taking some kind of opiate-based painkiller, which left him groggy. He was wearing clothes Paul had given him, which were far too large, with a white bandage round his head. The nurse who had dressed the wound had made a half-hearted effort to wash the blood out of his hair, so now it looked lank and dirty. He smelled of sweat and disinfectant. He'd been told he had to rest for seventy-two hours, because of the blood loss.

Paul was standing over by the doors onto the little balcony, looking at her, waiting for her to continue. The mood in the room was like something stretched tight between them. It was all her fault, of course, because Pasha was her brother – it was her family doing this to them. So it was down to her to find some way to stop it. But she couldn't. She had thought of everything, done everything she could. Now there was only this mounting feeling of depression and desperation.

She wiped a tear from her face and cleared her throat. Her mouth felt thick and dry. 'There are things I haven't told you,' she said, speaking to Paul. 'About Pasha and me. There are reasons I can't go to the police.' Her voice was trembling as she said the words. She looked at Chris again. She had her hand on his knee. She squeezed gently, hoping he would say something to help her. But his eyes were closed and he didn't react. 'I'm so sorry, Chris,' she said.

'It's not your fault, Lara,' Chris said, opening his eyes. 'Don't let the bastard make you think that. And besides, it's not so bad. It's a cut to the head. That's all . . .'

'He could have killed you.'

'I don't think that was what he wanted to do,' Paul said. 'He's not that stupid. And Chris is right – it's a superficial cut to his scalp. Scalp wounds bleed heavily, but it's not serious.'

Lara nodded. 'I know. I know. But I'm just so worried.'

'Finish what you started saying,' Paul said. 'Tell me why you can't go to the police.'

She took a deep breath, then started to tell him about the property transactions, about Pasha putting properties in her name without her knowing, about how he now had to sell those properties and needed her signature, about how she suspected the properties belonged to powerful criminal interests out in Pakistan, about Pasha's connections to Pakistan. Paul watched her intently whilst she spoke, his eyes on hers every time she looked up at him. She felt bitterly ashamed telling him it, though there was no judgement in his expression or reactions. Paul wasn't like that. He was as solid now as he had been when they were teenagers, when they had first met. The emotions she felt for Chris had always been obvious, overwhelming. By comparison, the thing with Paul had taken time to grow, been quieter. It was a friendship, a special friendship that she had missed through the last eight years. She had got on with Paul in a way she had never got on with Chris. She should have paid more attention to that.

'Would they really arrest you?' Paul asked her. 'After all, it's not your fault. Why would anyone blame you? Pasha didn't ask to use your identity, you didn't consent to it. Why would they arrest you for that?'

'To put pressure on me, to try to get me to give evidence against Pasha. And I can't do that. He's my brother, my flesh and blood. No matter what happens I can't give evidence against him. I can't betray him like that . . .' She broke off. She could see Paul frowning at her. Chris looked slightly angry. She knew what they were thinking – how much does Pasha have to do, how far does he have to go, before she would break that rule and turn against him? 'Not yet,' she said, quietly. 'I can't do that yet. I'm sorry.'

'I'll speak to him,' Paul said. 'I can't see any other way.'

'Don't be mad,' Chris said. 'He's a fucking psycho. He'll probably try to kill you too.'

Paul shrugged. 'I've dealt with worse,' he said. 'I think I can handle him.' He turned away from them and stared out of the windows. He looked at the grey day outside, then down at the street below, at all the little Londoners running around. This time a year ago he'd been looking at a very different scene, but he wasn't going to tell Chris and Lara anything about that. He'd let down a friend then as well, with catastrophic consequences.

Rob Ogle had served three years with him in Afghanistan. Of all the men he'd got to know in the army, Rob was the one he'd felt closest to. After the army they did a few private jobs together, in theatre, then Paul ended up talking to a man named Iskander Kom. Kom was trying to keep 'the foreigners' – meaning the Afghani Taliban – out of Chitral by arming local militias there. He had American backers prepared to sell him weaponry, but needed guards for his convoys.

Rob hadn't wanted anything to do with it. He'd been frightened. But Paul had persuaded him it was a safe job, that he would watch his back. Rob was a big hard man to look at, but the tours in Helmand had got to him. The fear of death was there, worming its way into his mind. He used to joke about it, to pretend he could cope. He said that if he was ever hit and left to bleed out, he would make sure his last words were 'the horror, the horror'. 'If I fuck up and forget,' he'd added, 'I want you to lie about it.'

One year ago, Thursday the twenty-eighth of May 2009, they'd come over the Khyber Pass, from Jalalabad, driving all night in a small convoy – two Humvees sandwiching two trucks – Paul riding shotgun in the front Humvee. Around nine they'd stopped at a village to the north-east of Peshawar, and Kom, who had been driving Rob's Humvee at the back, walked to a shop that sold freshly fried skewers of spiced meat. A quick snack for the six of them – Kom, Paul, Rob and the three others. Kom had used the kebab place before, and knew the owner. The trucks were parked in a line outside – the shop was in the front of a single storey, breeze-block building that served as a covered bazaar, with about twenty other stalls inside the place. The plan was to stop for a few minutes only.

Rob Ogle was back in his Humvee eating his kebab when the device went off. The meat was all over his face when Paul got to him. Afterwards they had worked out that the detonation had been right under his vehicle, in a covered drainage channel. The blast took the Humvee into the air and into the bazaar, straight through the shop where Kom had been buying the kebabs, demolishing the entire front of the building.

At the moment it went off Paul was standing on the other side of his own Humvee, partially shielded from the blast, about twenty feet distant. The shock wave had come under the Humvee and taken his legs away, flinging him about ten feet through the air. That was all he could remember of it – his legs being kicked out from under him, then lying in a dense pall of smoke and silence, face down, his eardrums gone. He couldn't recall the actual noise of the detonation, or Rob's truck going through the building. One moment he was standing by the open door of his truck, the next he was on the ground in the smoke. That was it.

He started to cough in the silence. Then picked himself up. There was blood all over his shoes, but he could stand, so he assumed – wrongly – that nothing was broken. By then there were people screaming. He could see an old man, his mouth wide open, blood running from his scalp, pulling at his hair, and crowds of younger men converging, all in shalwar kameez.

And still no sound.

He ran to the bazaar, because at first he assumed that both Kom and Rob had been in the kebab place. The dust dissipated quickly, but the clouds of smoke took longer. When he got to where the food stall had been he could see nothing but the twisted wreck of the Humvee, and dazed people scrambling out of the rubble. And still the total, unreal silence. He only realised that a bruised and shocked Kom was shouting at him when Kom started to pull his arm. Later he found out that Kom had wandered off, further into the bazaar, and so had missed the full force of it. Kom was trying to drag him away because he was worried about secondaries, a common tactic. But Paul had to look for Rob, so he shook Kom off, covered his mouth with his sleeve and stumbled up through a twisted pile of masonry and bent metal to where the cab of the Humvee was jutting from the mess.

Rob was in there, on his side. He was saying something, but Paul could hear nothing. His eyes were open and looked lucid, his skin was covered with bits of meat and kebab bread, his hair sticking up, but he looked unhurt. Paul could remember signalling to him that he couldn't hear what he was saying because his ears were blown, then telling him – without being able to hear his own voice – that he was going to pull him out.

That proved difficult at first – Rob was jammed in the wreckage somewhere – but then within seconds there were other men helping. They prised something off Rob, something that had been pinning him. Then Paul got him away. Another man took one arm, Paul held him under his chest. It was only as they got him out of the cab and down onto the jagged shards of shattered breeze blocks – in what had once been the back of the kebab shop – that Paul realised Rob was missing his lower legs. There were rags and blood where they should have been. At this point Rob was convulsing, with blood coming out of his mouth and nose. And still Paul couldn't hear a thing, though he could feel his own heart hammering with fear, feel now the acute pain in one of his ankles.

It took an ambulance twenty minutes to get from Peshawar. There was not much Paul could do whilst they waited. Both Rob's legs had been blown off below the knees. He tied tourniquets, but there was already too much blood loss, and in his panic he forgot all the rules so carefully drummed into them in the army. He didn't check for other injuries, so he missed the gaping wound just below Rob's left shoulder, even though the blood bubbling out of his mouth should have warned him that there was something internal going on.

In the end Rob Ogle bled out lying there on the mud outside a collapsed bazaar in some nowhere place in northern Pakistan. The shock set in whilst Paul was frantically talking to him, trying to keep him conscious. He was whispering something when it ended, but Paul couldn't hear what. Kom told Paul afterwards that Rob had been crying for his mum, just like everyone did.

That was one year ago. Chris was his oldest living friend now. If Paul hadn't persuaded him it would be safe then Chris wouldn't have done the Finsbury Park gig and wouldn't have taken the injury. Paul had let him down, taken Jules to the station, made the wrong call. And maybe Chris was right, maybe Pasha really was a lunatic, maybe the threat was worse than he was calculating it to be. Same now as a year ago. But he couldn't let that happen again. He couldn't lose another friend.

19

Andy had left Acton and was halfway back to Harrow when Luntley's number came up on the phone. Andy put it on the speaker and kept driving. 'Sorry, boss,' Luntley said. 'I know you're meant to be off and all that . . .'

'That doesn't matter. Go on.' He looked at the clock on the dash. After twelve thirty. He had told Helen he would be back by twelve. 'What's up?'

'I think you need to come back,' Luntley said. He sounded worried. 'Something's going wrong.'

Andy pulled the car over. 'Like what?'

'The Wimbledon probe – the one at Durrani's mother's house – it's been down all morning . . .'

'You already told me that. You said it was a technical issue.'

'Exactly. Technical Services have just told me it's not.'

'So what is it?'

'They think it's been moved.'

Moved? Did that mean tampered with? 'Is Durrani still in Richmond?' Andy asked.

'Yes. But he's started acting weird.'

'Like how?'

'I'm watching him now. He's running around the house with something in his hand – I can't make out what. Something small, about the size of a mobile. Maybe it *is* a mobile, maybe I'm overreacting, but he's not acting normally. I think he might be searching.'

'Searching?'

'It could be a detector of some sort. He could be searching for our devices.'

Andy screwed his face up. 'I'll come back now.'

By the time he got back it was all but over.

Luntley pointed urgently at the screens as he entered the room. There was only one surveillance screen still up. On it, Andy could see Pasha Durrani moving around on all fours in his living room, sliding a small, handheld black object across the floor and walls.

'He found the kitchen camera ten minutes ago,' Luntley said. 'We have no sound either. So he must have found the probes too. He's dumping us. No doubt about it. He knows we're watching and he's dumping us.'

'Did you call Snowden?'

Luntley nodded. 'He'll get back to us, he says. He's talking to Stanesby.'

'We need to warn the mobile team.'

'They're gone already,' Luntley said. 'Snowden pulled them straight away.'

'Fucking hell.' He bit his lip, trying to contain his anger. 'He should have consulted me first. I want them in place and ready.' He picked up the phone to call Snowden, eyes on Durrani. He was moving closer, towards the wall, coming for the camera. 'What's he got there?' Andy asked.

'Maybe some kind of transmission detector. I don't recognise it though.'

'Could we close down and evade it?'

'Or a metal detector? Who knows? We could close down. Yes. Not sure it would do any good though. He found the other camera without any problems. Ripped it out of the wall with a claw hammer. He was laughing as he did it. He's on to us, Andy. I don't think we're going to get round that.'

Andy got through to Snowden as Durrani's face loomed large on the screen. 'You know what's happening here?' Andy asked.

'I know,' Snowden said. 'I'm waiting for Stanesby to get back to me. It's his call.'

'We need to keep the mobile team on the target. If he finds everything else it's all we'll have.'

'I pulled them because that's the protocol. If he can ID our people then the risk is too high. He's not a petty thief. According to you he's a killer. I can't leave a team exposed like that. You know the rules. And it's useless anyway. If he knows we're watching it's not going to take long for him to get an eyeball—'

'He'll be loose and free if we don't keep them in place.'

'Like I said, Stanesby will decide. I'll tell you when I know.'

Andy hung up and watched. He was tense now, sweat running down his back. Durrani reappeared, holding something white in one hand, a small stool in the other. He put the stool down and stood on it, then held the white thing up towards the camera. For a moment Andy didn't know what it was, then the image came into focus. It was a piece of paper. Andy read the words written onto it: FUCK YOU.

'Well, I guess that makes things clear,' Luntley muttered. Seconds later something flashed in front of the camera and the image went black, the feed dead. 'That's us,' Luntley said. 'All closed down.' He pushed his chair back, took off his glasses and looked up at Andy, standing above the screen. 'He can do what he likes as of now. We have no sound, no image, no back-up mobile team.'

Andy nodded grimly.

'What do you think happened?' Luntley asked.

'You saw it all,' Andy said. 'You tell me.'

'He knew what he was looking for,' Luntley said. 'No accident. He got up and started trying to find the gear immediately.'

'You sure it wasn't a piece of kit sticking out of the wall?'

'No way. He knew in advance.'

They stared at each other. 'How would that happen?' Luntley asked, with heavy irony.

Andy looked away. 'Somebody told him,' he said. 'Somebody fucking told him.'

20

It was just before two by the time Paul got to Pasha Durrani's Richmond house. Lara had given him directions and described it to him in advance, and though he had realised then that it must be worth far more than Pasha could have legitimately come by, seeing it in reality made him think twice about his planned course of action.

To get to it you followed the road down from Richmond Hill towards Ham, then turned towards the river, walking into a very exclusive area of detached houses, each set in their own grounds and ringed by walls mounted with security cameras. Pasha's place was at the end of a long road that led back towards the river, and from its position Paul guessed it would probably back onto the river itself. There was a seven foot wall surrounding the place, with razor wire stretched across the top. At the entrance there was a heavy sliding gate and an intercom panel. Through a thin gap in the gate panels, Paul could see a long driveway, then the white front of a big new house. Looking at it, he realised that what Lara had told him was true: in this part of the world a house of this size would be worth five to eight million quid. For the first time the scale of it dawned on him. Despite Lara's words, despite Jimmy Chapman's warnings, he had somehow imagined Pasha as some kind of petty criminal. Completely wrong. With this kind of money involved Pasha had to be very highly placed. Paul started to wonder what exactly he had got himself into.

He didn't have a very sophisticated plan – press the buzzer and ask to speak to Pasha. That was about it. Suddenly that began to seem a bit reckless. But on the other hand Pasha's activities, whatever they were, would make him sufficiently exposed, he calculated, to make it unlikely he would try anything crude, at least not before Paul had a chance to explain his presence. Petty thieves shot from the hip, men with more to lose were more cautious. And he was counting on his explanation having some effect. He would very politely tell Pasha the position with Lara and Chris, very respectfully warn him about future police involvement, gently attempt to project himself as an impartial intermediary. Lara had thought this would do no good at all, that Pasha would take no notice, that Paul would be in danger. There was that risk, of course. If Chris was correct then Pasha had come alone to his flat last night, making the attack something personal. Seeing the house, the obvious wealth, that now seemed extremely unusual to Paul. People who could afford this type of property – the Jimmy Chapmans of the criminal world – were normally scrupulous about keeping their hands clean. They had no shortage of 'staff' for the dirty work. Which meant the business with Lara was either completely disconnected from Pasha's criminal activities, or he was getting very desperate about something.

Paul was still thinking about this when the gate started to slide open. He stepped sideways and walked a little away, pausing near a parked car. He waited.

Nothing happened. No car appeared. He waited a few minutes then walked back to the gate, now wide open and showing a clear view up to the house. He checked his watch

– two minutes past two. He glanced up at the CCTV camera, but, of course, that gave nothing away. He stepped over the line and started to walk towards the house. He got about twenty feet up the drive, with no sign of activity ahead. He was just beginning to think that maybe he could play it differently; maybe he could cut off to the left, into the tree line and the grounds, out of the line of sight, then circle round the back and take a look. He got as far as considering this, then heard the gate starting to close behind him. He turned quickly back, calculating the distance and the speed he would have to run to make it back, to get through before it closed.

That was the moment the kid with the gun stepped out. There were dense bushes to the side of the gates and he stepped out from between them, on a small path Paul hadn't seen, placing himself between Paul and the closing gate. He was a young white kid, maybe twenty years old at most. The gun was a short machine pistol, and it was pointing directly at Paul. The distance was about fifteen feet. Paul's eyes flicked quickly to the closing gate, then to the bushes the kid had emerged from. Paul had been careless, hadn't looked carefully enough. Now he saw there was some kind of low building behind the bushes, a gate-house. The kid had probably been in there all the time, watching him on the CCTV camera. He was walking quickly towards him now. He looked tense, jumpy, like he was frightened. The kind of gun he was carrying wasn't very accurate, but this was close enough even for an idiot not to miss. Paul put his hands up in front of him, palms out-wards, to show they were empty. 'Sorry,' he said, then laughed nervously. 'I'll just go right back out,' he said, nodding at the gate. But it was closed now, locking itself into place. 'I thought this was where Eddie lived. I see it's not—'

'Shut the fuck up.' The boy jerked the gun at Paul's chest. He was about ten feet away and closing. He stopped. 'Shut up and turn round. Hands on your fucking head.'

Paul frowned. 'Steady, mate,' he said. 'It's just a mistake. I'm not a burglar or anything – is that what you thought? There's no need—'

'Shut up. I'll drop you. I mean it. Turn round and shut up. No more trying to fuck with me. This thing is loaded.'

Paul raised his hands higher. 'Look. I've made a mistake,' he tried again. 'I was looking for Eddie Jones. You know him? He lives in one of these houses around here—'

He broke off, seeing that the boy was coming straight on, getting angry now, the grip changing on the gun. It looked like he was going to try and hit Paul with it.

'Now wait,' Paul said, raising his voice. He started to step backwards. 'This is just a mistake.'

The kid was coming quicker now, raising the gun to whack him with the metal stock. Unbelievable. Obviously he didn't know too much about guns. Paul could take it off him easily, he thought, but not without substantial danger that it would go off in the process.

'*Cut it out, fuck head! Stop now!*'

The words were shouted from behind Paul. The kid stopped at once, lowering the gun so it was pointed at Paul's chest again. He was looking behind Paul now, his face twitching. Paul could hear someone coming quickly down the drive towards them, shouting as he came:

'What's going on? What the fuck is going on?'

Paul risked a look back, then quickly put his eyes front again. There was a young man approaching from the house. He too was armed, but worse than that, Paul was almost sure it was one of the two young Asians he had surprised in the alley last night, threatening Jules.

'This fucker was hanging around the gates,' the white boy said. 'So I opened them—'

'You stupid little cunt. What did you do that for?'

'This is just a mistake,' Paul tried again. His hands were still in the air. He brought them down. The other man came round from behind him, then stared at his face. 'I'll go straight away,' Paul said, looking at him, praying he wouldn't recognise him. But even as he spoke he saw the man frown, his expression change.

'I fucking know you,' the man said. 'You were that fucker who chased us, last night.'

Paul smiled, then shrugged his shoulders.

'I knew he was trying something,' the white kid said. 'I knew it—'

'Shut up, idiot,' the other one said. 'Get back into your fucking kennel.' He brought his own gun up – a small handgun – and pointed it at Paul's head. 'What the fuck are you doing here?'

'I'm here to see Pasha Durrani.'

The two looked at each other. 'I told you to get back into the gatehouse,' the Asian said. 'Do as you're told.'

The white boy made a noise like a growl, then stalked off towards the bushes again, his shoulders slumped like a petulant teenager.

'And keep that gun out of sight,' the Asian shouted back at him. 'You.' He jabbed the gun closer to Paul. 'You turn and walk up to the house.'

'I need to see Pasha Durrani,' Paul said again, then turned slowly and began to walk. 'Is he up here? I just want to talk to him.'

'How did you find us here?'

'You should tell him I'm here. My name is Paul Curtis. He knows me.'

That was met with silence.

They reached the front door of the house, which was open. 'Shall I go in?' Paul asked. He could hear that the man had closed on him a little. Not that it mattered. He wasn't going to try anything with a gun pointed at him. Besides, he doubted Pasha would take this line with him. However, the trick was to get to see Pasha.

'Go through to the room beyond. Straight ahead. Keep your hands where I can see them.'

Paul went through the open door, into a hallway with a parquet floor. There were several doors off, pictures on the walls, furniture, but Paul wasn't concentrating on what the place looked like. He could feel the thrum of his pulse, raised, but not badly so. He was afraid, at some level, of course – enough to get the adrenalin into his system – but not so much as to be worried about it. It didn't seem possible that any of these clowns were going to try to shoot him, or do anything stupid. It was the middle of the day, in Richmond, England. He wasn't in Lahore or Peshawar. He would get to see Pasha and things would settle down.

The one behind him shouted something, which Paul didn't catch – maybe a name. In front of him another man appeared through an open door. Not Pasha, but another white guy, this one older, more muscular. He was stripped down to a pair of jeans, sweating like he'd been doing some heavy lifting, or exercise. His chest was thick with muscle, covered in tattoos, his hair shaved almost to his scalp. He had the face of someone who had been in a few scrapes – a flat, deviated nose, a ragged ear, a scar above his left eye. He wiped his hands on a rag, chucked it aside and stared at Paul with outright hostility.

'What's going on?' he demanded.

'I need to speak to Pasha Durrani.'

The white man looked at the one behind Paul, seeking an explanation.

'He was hanging around the gates,' the one behind Paul said, standing very close now. 'Your boy found him. I recognise him. He's the guy who came up when we were talking to the bitch in the pub last night. He chased us off.'

'My name's Paul Curtis,' Paul said, calmly. 'I'm a friend of Chris Napier and Pasha's sister, Lara. I'm here to speak to Pasha.'

'That right?' The white guy walked up to him, glanced behind at the Asian, then said, 'Keep the gun on him – if he fights, drop him,' then, without any warning, smashed his fist into Paul's stomach. Paul brought his hands down to block it, but way too late. It was a powerful, deliberate punch, from someone who punched a lot, who practised, who had hands as large and heavy as Paul's own. It came too fast to counter, aimed straight into the solar plexus. Paul doubled over at once, gasping for air, then sank to his knees. The pain was instantly disabling. Whilst he was struggling with it, the man went for him again. Paul saw it coming this time, tried to avoid it. But the man was quick, like a pro, using short punches that looked harmless, but were devastating. This one got him in the jaw.

He went over backwards, his head ringing, his vision blurred. The man was moving round him. He realised what was going to happen next at the exact moment a foot came down onto his head, cracking it off the floor. For a second everything went black. He rolled and tried to curl into a protective ball, the pain spreading quickly. He shouted incoherently, keen to give the impression he was beaten already. He could have tried to get up, he thought, could probably have started to fight, but didn't think it would help, not with the gun in the equation. They were going to give him a bit of a kicking now, he guessed. It wouldn't be the first time in his life. He'd miscalculated and now he'd pay. He'd thought that if Pasha was living in a place like this then he would be surrounded by people with a bit of sophistication, but instead he'd run into a group of savages. He could hear the Asian man laughing.

'Not such a cool fucker now, eh?' Then another stamp to the back of his head. He tried to say something, tried to get some words out, but his mouth was full of blood.

Then they were both going at him. Kicking so hard they were grunting as they did it. He rolled one way, then the other, trying to keep curled. His grasp of time quickly started to slip. He could feel his head being struck repeatedly, his motor reflexes going, everything being scrambled. Then a flickering blackness.

The next thing he knew there was vomit in his mouth and he was flat on his belly, a tremendous pressure across the back of his head. He could hear himself retching and gasping for breath.

'Now you'll fucking tell us who you are,' he could hear someone shouting.

'Get him up. Sit him up. I need to speak to him. He'll answer with respect now.'

Time stuttered and slowed. He'd lost consciousness, he realised, then come round again. Maybe he'd been out for a split second only, maybe longer. It was possible things had happened that he couldn't recall. That was bad. His head was spinning with a wretched, crippling dizziness. One of the blows had obviously hit him somewhere it shouldn't have. His vision was grey, his mind filled only with his own breath, his thundering heartbeat, the need to concentrate to stop the spinning, to stop himself vomiting again. He realised that someone was pulling him into a sitting position. He could hear a voice, but the words were very unclear. He kept still, panting, waiting for the sickness to stop. He wasn't able to do anything else. Above him, around him, an argument was taking place. Two or three voices:

'What the fuck have you done to him?'

'Whacked him. He was out front, snooping—'

'You stupid fucker. Is he dead?'

'He's fine. Just a few punches. I thought he'd take it.'

'It's the fucker who stopped us in the alley.' That was another voice. The Asian guy. Paul remembered him suddenly, then remembered how he had appeared with the gun, out on the driveway.

'What if he's a pig?' This voice was new. 'You idiot. I've told you about this. I've warned you many times—'

'He's no pig. Look at him. It's that fucker from last night.'

'You're a sick cunt, Don. You know that.'

'I needed it. I've been too tense, Rash. I needed to fuck someone over.'

'You need putting in a straightjacket. I left you for ten fucking minutes. We don't need any more trouble. We're supposed to be in Whalley by now. We're meant to get up there before him. What did you hit him with? Where?'

'I didn't hit him with anything . . .'

'He used his fists and feet, man. It was cool. It was like a movie—'

'You shut the fuck up as well. There's nothing cool about this.'

'Fucking hell . . .'

More hands on him, parting his hair at the back of his head. A noise came out of his mouth, a groan.

'Wait here. Watch him. I'll call Durrani.'

Did he lose consciousness again? He wasn't sure. He was aware of them talking around him, as if he wasn't there, then he heard someone shouting from further into the house. He kept his eyes closed, or he thought that was what he did. But when he opened them again they were all gone and he was flat on his back.

He struggled into a sitting position. His head was heavy, pulsing, an excruciating headache all across the back of it, extending forward into his eyes, but he could sit without vomiting, at least. He felt weak, dizzy, his body stiff. He managed to get his watch up to his face. Twenty minutes past two. He had checked it when he was at the gates and it had been two minutes past two then. He could hardly believe it. Only ten minutes had passed. He thought he'd been lying there for hours.

He could hear noises from outside now – a car starting, then driving away. Were they leaving? In that case, he had to do something. He had to get up, get out, run.

21

As soon as the door shut on Lara, Chris was regretting his words. *I don't think I can go on like this.* That was what he had said to her.

He stood looking at the door, hoping she would get as far as the lifts, turn round, come back, say something to reverse it all. All she had to do was walk back through the door and he would tell her he hadn't meant any of it, that it was all down to the concussion. But instead, after a few moments, he heard the lift humming in the shaft, descending with Lara inside. She had walked out on him, walked out in the middle of it.

She wasn't the kind to turn back. She had looked at him when he'd said it, then nodded quickly. That was it. No frown, no reaction aside from that little infuriating nod. Then she was turning to get her bag. He'd told her it was dangerous to go out unless Paul thought it was safe, but she hadn't listened to that.

'I'm going to my place to get my passport,' she'd told him.

'Jules will get it for you.'

'I'll get it. I'm not a prisoner.' Her voice had been frosty, hard.

'Or Paul will get it. I'll call him.'

'I'll get it.'

I don't think I can go on like this. It was the first time either of them had said anything like that, and it had broken a kind of bubble they'd been living in since they'd met up again, because the words implied that they could be apart, that they could split up, and neither of them had ever contemplated that before.

He turned from the door and went to the sofa. He sat down and placed his head in his hands. What had he done? It was absurd that he should have said such a thing. He knew what he was like, knew exactly how much he needed her. The idea of living without her filled him with panic.

He paced into the kitchen and ran a glass of water. He drank it down quickly, then stood by the kitchen window, looking out at the street below. Last night he had been lucky. Even the doctor had told him that. Blows to the head could kill. *That* was what should have been uppermost in her considerations – her fucking brother had almost killed him.

Forty-five minutes later he was still arguing with himself when the door began to open. He expected it to be Lara, returning. He had even planned a kind of apology, but wasn't sure whether he wanted to say it. But it wasn't her. Instead, the door opened and Paul walked in.

'Fucking hell. What happened?'

Paul stood beside the door and looked at him. 'I had a little reality check,' he said. The words came out slurred. The front of his shirt was wet, stained with blood. His face was bruised, one eye closing, his mouth swollen. There was blood in his hair, a smell like vomit coming off him. Chris walked quickly over to him.

'Did Pasha do this to you? Was it that bastard?' He could

hear his voice rising. 'If it was we call the police right now. Right fucking now.'

Paul shook his head, then leaned back against the door and took deep breaths. 'Not Pasha,' he said. 'His people. Pasha wasn't there.'

'Can you stand OK? My God . . . now she'll see what's happening. Now she'll see . . .' Chris took hold of him to steer him towards the sofa, but Paul stopped him, gently pushing the arm away. 'It's OK, Chris,' he said. 'I can walk. I got back here from Richmond. I'm not going to fall over . . .' He stood unsupported, swaying slightly.

'We need to get you to a hospital,' Chris said. 'I'm going to call an ambulance.'

Paul shook his head again.

'Your face looks bad, Paul. You can't see what I can. You've got to get it checked out. They break something in your mouth? You're speaking fuzzy.'

'They broke a tooth. Can you find me some painkillers?'

'You could have a concussion, man. We have to get you to casualty.'

'I will have a concussion, but it's manageable. For now. Trust me. I know about these things.'

'You black out?'

'Yes. But not for long enough to worry about. I'll be OK . . .'

'If you blacked out you have to get it checked. You know that, Paul. We have to get you to casualty—'

'Not now. Right now I've got to think about how to get even with these fuckers. Get me the painkillers, I'll clean myself up.' He started for the bathroom, limping slightly, then paused and looked around. 'Where's Lara?'

'She went.'

That stopped him. 'Went where?'

'To her place. To get her passport . . .' Chris looked at the floor.

'You let her do that?'

'I couldn't stop her.'

'How long ago?'

Chris shrugged, frowning. 'I don't know. Maybe an hour. She's a big girl, Paul. She can choose for herself.'

'I'll go after her.'

'What? Are you crazy?'

'Ring her and stop her, if you can get her. Call me a cab if you can't. I'll wash this shit off, change and go. You should have stopped her, Chris. He might be waiting for her.'

22

As she slid the key into the lock of her front door in Clapham, Lara was feeling a new confusion of emotions. Uppermost was still an anger with Chris. As she opened the front door she was thinking that it was like the end of something, some kind of dream she had been living for a couple of months. It was a thought that made her want to sit down and cry. She put her keys on the cabinet at the entrance to the front room, opened the door and stepped in.

'Hello, sis.'

She almost jumped through the wall. Pasha, sitting on her sofa, looking up at her, the TV remote in his hand, the TV just flickering as he switched it off. Sitting in her front room like he owned the place, like it wasn't a matter of only a few hours since he had physically attacked her boyfriend.

'I've been waiting for you,' he said, casually. 'You and I need to talk.'

She tried to run, immediately. But he was ready, his foot out and kicking the door as he stood, slamming it so that it glanced painfully off her head and barred her exit, then his hand jarring her back against the wall.

'Let's not fight again,' he said. He was breathing rapidly, already angry, face very close to hers. He put a hand up, flat against the wall next to her head, between her and the door. 'I'm your brother. You've nothing to fear. I won't hurt you.'

She got control of herself. 'Get out of the way, Pash,' she said. 'Get your fucking hands away from me.'

He shrugged and moved back a couple of steps. She rubbed her head. It would bruise where the door had hit her. 'You attacked Chris,' she said. She felt like hitting him. 'You attacked him with a broken bottle. You're a fucking animal, an animal . . .'

'A little cut,' he said, looking straight at her. 'Nothing serious. I was careful, believe me.'

'He had ten stitches. He could have been seriously injured.'

'You should have listened to me.'

'What do you want?' she asked angrily. 'What are you doing here?'

'It's time for you to make choices,' he said. 'Important choices.'

'I don't think so. Get out. This is my house. Get out. Leave me alone.'

'Not a chance of that.' He glanced around the room. 'I've got things to tell you. Things you have to listen to. You want to do it here? Or up in Lancashire?'

She laughed, trying hard not to appear frightened. 'How do you think you would get me up to Lancashire? Drug me? Asphyxiate me again?'

He shook his head. 'That won't be necessary. When I'm finished talking you'll come of your own free will.'

She wanted to laugh again, but couldn't. 'I shouldn't have come back here—' she started.

'Well you did. As I knew you would. So sit down and listen.' He pointed to her own sofa. She stood her ground, staring at him. Opening the door and trying to run would be useless. So what to do?

'Come on, Lara. Please don't make this harder than it

already is.' He looked at the ground as he spoke, his voice suddenly tired and sad. 'I don't want it to be like this. Believe me. I don't want it to be anything like this between us. You're my sister, Lara. I love you. You know that?'

He looked up at her, his eyes softer. A hint of the Pasha she'd grown up with. It melted her resolve a fraction.

'What do you want to say?' she asked.

'Sit down. I'll tell you.'

She sat down, reluctantly. 'Not for long,' she said. She sat on the edge of her sofa – the old yellow thing she'd got from Jules's parents – and looked up at him. He remained standing, then began to pace. He looked slightly dishevelled, she thought, his hair a bit lank and greasy. The knees and bottoms of the jeans he was wearing were stained with dirt or dust. His hands looked dirty too. How long had he been waiting here for her, she wondered?

'Do you know how we got here?' he asked after a moment. 'How we got into this position?'

She wasn't sure what he meant, but shook her head.

'We were a nice family,' he said. He sounded angry about it. 'A father who was a mad doctor—'

'Don't say things like that! Don't start with—'

'Shut up, Lara. You worship his memory but you were too young to really know him. Not like I did. Maybe he seemed OK to you. But he wasn't. You know why he was struck off?'

'Racism. They didn't want a—'

'Like fuck. He was struck off because he was prescribing drugs that were banned.' He turned to her and smiled. 'He was a drug dealer. And not the first in our family.'

'Don't be stupid. He gave prescription medication to addicts . . .' She'd heard the story before, of course.

He laughed. 'OK. Believe your little dream. It doesn't

really matter what he did or what he was like. It was so long ago.' He stopped pacing and sighed. 'We had a father who was mad and a mother who wasn't much better. A religious fanatic married to an atheist. For fuck's sake. Maybe it was good he killed himself. Maybe they both should have.'

She kept her mouth shut at that. It was peculiar to hear him speak like this about either parent, but especially their mum. It was on the tip of her tongue to make some comment about *him* being a 'religious fanatic'.

'Anyway,' he continued. 'He killed himself and there we were. Stuck up in Manchester with nothing. No money, no house. Fuck all. You won't remember it as it was. You were fifteen. I didn't want you to know what it was like. So we kept things from you – the worst of it. But it was fucking desperate, Lara.' He walked over to the matching yellow chair and sat on it, like her, right on the very edge. 'So this is what happened,' he said. 'I'll tell you now what happened.'

She frowned. What was he talking about?

'The brother came,' he said, waving a hand dismissively. 'Dad's brother. A miserable old fucker who thought he should have my mother because that was the way they did it several hundred years ago back in the old country. Husband dies, brother gets wife, looks after her and family. You know, she would have gone along with that?' He glanced at her, checking she took that in. 'You think she wasn't mad? You reminded me, not so long ago, that she is half white, my mother. Yet she would have gone along with that.' He tapped a finger against his temple. 'Talk about an identity crisis. She has a screw loose.' He paused. 'I wouldn't allow it, anyway. But we went south when the mortgage company took the house. So we ended up with the brother anyway.' He stopped and shook his head for a long while, staring at the floor. 'I was different then,' he said eventually, slowly.

'Still young, I suppose. It was all religion with the brother. Religion and what it was to be Pathan. I swallowed all of it, I guess, and some of it stuck. But there were limits. He wanted to be a father figure, but I wouldn't let him.' He looked up at her and smiled awkwardly, then looked at the floor again. She thought he was thinking about it, thinking about what he should say to her. 'We were so close, you and I,' he said, finally. 'Do you remember how close we were?'

'When?'

'When we were kids.' He smiled again. 'My little sister.' There was a far-away look in his eyes that unsettled her even more. 'My gorgeous little sister. Everybody wanted a bit of you. It was always like that. You were always gorgeous, Lara.'

She moved in the seat, looked away from him. He was being . . . what was he being? She couldn't read it.

'I only ever wanted what was best for you,' he said. 'Father died, so it was down to me—'

She opened her mouth to contradict him, but he held a hand up. 'I know you don't think it was like that,' he said. 'But for me it was. I had to look after you.'

Another silence.

'So,' he said, like he didn't want to go on. His eyes were down again. 'So a man came from Pakistan. And he was OK. That was the thing. He seemed OK. He had money. He was from a wealthy family. The Asuris. They would help, they said. And in return?' He looked up at her, looked directly into her eyes. 'In return he wanted you. Not for himself, but for one of his sons. Shamsuddin. It was a tribal thing. Some kind of plan to make the clan stronger by marrying into our family. I hardly understood at the time. But it didn't seem like a bad thing that I was doing—'

'I wasn't yours to give away like that.' She could feel the anger rising again.

'Listen!' he said, raising his voice. 'I had nothing else to give. That's the first thing you have to grasp. You were what he wanted and we had nothing else to give. We were about to be kicked out of the house in Wimbledon. We hardly had enough money to heat the—'

'What happened to father's money? There was—'

'There was nothing. Father's money went back home. All of it.' He laughed bitterly. 'You didn't know that. He sent me to a shitty little comprehensive and meanwhile he was sending his salary to Pakistan. Not to his family there either, but to a charity that provided education to village kids. People he didn't even know. It's funny, I think.'

That was news. She waited for more.

'So what was I to do?' he said. 'I said yes. But . . .' He held the hand up to silence her again. 'Remember what I say. Firstly, there was no other thing I could think of to do. Secondly, I put conditions in. I said that it couldn't happen there and then, which was what they wanted, but only after you had finished school. They were to pay for the school. You knew where the money came from to send you to that school?'

'I knew the family paid. I knew that you sorted it for me. I've always been grateful . . .'

'The man you're meant to marry paid.'

Had she known that? Had she turned a blind eye to it?

'You knew the deal as well,' he said. 'I told you.'

'But it was absurd. I didn't think it was real. I was too young to grasp it. I was—'

'You didn't think it was serious?'

'No. You didn't ever explain it that way.'

'No. Because I never ever thought it would come to this, Lara. Never. Because I have worked fucking hard. I have done things for them that you wouldn't believe. I have been . . .' He stood suddenly. '*I've been mired in their fuck-ing filth.*' He hissed the words, then started pacing furiously, one side of the short room to the other. 'Everything they wanted from me, they've had. I've made them enough to repay your fucking stupid school fees twice over. More than that. Much more. They've had their money, had their pound of fucking flesh. But no. I thought it had gone away. You finished school and I heard nothing. Years passed. Three bloody years. Then they come at me with it, out of the blue. *The marriage arrangement.* She's my sister, I say. Respect-fully, I say this. I say everything with the greatest respect, always, because you cannot imagine the kind of people we're talking about.'

'You just told me he seemed all right . . .'

'He seemed OK when I was younger, when I was desper-ate. It took a while to get the measure of them. Three years later they demand my sister. So I say she has her life now. She has a career. And I have paid you, with respect, I have paid you six times. But, they tell me, "You know our code, you know about honour." Honour! Fucking honour! That's what this is all about. A contract is a contract, they tell me. A sacred thing.' He stopped pacing and stood in front of her, his face twisting with the difficulty of it. 'I tried to get rid of it, Lara. I didn't think it would ever come to this. You have to believe me. I tried.'

She stood up. 'You should have told me. There might have been something I could have—'

'Nothing. Nothing. Nothing. There's nothing anyone can do.'

She stood in front of him, awkwardly. He was so agit-ated, so full of guilt, she wanted to help him somehow. But he didn't move towards her.

'They want their bride,' he said. 'They want their virgin.'

He was chewing his lip, his face bright red. 'That's what they have to have.' He looked sideways at her. 'Can you give them that? Can you give them that for me, Lara?' His voice was charged with tension, cracking.

'Give them what, Pash?'

'All of it. The marriage, the . . . the status . . .'

'The status?'

He hissed something through his teeth that she couldn't pick up.

'There are ways around it, Pasha. We can go—'

'Did you hear me?'

'I heard you. I'm trying to tell you.' They could go to the police. Was that what she wanted to say? They could get him out of it. But no, she knew even as she thought it that there would be reasons why that wouldn't work, reasons to do with what he had 'done' for them.

'There must be—' she started.

'Are you a fucking virgin still?' he demanded. 'That's what I need to know.'

It felt like he'd slapped her. She was stunned. 'What?' she asked, stupidly.

'Your *honour*. That's how they talk about it. Is it intact? Literally intact? If it's not then we're dead. You understand that. That's what they do. That's the way they work. They practise the exact opposite of mercy. If you're not demonstrably a virgin then they will kill us. All of us. Are you a virgin?'

'Pasha!'

'Answer me! Tell me the truth.'

'I will not. It's nothing to do with you whether—'

Suddenly he had hold of her face with one hand. 'You're not listening, Lara. You're not listening or taking it seriously. I did what I did. It was back then. I wish I hadn't done any of it. But it's done now and this is where we are. THEY WILL KILL US. Do you hear me? THEY WILL KILL US.' He forced her to the sofa and pushed so that she was driven back and banged her head off the wall. She cried out and rolled off the sofa, onto the floor, on her hands and knees. He moved behind her, grabbing her hair with both hands and dragging her back onto her knees. 'I'm trying to keep us both alive, Lara. Both of us. It's not just me they'll kill. Maybe not even me. It's you. You! They will come over and find you and they will cut your fucking throat. THAT IS WHAT THEY DO.' He had a hand round her throat now, the other wrenching on her hair. She started to cry. 'LIKE THIS!' he screamed. He chopped at her throat, making her choke. 'They will kill you. Cut you open like a pig. You! My own sister.' Suddenly he released her and she slumped forwards, sobbing. He paced to the wall by the fireplace and leaned his head against it, gasping for breath. She waited until she could breathe properly, then pulled herself onto the sofa.

'Have you slept with that fucker?' He asked it in an urgent whisper. 'Please answer me.'

'NO! NO NO!' she screamed. 'I didn't. I haven't.' She bent forwards and put her face in her hands. She felt terrified of him. He was mad, completely mad. And up to his neck in it. She didn't know what she could do to stop him now. She felt disgusting. She could not believe she had answered him. She felt the sofa move beside her and flinched, thinking he had come over to hit her again. But he was sitting next to her, pushing his head up against her like a little kid, crying. 'I'm sorry, Lara,' he was saying. 'I'm so sorry. I don't know what I can do except this. I'm sorry.' He was sobbing uncontrollably. She felt a dizzying confusion. She wanted to put an arm around him to help him, but he was dangerous. He was living in a reality she didn't even recognise, and trying to drag her into it. 'They're coming to the Lancashire place,' he said, still sobbing. 'They'll be there on Sunday. You have to be there to meet him. They want to see you. If you come up with me then I will try to bargain with them, get more time. It's all I can do. But you have to come up with me . . .'

She started shaking her head. He felt the movement and pushed himself off her, then started pleading with her. 'He's not that bad, Lara. He's thirty-five. Not so old. He's not religious. He's not like the father, or the uncles. He's educated. He doesn't expect you to follow religious rules. He even looks OK. I have photos I can show you. He has money and status out there. You will be able to talk to him as an equal, to arrange things, to live over here, at least part of the time. I am arranging a place for you here, a real place for you to live, a place you will love.' She was still shaking her head. 'You can wear what you want. He has guaranteed that. And you'll have money. More than you could ever earn in the job you have now. They live in a fucking palace in Islamabad. The family land is out west, but you won't be expected to go there. You can live here. You can live in this country. You can work still. You can be a lawyer. And I will make it up to you. I am buying a place that—'

'No,' she said. She spoke quietly. But he kept talking. So she said it louder. 'No! I said no. I mean no.' He stopped talking. 'I will never do it, Pasha. I would rather die—'

'For fuck's sake!' He leaped to his feet. 'You will kill yourself and me and mother. Three people. Do you get that? Not just you. You are making choices about other people's lives too.'

She shook her head vigorously. 'No, Pasha. I'm not. Those were choices you made. Not me. I had nothing to do with this.'

'You took the money . . . you went to the school. You'd be in some sweat shop in the East End now, sewing cloth. I rescued you.'

'You did what you thought was right. I can believe that now. But I have to do the same. I cannot consent to this. It has nothing to do with me. I won't come to Lancashire. I won't come anywhere with you. You will have to come to some other arrangement with them.'

He stopped crying and took a breath. 'OK,' he said. 'Look at me. Look closely at me, Lara. I'm going to tell you something else now. I want you to look closely at me so that you can decide whether I am telling the truth or not. You understand?'

'This is a waste of time, Pasha. I won't change my mind—'

'You have no idea what the world out there is like, Lara. You're like a little child. Two days ago – because of what I do, because of the world I live in – two days ago I gave an instruction for someone to be killed. Look at me. *Look at me!*' She didn't want to. He stepped towards her and grabbed her jaw again, forcing her to face him. '*Look into my eyes!*' he hissed. '*See the truth!*' She looked, briefly, and saw the expression she had seen when she had first come in, the expression she had been unable to read. It was fear. 'It happened,' he said. 'It was done. A life was taken. The same will happen tonight. Another life.' He took a huge breath, ran his hands through his hair. He was sweating. He looked completely desperate. 'That's part of what I do,' he said, voice shaking. 'Seven years ago I did it myself.' He stepped back, letting go of her. He held his hands up. 'With these fucking hands. I shot someone. Do you understand that? *I* did that. Me. Pasha. Your brother. That's what I'm in, that's the filthy fucking cesspit I'm swimming in. I kill people,

Lara. I kill them. If I have to then I do it myself, or I pay others to do it for me. Do you understand that?'

She was horrified, speechless. He was telling the truth. She knew it without looking at him, just from the way he was speaking. And from the suspicions, from everything that had been rumoured about him. Six months ago, in chambers, there had been a case that police from a specialist squad had asked she not be given. They had feared a 'conflict of interest'. She knew what Pasha was doing then, but just couldn't admit it.

'I would not lie about these things,' he said. 'I'm not proud of them. I don't want to tell you about them. But I need you to understand the character of the world you are part of, whether you like it or not.'

'I'm not part of it—'

'Shut up! Shut up and listen!' He took out his mobile phone and held it up. 'I can call someone now,' he said, speaking very quietly. 'They will go to Camden and find Christopher Napier. I know where he is because one of my people has just followed a very careless idiot called Paul Curtis from my Richmond place to Curtis's flat. That's where Napier is. If I call them and give the order they will go in and kill him. It's that simple.'

'Oh, Pasha. Please don't say that . . . please . . .' She could feel her legs starting to shake, the tears springing to her eyes again.

'Either you come with me now,' he said, 'or I do it. I said you had an important choice to make. Well, that's it. You want Chris Napier to live or not?'

23

Jeff Fletch was driving a sleek, black BMW saloon. Andy waited for it to pull up to him in the Acton car park, then got in the front passenger seat. Fletch looked grim. He leaned over and shook his hand with too tight a grip, then pulled out. 'We'll go for a little drive,' he said.

They drove about a mile, to an ordinary residential street, still in Acton. Neither of them said anything until the engine was switched off. 'Did you tell them it was me?' Fletch asked.

Andy shook his head. He'd been in a fraught meeting when Fletch had called him. Stanesby, Hemmings, Snowden, Pearce, DS Exeter – all the supervisors sitting round a table trying to work out who on their teams was bent, who was most likely to be selling information to Durrani. Andy had said virtually nothing unless he was specifically asked a question. He had wanted to get out, get back to Helen and the kids. He had no confidence whatsoever that the leak wasn't one of the people sitting round the table with him.

'Good,' Fletch said.

'Is it? I don't know what's good, what's bad. Or who. Not any more.'

'You look worried about that.'

'That's right.' He stared out of the window, put his hand

up to his mouth and started chewing the edge of a finger. 'I'm used to things being a little clearer than this.'

'You can't trust anyone you've been working with,' Fletch said. 'You realise that? Someone on your team has compromised you.'

'Obviously.'

'Any ideas who?'

Andy shook his head again. 'That's what they're trying to work out in there.'

'OK. Well, we'll leave them to it. This is what *we* do now. Time is crucial. Durrani has lost his solicitors thanks to decisions made by your superiors, so he can't complete his property deals on schedule. That will anger and worry the Asuris – and Khan. Your friend Mark Johnson is due to report back to Khan on Sunday. If he has managed to get a copy of the original valuation on the Brighton property, plus some proof that Durrani was paying the surveyors to undervalue it substantially, then I think Durrani's life will become very difficult on Monday. Time will have run out for him. That his co-conspirator Ross has been murdered will only add weight to what your friend can tell Khan. Khan will naturally assume Durrani killed Ross because Ross got cold feet. That will render Durrani a liability in their eyes. A liability and a fraud. You get the picture. So it is absolutely essential that you get whatever information you can from Mark Johnson as soon as possible, and certainly before Monday. Whatever he has now, right now, we need it. We need enough to bring Durrani in this weekend and we need to absolutely prevent Johnson giving any information to Khan, even if that involves payments to Johnson. You understand? That's the only way to get this thing back on track. We've been outwitted. Fair enough. It happens. It happens all the time, in fact. But you haven't got to let it skew things. You treat it as part of the job, part of the world we move in. That's all. Someone is dirty. That shouldn't be a surprise. The key thing is to defeat them. So you keep a clear eye on the target, make alternative arrangements, stick to your original goal. To do that we need to reel Durrani in, as planned. Can I be sure that you understand that? That's how we move on from here. You understand?'

'We don't know where Durrani is. We have nothing on him. No cover. All we've got left is a team watching Christopher Napier. We haven't even got cover on Durrani's sister. It's all been pulled . . .'

'I realise that. But finding Durrani is something I can handle. What I need from you is the information from Mark Johnson and the guarantee that Johnson will *not* give the information to Khan. Can you do that?'

'You think I should trust you? Why you? I can't trust anyone else.' He turned and stared at Fletch, the muscles in his face bunched tight with tension.

Fletch shrugged, as if the question were irrelevant. 'You don't need to trust me,' he said. 'If it makes you happier, then assume I'm bent – don't tell me anything you don't wish to get back to Durrani. I don't need to know anything. I just need you to call Johnson and do as I've asked.'

Andy looked away. 'And what do I tell them when I go back into the meeting? Stanesby is there.'

'Don't go back. Go home. Call Mark Johnson now. Let me know what he says.'

'That's not the way I usually work.'

'Well, this isn't a normal set of circumstances. Let me worry about the sensitivities of your superiors.' He paused, then looked away and spoke very quietly, almost to himself. 'Besides, I doubt there will be many of them left once this affair is over.' He looked back at Andy. 'Don't mistake my demeanour for calm, Mr Macall. I am absolutely fucking livid about this. Durrani is *my* operation, *my* target. He was a key opportunity for us to establish connections in a vital area of interest. And by us I mean ourselves *and* our alliance partners. The effort to get Durrani on board is a joint US/ UK operation. It is *that* significant. If it gets fucked up then I will make sure somebody pays. You understand what I'm telling you? Somebody will fucking pay for this.' He took a breath, his face suddenly bright red. 'But don't let that concern you. Can you do what I'm asking?'

It was the first display of real anger he had seen since Durrani had held a sign up telling him to fuck off. Andy nodded. 'Yes. We're already halfway there, in fact.'

Fletch raised his eyebrows. 'Meaning?'

'Meaning Mark called me about an hour ago.' So far he had told no one about the call. 'He has the material already.'

He saw Fletch's eyes light up, then his whole body seemed to relax a little. He even smiled, fleetingly. 'Thank God,' he said. 'When can you get it?'

'I don't know. I need to call him back.'

'Make it quick. I don't want to leave anything to chance. We're exposed as it is.'

'I'll try for tonight.'

Fletch nodded again, this time obviously pleased with him. 'Good,' he said.

'The other part is harder,' Andy added. 'Mark has to present *something* to Khan, obviously. So he may need an incentive to fudge that.'

'I imagined it might come to that.' He gave the unpleasant thin smile Andy remembered. 'But that's not a problem. I told you this was a joint US/UK operation and I meant it. I have very large sums available to buy success. I can transfer money to his business account within twenty-four hours. How much do you think will suffice?'

'I don't know. I'll ask.'

'You do that and I'll find Durrani. That a deal?'

'If you want to call it that . . .'

'I do. Our deal. Between me and you. That's vital. Don't go fucking things up by telling Snowden, or Stanesby. Or anybody. This is our little operation now. We keep it tight. We tell no one. We pull in the prize.' He almost looked excited. He leaned over and started the engine. 'I'll drop you back at the car park. Get in your car and drive away. No stopping to chat. I'll take the fall-out. That clear?'

As they drove, Andy called Mark. They quickly agreed on a meet in the same place as the first time – the wooded area off the A636, just north of the Woodall service area, at ten that night. He passed this on to Fletch, but not the location.

'Where are you meeting?' Fletch asked immediately. 'You should tell me that also.'

'Should I?'

'Yes. For your safety. In case I don't hear from you again. In case I have to get sniffer dogs out looking for your body.'

Andy scowled. 'Are you being serious?'

Fletch didn't smile. 'Durrani killed Ross. Isn't that what you think? The stakes are high for him. You think he thought Ross was responsible for exposing him to his solicitors, so he killed Ross, but the possibility of Mark Johnson exposing him to Khan and the Asuris carries an even greater threat for him. Your friend Johnson needs to be very careful, I would think. Now where are you to meet him? You need to tell someone, and it can't be any of your team or supervisors.'

Andy hesitated for a moment, then told him.

*

Andy's mobile started ringing before they were even back at the car park. Snowden. He ignored it. It rang four more times as he drove back to Harrow. Three times it was Snowden, once Hemmings. Then there were texts, increasingly angry, all from Snowden. He sent one back saying he had a domestic crisis and would ring later. That prompted another flurry of unanswered calls.

Then he was back home, the kids running at him, shouting, excited, Helen standing there in the hall with bags packed. He frowned, crouching down to hug Magnus and Sophie.

'Brighton,' Helen said, reading his puzzled expression. 'Remember? The big beach trip.'

'Shit,' he muttered. He saw Helen's face drop.

'You're kidding me,' she said. 'They've been going on about it all day, Andy. And it's not the beach they're looking forward to. It's time with you.'

'You coming with us, Dad?' Magnus asked. 'You said you were.'

He thought quickly. Helen looked like she was going to throw a complete fit. His intention had been to finally tell her about the threat, ask her to move to her mum's for the night, until he could get back from meeting Mark. 'Maybe you could all still go,' he suggested. They had booked a guest house for two nights. 'I have a problem with tonight though—'

'What kind of problem?' Magnus demanded.

'A work problem, son. It happens.' He looked up at Helen. She was fuming, trying to stop herself exploding in front of the kids. 'Let me and your mum talk about it a minute,' he said. 'We'll sort something out.'

Magnus was persuaded to entertain his sister for a bit.

They went into the kitchen. Helen stood with her arms folded, face set.

'There's a police guard in the street,' he said. That changed the parameters. The anger vanished at once.

He told her about it, about Durrani, the operation, the meeting in the petrol station, the loss of cover, the uncertainties. 'To try to get him back under control I have to go north tonight,' he said. 'I have to meet someone. I was going to ask you to take the kids to your mum's, so I didn't worry. But you could go to Brighton, as planned. That would do just as well. Maybe better. I could join you all there tomorrow.'

Now she was beginning to worry. 'Wouldn't we be safer staying here?' she asked. 'If you've got cover outside. You sure they're there? I haven't noticed. Christ, Andy, you should have told me all this earlier. You should have told me.'

'I didn't want to worry you until I was sure. The uniforms are there, yes. I checked on the way in. But police cover doesn't make me feel as safe as I need to be. There's an additional problem.'

She frowned, not understanding, so he told her about the possible leak. 'Maybe it would be better to go to Brighton,' he finished. 'You go there and I tell the boys outside you've gone shopping and will be back soon. You drop off the police radar. I'd feel safer that way.'

'Are you crazy, Andy? Is this that serious?'

'I don't know.' He shook his head. He could feel his heart going too fast. Just thinking about it was releasing adrenalin. He ran a hand through his hair. He felt strung out. He tried to slow his breathing a bit. Helen saw what was going on and ran him a glass of water. He drank it down. 'I've never been in this position before,' he said.

'We're dealing with someone who kills and who has a lot to lose. And the system is leaky. Durrani has help from the inside.'

Magnus pushed the kitchen door open and came in. 'Are we going now?' he asked. 'Are you coming, Dad?'

Andy nodded. 'Yes. Let's go. I can't come tonight, but I'll be there when you wake up tomorrow. We'll get up and go straight down to the beach. I promise.'

24

Paul stood leaning over his sink, cold water dripping from his face and hair, nursing his anger whilst he stared at the image of his battered face. Silently, he took an inventory of the damage. His left eye was swollen closed, leaking tissue fluid and tears down his cheek. His lips were fat, cut, bloody. There was a long scrape across his left cheek – clearly showing the tread pattern from someone's boot. Inside his mouth a tooth on the left side had broken and gashed the inside of his cheek. He had bitten his tongue. Both nostrils were blocked with blood. He had a tender pulsating bump about the size of a half egg to the rear left of his skull, a splitting headache that painkillers had failed to dull. A stiffening left leg. Various other bruises throughout his body.

But none of that mattered.

Lara was gone. Vanished into thin air. They had to find her. She had not been at her flat when he had got there, and there had been no sign that she had been there, no sign of any struggle. Chris had texted and called her every minute once Paul reported her absence, finally getting a response after a few hours – a short, uncharacteristic text saying she wanted to be left alone, after which her phone was dead. They'd had a fight, Chris had confessed, but Chris was sure that wasn't the problem.

Jules had agreed and driven straight to Lara's flat to help Paul search it. Lara's passport was nowhere to be seen, but they had recovered an address book. Paul had been suffering a little memory loss then – the details of the kicking had been absent. But the word 'Whalley' in the address book had brought back that someone had mentioned the place, as if Pasha might be there. Jules had recognised the name immediately, because she'd been there, with Lara, to see her brother, about three years ago. Whalley was in Lancashire, it seemed. Paul was guessing that was where Lara and Pasha were. So that was where they were going, in Jules's car, as soon as he could sort out a couple of other things.

He pushed himself off the sink and walked back out into the flat. Jules and Chris were sitting in the same position he had left them in, huddled together on the sofa like someone had died.

'I have to check something downstairs,' Paul said. 'I'll be back in a minute.'

He took the lift down to street level and walked out the front doors. A couple of people stared at him, but mostly people averted their eyes. He looked rough now, dangerous. The day was relatively warm, sometimes sunny, sometimes grey and colder. The street was full of traffic and pedestrians, noisy and normal. Paul stood near the front door looking at it all through his squinting eye, waiting for movement from the parked cars on either side of the road, or the people standing opposite on the pavement.

Was he being watched? That was the question. He'd got a feeling about it on the way back from Richmond, then again as he'd got back here from Lara's flat, with Jules, in Jules's car. On the Richmond trip he'd been in poor shape, not very observant. Nevertheless, he'd had a suspicion that a young white guy had been both on the street in Richmond where he'd got the cab from, and later in this very street. No one he'd seen before. But had he recognised him in the two places? He wasn't anywhere to be seen now. And if any of the men in the cars were actually watching him then they certainly weren't making it obvious.

He turned back and went through the entrance again. He stood for a while in the shadows there, watching still. His fear was that Pasha would have a real go at Chris. That had seemed unlikely a few hours ago, but with Lara vanished and his surprising reception stamped, literally, into his brain, he didn't wish to take any chances. It would be Chris they were after, not him. They'd already had a chance to cripple him. So Chris would have to come with them to Whalley – there was no question of leaving him here unprotected – but it would be better, perhaps, not to just drive out with Chris in full view. Just in case.

He took his phone out and dialled Jimmy Chapman's number. He'd already tried to get Jimmy four times that afternoon. Now finally he answered. Paul spoke quietly to him, urgently, explaining his need. He wanted a gun.

'You in trouble, son? Your voice sounds funny.'

'Not really. Bit of a fat lip, that's all. Nothing I can't handle. But I need cover.'

'Maybe you should tell me about it.'

'I can't do that, Jimmy. Not right now. I need your help, if possible, with no questions. I'm sorry to ask like this.'

There was a long silence. The number he was calling was a Spanish mobile, so he guessed Jimmy was somewhere in Spain.

'Your mother will kill me if she finds out . . .' Jimmy said, eventually. 'You sure you don't need help – I mean manpower?'

'Just a clean weapon. I know what I'm doing.' His tongue

caught in his swollen mouth and the words came out indistinct, all rolling into each other. Jimmy missed it. He repeated it, but more slowly.

There was another silence, then the muffled sound of Jimmy talking to someone, covering the mouthpiece.

'Where are you now?' Jimmy asked.

'London. But I have to go north – to Lancashire.'

'What kind of thing you want?'

'Something small. A handgun.'

He waited whilst there was more talking off line. 'Did you say Lancashire?'

'Yes.'

'Which bit?'

'Near Blackburn.'

'Hang on a minute.' The line seemed to cut. Presumably Jimmy had silenced the microphone. He came back after about thirty seconds. 'Can you be at Blackburn Travelodge, on the M65, in about three hours?' he asked, sighing.

'Yes.'

'We'll do it there then. But you better know what you're into, son, because I don't like this. Your dad will be turning in his grave.'

25

Pasha cut the call from his mobile and placed the phone in his pocket. Unsteadily, he crossed the two steps to the window and leaned heavily on the sill. His heart was going crazy. He felt so dizzy he thought he was going to fall over. All day he had been hoping not to get that call, and that the next call wouldn't be necessary. Nothing was working out now. Everything that could go wrong was going wrong. He glanced back across the room at where his sister was sitting on the bed, head in her hands. She didn't look up.

He selected Caserne's number and called him. Caserne answered before Pasha even heard it ring. He'd been waiting, obviously. 'Do it,' Pasha said.

There was a pause, then, 'Sure. No problem.' That irritating French accent. 'I'm already there. I'm waiting. When will he get here?'

'Just before ten. After, go straight to the place in North Yorkshire. The place I told you about. You remember how to get there?'

'Yes.'

'I'll meet you there with the ID documents as soon as I can. And trash this phone now. OK?'

'OK.'

He cut the line, then almost collapsed against the sill, sucking a huge breath into his lungs. That was it. He'd done

187

it. So easy to do. But his legs were shaking like jelly. Easy to say the words, but his body knew what he was doing, knew the horror of it.

He tried to get his nerves in order by staring out at the garden below. This place was the safe house, the place he had been assured they didn't know about – 'they' meaning any and every security or law enforcement agency that had recently been poking their noses into his affairs. The whole point of the place was that it was low profile – there was no security, no cameras, no fences, nothing. You could walk in and out. There were his men downstairs, of course, four idiots, two with guns. But they wouldn't help much, not if push came to shove.

Why had he ever thought he could trust Ross, he wondered? The miserable fucker had added countless layers of fear to his life – if Ross really was to blame, that is. They had told him it had been Ross, but Ross hadn't admitted anything, not even when he'd been bleeding to death. And if it hadn't been Ross it had to have been the surveyor – a very old friend called Ali Kapoor. It seemed unlikely that Ali would have betrayed him. Yet only Ali and Ross were in on the scheme.

Pasha put a fist into his mouth and bit down onto it, waiting until the pain was stronger than the unwanted, insistent images: Ross lying in the leaves, begging for his life, going on about his daughters and his wife. Caserne had fucked it up – cut too deep, severed an artery. Because he was a fucking butcher, used to cutting up cows. They'd tried to get a tourniquet on him, to save him. Or rather he had; Caserne had stood there watching whilst he'd struggled to save Ross's miserable life. All the blood rushing out. It had been incredible – one little cut, then all that blood, something controlled turning into something desperate in a split second. Had Caserne known? Fucking Caserne. Could he be trusted not to fuck this one up? There was no one else he knew to do it.

And all because he had wanted something to give to Lara, some way of making all this sweeter for her. Her dream house. The asking price was as low as he had been able to force it – with considerable leverage – but still much more than the money that would come to them when she married Shamsuddin. So the fraud on the Asuris was supposed to make up the shortfall. Now he was going to have to think of something else. Worse, now he was going to have to explain to the Asuris that there was a delay. In fact, he was probably going to have to beg Khan to assist him, to 'recommend' new solicitors. Because the solicitors he'd just lost were bound to pass on a warning to whoever took over the files now, which meant it couldn't be just anyone. It would have to be a bent firm, someone on Khan's obligation list.

'Can you leave me now?'

He turned round to find his sister standing, her face streaked with smudged eye liner. 'Can you get out, please?' she repeated.

'I'm going,' he said. His voice sounded hoarse. That was all the adrenalin in his blood. He held his hands out in front of him and looked at them. They were shaking like he'd just been in a car crash. That was the effect of the phone call. And the rest of it. He looked down his mental list of impending problems. There were too many to keep track of. What did he have to do tonight? For seconds he could think of nothing and his mind was a complete blank. Then it all came back, with the attendant feelings of panic. He had to get out of here, as soon as possible, taking everyone with him except Lara. They would all go to a restaurant in the next village, a place he knew well, where the owner knew him. He would make sure that he was seen, recognised, recorded. That would be his alibi, just in case, his personal alibi. It meant he would have to leave Lara here, with just one guard, perhaps. That was a risk he needed to assess.

'You like the room?' he asked.

She turned away and looked at the wall.

'I had them set it up for you.'

She said nothing. She was trying to control herself, he knew. She was trying not to break down. He had probably made her the most miserable she had ever been in her life. That was his achievement. The woman he loved most in the world, and he had done this to her.

'There's everything I thought you might want,' he said, uselessly. He hadn't wanted her to feel like a prisoner, so he'd set it up as comfortably as he could, with pretty pictures, a widescreen, a computer, though no net connection. He didn't trust her that much. But she could work on the computer, if she wanted. He'd tried to get her to bring work stuff from her flat, to regard the trip as a short holiday – within five days she would be back in town, after all – but she hadn't gone for any of that. 'What's the point?' she'd demanded. 'You're going to marry me off. I'm going to spend the rest of my life locked in a house in some shit hole in Pakistan.'

'Not true,' he'd said. 'I told you, you can live here. You can work here.'

'I don't fucking think so.'

She had ideas about Shamsuddin Asuri that bore little relation to reality. She hadn't met him recently, as Pasha had. Asuri ran a bank in Lahore. He was a quiet, cultivated, careful man, albeit thirteen years older than Lara. He had little to do with the tribal politics of the region, still less with any kind of fundamentalism. That was the province of his father and uncles, who were a completely different species. And he'd had a thing going for Lara – a straight-forward attraction, as far as Pasha could gauge it – since he'd first seen her at sixteen. That wasn't the reason he wanted to marry her, of course, but it helped. The reason he was going to marry her was because he had been told to, because greater tribal interests were at stake, because Lara – though she didn't know it – occupied a particular place in a complex tribal jigsaw. And because, like Pasha, Shamsuddin Asuri was scared of his father and uncles, scared of what they were capable of.

'Leave me, Pasha,' she said again now. 'I'm not going to run, or try to get away. But I need to be alone. Please.'

He met her eyes and tried to read them. Was she telling the truth? She looked defeated, broken. He felt utterly disgusted with himself.

26

'What are you thinking about?' Jules asked quietly.

Paul looked up at her, trying to free his thoughts from Rob Ogle and the stumps of his legs, the silent screams as he had hauled him out of the twisted cab, the total, unnerving silence of that moment. He shook his head. 'Nothing.'

'Tell me. You can tell me.'

He forced himself to smile at her. Probably she thought he was worrying about the next few hours, about what he was going to do. 'I was thinking about Pakistan,' he said. He cleared his throat. The swelling in his mouth was already less, but the words still sounded thick to him. She reached a hand across the table and squeezed his fingers.

'It's not like you think,' he said. He closed his fingers around hers, letting himself enjoy it for a moment. 'Contrary to what Lara would have you believe, or your experience with her brother, not everything about Pakistan is bad.'

He looked around them. They were in the service station restaurant, at a plastic, fixed table, on plastic, fixed benches. He picked up his coffee and took a very wary sip, carefully guiding the tepid liquid past his smashed tooth. He needed caffeine. He'd slept for almost three hours on the way up, letting his brain shut down, recover. Chris was still sound asleep now, out in the car. Paul looked to his left, through the windows, squinting through his one good eye, and could see the car there, in the front row of the car park.

He needed to get his brain in gear. This was the place where he was meant to meet Jimmy's man, and anyway, they were only about thirty minutes from Whalley now. He needed to be sharp. But his brain kept coming back to what had happened a year ago.

To keep the thoughts at bay he started talking to her about Pakistan. He tried to think of innocuous memories. He told her about Tirich Mir, about Chitral airfield, landing there by night, getting off the plane into a brisk mountain wind, everything suddenly clean, cool, dry. Not like Pakistan at all. He told her how he had stared at the immense outline in the distance with open mouth, stunned. Twenty-five thousand, two hundred and eighty-nine feet. Tirich Mir. The highest mountain in the Hindu Kush. The Lord of Darkness. It hadn't seemed twenty-five miles away. It had dwarfed everything, a terrifying presence at the end of all views.

'I was there working for a guy called Iskander Kom,' he explained. 'He was trying to arm militias in Chitral, to keep out the fundamentalists.' She looked more interested in that, so he went on a bit. He could see her thinking about what he was saying, what he might be leaving out.

She was doing well, he thought, all things considered. She was a posh, middle class woman with little experience of violence or crime, and now it was coming at her in spades. Her best friend kidnapped by her brother, maybe. Chris bottled, strangers threatening to kill her. She'd allowed Paul to conceal both Chris and herself beneath blankets in the rear of the car whilst he had driven out of the garage in Camden, just in case there was someone waiting. In the context, that must have been frightening. Then she'd driven up here, allowing him to sleep, and she was sitting there now, apparently calm, composed, though she knew that at any minute a man was going to walk in and give Paul a gun.

'Lara would rather die than go to Pakistan,' he said. 'But I think it's the most beautiful place I've ever seen. In most of the country I met only honest, ordinary people who were trying to keep their heads above water. Not everyone over there is a fanatic.'

She smiled at him. 'I realise that,' she said.

Of course she did. She was an educated, intelligent woman. He shrugged his shoulders, then remembered that Rob Ogle had been right beside him on that trip to Chitral. They had stood together on the runway.

There was a bit of an awkward silence, her fingers still there, in his hand. Then she looked away and moved her hand. He focused his eyes behind her. A man had just entered and was standing by the coffee machines, a blue holdall in his hands. He matched the description Jimmy had given him. It was just a matter of him putting the hold-all down and walking out, leaving it.

'We're clear about what's going to happen when we get to Whalley, right?' she asked.

Paul kept his eyes on the man. 'I'll check it out,' he said. 'See how it looks.'

'Then we go to the police.'

He nodded. 'If we think she's there, against her will, then we go to the police.' There wouldn't be any other option, assuming there wasn't just Pasha and Lara in the building. The man walked back towards the wall by the entrance, put the holdall down next to the wall – without making eye contact – stood for a moment beside it, then turned and walked out the way he had come.

'OK,' Paul said, standing quickly. 'That's it.'

'What?' She looked alarmed.

The restaurant wasn't very full, and no one seemed to have noticed the bag, but he didn't want some innocent bystander wandering up to it and raising a bomb alert. 'You wait here,' he said. 'Wait a minute or so, then come out to the car. I'll already be there. If I'm not then just drive off without me.'

27

Lara stood alone in the room, locked in. When they were little, she remembered, birds had fallen down the disused chimney in their house in Manchester. They could hear them flapping desperately behind the walled-off fireplace, trying to get out. The noise went on for days, getting fainter and fainter. Finally it stopped. Even Pasha used to hate it, even he used to know that they were listening to the last struggles of something stricken with terror, buried alive. He wouldn't feel those things now though.

She was locked in with a guard downstairs. Pasha had been gone over an hour. He wouldn't be back until after midnight. Time enough.

She emptied the bag she'd brought onto the bed. Her pulse was racing as she scattered the contents, knocking things off the bed and onto the floor as she tried to find the pill bottle. He had given her very little time to pack in Clapham, but she had found the bottle in her medicine cabinet. She picked it up now, unscrewed the top and carefully poured the pills onto the bedside table, keeping them from rolling with a shaking hand. They were a relic from eight years ago, something she had kept to remind her. To remind her, she had thought, never to go there again. But everything came back in a circle, and here she was. As a teenager she had assiduously hoarded these pills after her father had died.

She started to count the pills carefully. They were some kind of sleeping pill or tranquilliser, she didn't know what because the label on the bottle was now too faded to read. She had collected two full bottles' worth over a year or so, then taken an entire bottle, locked into a toilet cubicle in the new school, in London. Jules had found her though, saved her life when she had not wanted to be saved. Because she had been serious – she had intended to take her life, albeit with poor juvenile planning.

She held the pills in her hand and remembered the devastating, crushing depression that had crippled her in the months after her father's suicide and the move to London. She could feel it starting again now. But this time she wouldn't let it go so far. She had a way out. In fact, it was the only way out. It was just a matter of getting a glass of water, sitting calmly on the bed and taking the pills.

28

In the end, too worried to leave anything to chance, Andy had driven Helen and the kids to Brighton himself, which meant it was after eight thirty before he got clear of the city again, to head north. By then it was already getting dark. Expecting to be back that night he was in the Verso. He sent a quick text to Mark's mobile number, saying he would be a little late, but as he got to Yorkshire and took the exit to double back under the railway bridge he was running about half an hour over.

He had marked the location on his satnav, so found it easily enough. He turned carefully onto the dirt track into the trees, headlights on. A hundred yards ahead he could see Mark's Range Rover parked where it had been last time, driver's door once again open. He pulled in behind it, cut the engine and lights and waited impatiently for Mark to appear at his door. After about a minute he switched the headlights back on, looked more carefully at the Range Rover and decided Mark wasn't in it. He scanned the wall of trees, but could see nothing in the half light. Maybe he'd gone for a piss in the bushes.

He waited a couple of minutes longer, then switched his lights off and got out. With the lights off it was darker than he'd thought.

'Mark?' he said, trying to resist the urge to whisper. He

could hear a low-level hissing noise off in the distance – the M1, he thought, on reflection, and not a stream.

'Mark! You there?'

The night was still, windless. The Range Rover began to look like something vaguely abandoned. He walked over to it and looked through the open driver's door. An empty seat, an empty vehicle. He looked round quickly. The scene began to change, moving from some harmless image of a parked car to something not quite right. The hairs on the back of his neck began to stand on end.

'Stop pissing around, Mark!' he said, a little louder, looking uselessly into the darkness past the trees. But already he knew in his stomach that Mark wasn't messing around. Mark wasn't here.

He took a deep breath, trying to calm himself, then switched consciously into another mode – a more careful approach. He had to be calm, assess the situation properly, if only because the increase in his heart rate compromised his awareness. He could feel his heart thumping, hear the rush of blood past his ears. Underneath he was starting to panic, which was silly, and counterproductive.

He tried to think his way through it, keeping dead still by the open Range Rover door. He was alone here and something wasn't as it should have been. The woods around him were dense, hushed, more threatening by the second, but he had to stop himself thinking that way. He couldn't see far enough into them to be certain that someone wasn't out there, watching him.

He walked quickly back to his car, concentrating on the sounds he could hear, on any little movement in the periphery of his vision. He opened his passenger door and from the glove compartment took out his torch, then turned back to the trees on the other side and saw something before he even had a chance to switch the beam on. A vivid colour.

His heart started pounding again. It was blood he could see. It was all over the gravel by the passenger side of the Range Rover. He switched the torch on and shone it there. *Blood.* He said it to himself, trying to take it in properly. There was a clear trail of it from near the car over to the trees. Suddenly he felt paralysed. He swallowed hard, his throat and mouth very dry. He wanted to shout 'Mark' again, but couldn't now, because now everything was screaming *danger, get out!!* He walked slowly back to the driver's side of the Verso and closed his eyes, listening hard. He could hear nothing at all, but he had a clear sense that someone was watching him, that someone was out there.

Which meant something had happened to Mark, because it wouldn't be him out there.

He fought with the information for a while, knowing full well that there was no such thing as a reliable sensation of being watched. He considered the options. Was it likely there was someone there? Worst case scenario was that someone had come here and attacked Mark, in which case they wouldn't be hanging around.

Could he phone someone, now, tell them what he was doing, where he was? He took his mobile out and looked at it. He had a signal. But something stopped him. He kept the door of the Verso open and walked deliberately away from it, over to the blood. There was more of it, leading off into the trees. Whoever it was they were going to be in trouble. He stepped forward, keeping away from the actual splashes, and stood by the first tree. The undergrowth beneath it was waist height. It was flattened down and matted with blood as far as he could see into the darkness. He could actually see a parting, a trampling of the fern, where someone had passed through, spilling the blood all over. He took a route to the right of it, shining his torch all around, then took a few steps in. Almost immediately he saw legs. He stopped.

They were sticking out of the bushes and the shadows, about ten feet ahead, flat out. Perfectly still. Around him he could hear nothing. Just his own blood in his neck, his heart in his chest. Now he felt sick with fear.

He waited a long time. Too long, he knew. Whoever was lying there might be injured, not dead, might need urgent help. Now was the time to make that call.

But something still held him back. Instead he found himself inching forward against the fear, senses strained to a tight wire of attention. He circled slightly, working his way to get an angle through the vegetation, coming around slowly towards where he guessed the head would be. After a few minutes, by crouching low, he could see the chest, about ten feet away in the beam of the torch.

There was no discernible movement. But he'd heard about people being caught out like that – no sign of life at a distance, then eyes open when you got close, breathing shallow, pulse present. Then the urgency, the mad, desperate rush to save them. Some were lost like that. Time was always against you. You couldn't assume anything. Or better, you should *assume* they're alive and need urgent assistance. That was the rule.

He stood up and walked forward, decision made.

He was almost right there, above the place where the chest was, buried in the plants and twisting brambles. He checked again all round him, shining the torch slowly a full 360 degrees, then stooped and cleared the foliage.

It was Mark.

He took a deep breath, a riot of thoughts and fears

suddenly swamping him. It was Mark and he was dead. He could hear himself gasping for breath. It was *all* he could hear.

He crouched low, legs trembling, and looked without touching. There was no need to touch to see he was dead, no need to check for vital signs. The throat was slit open in a big, bloody gash. There was blood all over the face, all over the plants around him, all over the ground he was lying on, all over his clothing. The same Barbour he'd had on two days ago.

He could feel his stomach tensing into a taut, constricted ball. Physically, he was acting as if he'd run very fast from somewhere, the noise of his breathing furious in his ears. If someone was still here – if whoever had done this really was watching from a distance – he could run up at liberty and take his best shot. Andy wouldn't hear a thing. He straightened quickly.

He had to look for a pulse. He knew that. Just to be absolutely certain. He bent over again, swearing under his breath, not sure what he was feeling or doing. He put his hand out and flinched as his fingers found the skin. It was unyielding, lifeless. But not cold. This hadn't happened long ago. Maybe less than an hour, even. The smell was in his nose now, the smell of fear and struggle, the stink of faeces, the sweet, awful stench of congealing blood. There were knife wounds all over the torso, the stomach and bowel contents had seeped out with the blood. There were insects buzzing already, homing in on the odours.

He stood up again and took deep, measured breaths, turning his face away. He wanted to lean against the nearest tree to support his shaking legs, but didn't want to touch anything else. It was a murder scene. He was contaminating it, leaving his DNA all over. He kept shining the torch around, looking for movement.

His head was spinning with questions now. He had to try to think a way through it, work out what to do.

It was Mark and he was dead.

He tried to compute what that should mean.

'Jesus Christ!' he whispered. 'Jesus fucking Christ!' His voice was trembling.

He *was* frightened. Very frightened. He turned round yet again, scanning the shades. Nothing.

Time to make the call? He took out his mobile but almost immediately felt too unsafe. He made his way quickly back to the car. Call the local police? He wanted to. But something kept jarring. Mark had been careful about his personal security. So how had this happened? How had Durrani – if Durrani was behind this – found out about the meet in this place? It seemed inconceivable that Mark would have allowed someone to follow him here. Had he, Andy, given it away? Had he slipped up somewhere, allowed the information to get to whoever was leaking information to Durrani? Who had he told?

Fletch.

He had told only Fletch. So was it possible that this had happened because information had leaked from Fletch, from MI5? *Think it through.* He tried desperately to get his brain to focus, but then, far off, from somewhere to the north, he heard sirens. An ambulance? No. It was police, getting rapidly closer. Immediately it was as if he had a thought planted in his head direct from Mark's brain – *someone was setting him up.* The sirens were coming here.

He was being set up.

It was right out of one of Mark's conspiracy plots. He pushed it away, but he got quickly into the car as well.

Suddenly, in all the jumble of confusion he was experiencing, one thing alone seemed clear. Mark had come here to hand him a file on Pasha Durrani. That file wasn't on the body, wasn't in the woods, wasn't obviously in Mark's car. So if this was Durrani's work then he had taken the material. If Andy waited here for the local force to arrive then he would be stuck here for hours and Durrani – assuming it was him – would have a clear run at covering his trail.

There had to be a back-up file, either paper, or on a computer in Mark's work place. So he had to get that quick, before Durrani had the chance to do the same. He had to get to Mark's office and Mark's home before anyone else did.

He started the engine and turned quickly in the limited space. The rear end of the Verso banged into something – a tree? – then he was facing out. He drove quickly over the bumps and onto the road. As he accelerated away he could see blue lights flashing in his rear-view mirror. He thought they would speed up, come after him, but they didn't. They were turning where he had come out. He'd been right. Someone had to have called them to the scene, to get them there whilst he was present. Which meant it *was* possible that someone had been out there, watching him.

29

Just after eleven. Dark. A half moon obscured by patchy cloud. Paul crouched low on the ground, just the other side of the wall, behind bushes and a flower bed, but only seven or eight yards from the side wall of the house. He let his breath settle. Normally, scaling a wall a little over his own height didn't wind him so much, but his head was far from normal, and there was enough intermittent pain from his lower right chest area to make him wonder whether he'd cracked some ribs there.

He'd dosed up on the strongest painkillers he could find, a bottle of 75mg diclofenac, which had been lying in the bathroom cabinet of Lara's Clapham place. The cabinet had been virtually the only area of the house which looked as if someone had gone through it in a hurry. He'd asked Jules about that – whether Lara had an illness that required her to take medication. He was thinking of diabetes, or something similar that might affect the urgency of locating her. But Jules knew of nothing. She had looked worried by the state of the cabinet though, and then, a little later, had confided to him that when she had first met Lara, at St Paul's, Lara had been depressed enough to have taken an overdose of tablets in the toilets at the school, locked in a cubicle there. Jules had found her and raised the alarm. For some reason the information hadn't surprised him at all.

There was no change within the house that might suggest anyone had seen or heard him, so he crept carefully forward, going round the bushes to avoid noise. He'd already circled the house using the street, the gardens of the neighbouring properties and the open fields behind. The place was a fairly large, normal detached residence. In fact, the only thing unusual about it was that it looked too ordinary for the area it was in. Whalley, Paul had discovered, was a serious bolt hole for the top slicers of the region. The village was tucked away in what Paul considered the middle of nowhere, in a place called the Ribble Valley, which was probably chocolate-box scenic, but it had been too dark for them to see much on the way in. The houses in this part of the village – the edge – were all massive, all walled, all surrounded by a lush, mature screen of trees and bushes, all backing onto fields or woods. Most had the usual array of cosmetic security measures: walls with embedded glass shards, prominent alarms and camera systems. The cameras were meant as a deterrent, Paul guessed, since their locations were all obvious and their coverage less than comprehensive. They'd been easy enough to avoid.

The house Jules had pointed out to him, the one he was creeping up to now, was also unusual in that it had no observable security systems at all – no cameras, no barbed wire, no alarm box. There wasn't even an intercom on the front door. A far cry from the Richmond address where he'd got his head kicked in. The wall Paul had just slid over was the only barrier he had come across so far. If he wanted to he could walk right through the front gates and up to the front door, unchallenged.

He'd left the gun Jimmy had obtained for him with Jules and Chris, back in the car, parked two streets away. A small H&K, with two clips. He'd wanted it more to feel safe –

because that was how he was used to ensuring his personal safety – rather than to take the silly risk of humping it around with him. His plan now, as he had repeatedly reassured a very anxious Chris and Jules, was simply to scout this place, to discover what he could without being detected.

So far he'd discovered that the house looked relatively empty. There were no cars parked up outside it, no cars in the big double garage. There was a single light on downstairs, in the room he was approaching now, which he guessed would be the living room. It already seemed highly unlikely that either Lara or Pasha was here. Perhaps no one was here.

He made the house wall and edged along to a window, curtained. He waited a few minutes then inched his head up. The curtains were thin enough to see vague shapes within. He could see the rectangle of light from a TV set, some chairs, perhaps. The TV was on – he could hear it faintly. It was possible someone was sitting in one of the chairs watching it. He would have to assume that. There wasn't a room full of people though. One person, at most two.

He ducked back down and considered his options. He'd tried the rear doors – locked – and looked for open windows – no joy. Which meant he couldn't break in without being challenged. What was the best way to play it? It was possible that Jules had remembered the wrong house. As far as he could see the only sensible thing to do was to walk up to the front door, ring the bell and see who was in. One or two people he could handle. Especially with the gun. He would need to go back to the car and get it. He waited a few more minutes, listening to the sounds around him, then retraced his steps and climbed the wall again.

Jules and Chris were out of the car, coming towards him as he turned into the street.

'We were too fucking worried, man,' Chris explained in a stressed, exaggerated whisper. 'We couldn't wait in there.'

'You said five minutes,' Jules said. 'It's been nearly fifteen.'

They sat in the car whilst he took a long drink from a bottle of water, then explained to them what he was going to do.

'Just go up to the door and knock? Are you fucking mad?' Chris asked.

'And what are we meant to do?' Jules added.

'I want you two to stay here so I don't have to worry about you.'

'So what was the point of us coming?'

He turned and looked at Chris, who didn't look fit enough to participate in anything involving exertion. 'Jules drove,' Paul said. 'For which I'm very grateful. And you'll both be needed later, when we find Lara. Meanwhile, I'm going to check whether she's here. That's why we've driven all this way.' He turned back to Jules, in the front passenger seat. 'You sure that's the place, Jules? I think there might be one person in there. It's like a normal house, not what I'd expected at all.'

She nodded. 'That's the place. I drove last time too. I remember.'

'OK. Give me ten minutes this time, then call my mobile. If you can't get me then call the police. Don't get out of the car. OK?'

He got out and went to the boot, opened it and unzipped the blue holdall. The gun was lying wrapped in a towel. He unwrapped it and, leaning into the boot, tested the mechanism again, then he slotted a clip in, put one in the breech, operated the safety. He pushed the gun down the back of his trousers, tightened his belt, pulled on his leather jacket and set off.

At the house he walked straight through the open gates and up the drive. The distance from the road to the front porch was about twenty metres. He stepped up to the door and looked for a buzzer, or a spyhole. There was a bell, but no spyhole, and no window that looked onto the small porch space he was now standing in. He checked the position of the gun, took a breath and pushed the bell.

There was movement pretty quickly from inside, then the sound of a handle turning. No precautions, no questions from behind the safety of the door. Whoever it was didn't even switch on the porch light directly above Paul's head. The door began to open. Not slowly and cautiously, but as if pulled by someone who had nothing to fear. So what Paul was expecting was to see a middle-aged woman or man – the person who lived here, the person who had been sitting happily watching Friday night TV. He even started to prep his apology. The door stopped, halfway open, a face appeared, peering round it, staring at him.

It was the big white guy, the one who had given him the kicking.

There was a split second of stunned silence, then the man's eyes widened in delayed recognition. He was half a breath behind Paul. That was all Paul needed. The man had the door across his body, one hand visible, his mouth opening to say something.

He kicked the door. He leaned back into the kick and gave it everything he had. The man saw it, started to react, moved backwards, but a split second too late. The edge caught his head before he was clear. The impact was heavy, with a loud cracking noise. The man reeled back into the space behind, shouting in pain and shock. Then Paul was up the last step and in. He got the door past the guy's stumbling body and closed quickly on him. The guy was up against the wall opposite, hands up to his face and blood already coming. Paul started punching.

The anger was like a drug. He let go, let it come, let it flood him with aggressive energy. He leaned in and went at it with all the strength he had. He targeted the head and face, cutting under the arms that came up as protection, then going over them, using short, heavy jabs, right and left, six-seven-eight times, looking for his moment, watching for a gap. Then, as the arms came down a little and the head started to jerk back he took bigger swings. The man was quickly cowering, sliding backwards down the wall, his legs kicking out, connecting with Paul's legs, but not hard enough. Probably the first blow, from the door, had stunned him enough for Paul not to worry. But you couldn't assume. The man was big, and Paul had felt what his fists and feet could do. He wanted to flatten him. He wanted him out cold and suffering. So he kept going until his fists were stinging and there was blood all over his knuckles, all over the wall behind. Then he stepped back and started to kick. When the body sprawled and the shouting stopped, he paused, taking a gasping breath. 'Not so fucking clever now,' he muttered, looking down at the panting, twitching form. Then he leaned back and kicked twice more, aiming more carefully. That did it. The head snapped back, the body flexed with a spasm, then went completely limp.

He bent over and moved the head from side to side. There was no resistance. The eyes were closed, the breathing shallow, rapid. He was out, but probably not for long.

Paul searched the motionless body. There was no gun

anywhere. He took a mobile phone from the man's pocket and crushed it with his heel. Then he wiped his hands on a dry part of the guy's shirt, stepped away, walked over to the room with the light on. The TV was still on, some hospital drama showing. No one else in the room though.

He went quickly through the ground floor as he caught his breath, checking each room. It was hard physical work thumping someone into unconsciousness, and his balance felt uncertain now, the headache pounding at him again.

He ran quickly up the stairs, switching on the lights. The house was a nice size, way bigger than he would ever be able to afford. On the first landing he saw doors off for six rooms, all closed. The stairs continued up a flight. He started opening the doors, one by one, switching the lights on, looking. The first was a bathroom, then a toilet.

The third opened onto a bedroom, with a double bed, a table with a computer, a few chairs, some open suitcases on the floor, clothes. The bed hadn't been slept in. He stepped in and checked the fitted wardrobes, not quite sure what he was looking for – a woman's clothes? The room smelled a little of aftershave, there were a couple of men's shirts and trousers in the wardrobes, but mainly they were empty. A door was open onto an en suite bathroom of luxury proportions, but there was no one in there, and no sign it had been recently used.

He moved on, sucking the air in to try to clear his head. The next room was at the end of the long landing. When he got there he found the door locked. He knocked. No response. He waited a bit, listening to the silences around him and feeling a sudden deep panic in his gut. From downstairs he thought he heard groaning. It occurred to him for the first time that he could have fractured the man's skull, caused serious damage. He had really gone at him. Maybe he was groaning because he was dying.

He stood back and kicked the door in. It gave easily, at the first kick. Immediately he saw a body on the floor within. He crouched, automatically pulling the gun and holding it out in front of him. He was shaking now, worried. He inched in, still crouching, the lights still off. The person on the floor was a woman, he thought. He called out to her, but she didn't move. Right at that point he knew it was Lara, without seeing her properly. He stood up and found the light switch. Then stepped forward, towards her, scanning the space quickly. Small room, one bed, table, chair, laptop.

Then he was down beside her. It was Lara. She was flat out, half on her side, half on her back, lying in a pool of vomit. He could smell it strongly now. He moved her carefully onto her back and looked at her face. It was deathly pale. He started speaking her name. But there was no response at all. The breathing was very shallow, the skin damp to touch, but burning. Like she had a fever. She was wearing the same clothes he'd seen her in this morning. He started asking her if she could hear him. There were little objects in the vomit – capsules of some sort, he thought. Many of them. He recalled what Jules had told him.

He looked frantically around him. He had to get her out of here before the guy downstairs recovered enough to do something. He shoved the gun into his waistband, then stooped and slid his arms under her, very carefully. Then he stood, picking her up, the pain flashing through his ribs. His head was spinning again. He had to get out with her, get to the car, get her to a casualty department. He turned towards the door and started to run.

30

Before he got to the stairs he heard the shout, then the noise following it. He had time to realise that it was Jules who had shouted, that the shout was a cry of pain, that the noise following was a blow, then there was a loud crack.

A firearm. Someone had fired a pistol, from the bottom of the stairs. He had a moment of frozen shock, rooted to the floor, then he was moving again, really frightened. As he turned onto the stairs he could hear the noise of desperate struggling, some shouted warnings, at least two terrified voices all screaming or shouting at the same time, then he was halfway down and could see it all happening in front of him.

Immediately, everything speeded up. All the firefights he had ever been in were exactly like this. Surreal. Racing and in slow motion all at once. There was never any time for fear. Never any time to decide. They trained you so you could react competently without having to stop and think. That was what he was doing now. He was going down onto his behind, easing Lara to the floor, getting a hand free, feeling for the gun. At the bottom of the stairs the guy he'd decked was moving towards him.

The details came all at the same time. The guy had Chris by the hair with one hand, pulling him forward, across his body, in his other hand a black automatic. Chris was stumbling, his face contorted, his mouth open, shouting. The guy was screaming at Paul through a bloody mouth, telling him to put Lara down, to get his hands in view. His eyes were bruised, he was staggering, struggling to hold Chris and balance, but he was up and armed. He was dangerous. He wasn't anywhere near dying. And behind him, just in front of the open door out onto the driveway, Jules was crouched over, her hands up to her face, screaming, blood coming out of her mouth.

It was a split second of time, the whole thing appearing like that, like some horrific frozen tableau. Everything was completely unexpected – the gun, Chris and Jules, the big guy moving around with so much energy.

Obviously Chris and Jules had ignored him. They'd got out of the car and come for him.

The gun had fired. Had Jules been shot? Was Chris shot? He couldn't see. As he tried to wedge Lara's prone form against the banister, halfway down the stairs, his hand found his own gun. He was totally exposed, higher than the guy, a prominent, easy target. The guy had the gun pointed not at him, but at Chris's head. He was pulling Chris's head to his chest and screwing the barrel of the gun into it, into the bandages. Paul could pull his gun, but then the guy would be forced to react. And Chris would certainly be hit and killed if he fired now. Paul's finger found the safety and clicked it off, his knee pressing against Lara's back to stop her from sliding down the stairs.

'*Get away from her. Get fucking away from her . . .*' The guy was still screaming it, still moving towards him. He couldn't shoot with Lara there, Paul realised. His boss's sister – he couldn't risk hitting her. Paul sank his head lower, closer to Lara, hand still on his gun.

Then there was frantic movement. Chris fighting, jamming

his elbows back into the guy's stomach, kicking back at his shins with his feet, wrenching himself away.

The guy reacted as Chris got free, a huge clump of his hair coming out in his hand. But he didn't pull the trigger. Instead, as Chris fell back he brought the gun up and pointed it directly at Paul. Paul was looking straight down the barrel, the distance no more than ten feet.

The guy fired twice. Two shots in quick succession. Paul saw the flashes, saw the recoil, then closed his eyes and ducked, though he knew that was useless. He heard splintering noises above and behind him at the exact time that he realised both shots had missed.

Then Paul's gun was out. He was on autopilot. But as he opened his eyes and sighted, Chris lunged at the guy and caught his legs. The guy kicked at him, but Chris had him in a rugby tackle and was dragging one leg to the floor. The guy's face – streaked with blood – creased with anger and he started to move the gun back down, to bring it to bear on Chris.

Paul fired. He wanted to shoot at the legs, but couldn't, because of Chris, because he'd never fired this gun before and didn't have a clue how it would behave. He aimed as low as he could, but the kick was unreal. His hand snapped back and he knew the shot would be high. As his eyes focused past the muzzle flash he saw the guy dropping backwards, a massive gout of blood high in the air above him, then he was down on the ground, the gun dropped, the blood splashing across the wall seven feet behind him. Paul started to shout at him, to warn him to stay down or he would shoot again, but then saw the legs fluttering and kicking, the spasms rippling up through the body.

He stood quickly as Chris crawled away, then placed his gun on the stairs and picked Lara up. She was making a groaning noise, saying something, moving. He took her down the last ten stairs and placed her on the floor.

He stood over the guy in a daze. The shot had got him in the side of the head, near the temple. Not his intention at all. There was a hole there, then the exit wound, which Paul couldn't see. But he could see the mess. The guy's eyes were open, looking right at Paul. His body was twitching like he was still alive. His chest was heaving up and down, blood frothing up through his mouth, down his nose, out of his ears. Behind him Jules was still screaming.

This is the problem with guns, he thought.

He walked over to Jules and placed a hand lightly over her mouth. Her eyes were wide with fear. With his other hand he stroked her hair gently, then said something to her, pointing back to Lara. Maybe he said *Go to Lara, check Lara.* Maybe not. He felt detached from himself, as if he were watching all this from a distance. Lara had rolled herself into a sitting position and was looking at them. She looked like she was in shock. Everyone did. Paul glanced outside but couldn't see anyone coming. Not yet. And no sirens. He could hear himself asking if anyone was hit, if anyone had been shot.

Jules stopped shouting. It seemed no one had been hit. Incredibly. He could see the holes in the ceiling and walls. If they were safe and alive it wasn't because the guy had wanted it that way. He had fired a gun at virtually point-blank range. He had tried to kill. Paul listened to his own thundering heart. Suddenly, he wanted to just sit down and weep. But he couldn't do that. 'We have to get out of here,' he said. 'Now.'

31

Andy drove badly. His hands were shaking uncontrollably, his legs felt weak. He wanted to pull over and vomit, but he was worried about being followed. After the police car turned off behind him – driving right onto the track where Mark's Range Rover was parked – there was nothing in his mirrors for a few seconds, then headlights at a distance, gaining quickly. He sped up, taking a deserted country roundabout too fast, putting the wheels onto the verges. The back end was slipping as he came off, but he got it back and held it in a straight line downhill. The road was narrow and dark, empty as far as he could see ahead.

He had no idea where he was going. He knew his 'plan' – to get to Mark's offices in Manchester – but the plan got lost behind a welter of overpowering reactions and emotions. So he just kept driving furiously, trying to put the headlights in his mirrors out of range, not computing his actions, not working out where he was going.

Nothing like this had ever happened to him and he had no idea how to deal with it. He screwed his face up thinking about it, trying to get a sense of what was going on. But the connections wouldn't come. He could only think of Mark as someone living, as he had seen him a couple of days ago. But Mark was dead. He had the image of his mutilated corpse flashing in front of him like something from a horror film, he had seen the bloody mess where his eyes had been, seen the trampled, blood-spattered trail through the undergrowth where he had run to try to escape. The stench was still in his nose. There were smears of blood on his fingers, which he'd wiped on his trousers, not thinking.

What the fuck had happened? How had someone managed to come up on Mark, out there, in the middle of nowhere? Mark had been obsessed with security.

He leaned forward and switched on the satnav, the car swerving dangerously as he took a hand from the wheel. All around him, as far as he could see, there was still nothing but fields, in darkness. He had to find out where he was, pause, take stock, locate a route back to the motorway. Maybe he was doing the wrong thing. Acting on impulse he had decided to flee the scene, on the basis of some silly fear about being set up, then with the idea of getting quickly to Mark's offices. Maybe he would be able to explain that, later – why he had made all haste for Mark's offices. There was nothing particularly unusual in that, perhaps. He was a police officer, he was investigating. You *could* look at it that way. But he wouldn't easily be able to explain why he wasn't calling someone to tell them what had happened and what he was doing. If not the locals then he should be calling Snowden, his own boss.

But Snowden, he knew, would simply tell him to call West Yorkshire Police, or he would call them himself. Plus, he would probably record the call on one of several computer databases. Andy didn't want that. All the SO15 systems were meant to be secure. They were, if you assumed that it was safe for SO15 personnel to access them, as you had to. But somehow, someone had discovered about Mark's arrangement to meet him, had even found out where. The leak could have come from Mark's side, but

Mark was being a lot more careful than Andy. He had the vested, personal interest in his safety. Andy hadn't taken Mark's fears seriously enough. The previous meet – in exactly the same place – had gone onto systems that were accessed by SO15, SOCA and the Security Service. So it was possible that whoever had tipped off Durrani that he was an SO15 target had also given him information about where Mark was to meet Andy. And then there was Fletch. Andy had told Fletch the specific time and place. He needed to think very carefully about that before giving even more away to Snowden.

He came round a long bend as the satnav was still searching for a fix and accelerated down another long gradual incline. He was about halfway down when the headlights turned the corner behind him and started to follow. Now he could clearly see that the car was gaining very rapidly.

He began to curse and swear. It could be police, or it could be whoever had been sitting out there in the trees, watching him. Which was more likely? Maybe there had been two police response cars – one had turned off up the dirt track, the other had come after him. Almost as soon as the thought crossed his mind he heard a siren wail behind him, then blue lights flashing.

His heart started to jump. His eyes flicked across his bloodstained fingers, his mind seeing all over again, and from a different angle, the absurd sequence of his actions. He had been at a murder scene and he had fled. That was how they would see it. He knew. He had their mindset. He was one of them.

The sweat was pouring off him, he was trembling and frightened and shocked. He hadn't a clue what he was doing. Instead of thinking about it any further, he tried to lose the pursuit car. Still flat out downhill, his speed reached

120 as he took another bend and the road levelled out. At the exact time he saw a turn-off approaching he realised the flashing lights had dropped behind and were out of sight. He could turn now, if he was quick, kill the engine, get the car off into some trees, let them pass him.

He braked viciously, the rear wheels instantly locking and skidding. The turn was to his right, almost at a right angle. If he could get round it he could see a narrower road, climbing back up the hill, quickly disappearing into the shadow of trees. He just had to get the car round the corner before the headlights appeared again.

His speed was forty-five as the turn came up. Still nothing in the mirrors. He turned the wheel, realised he hadn't put enough lock on it, braked harder, pulled the wheel over.

There was a moment where he knew he'd lost it, that the wheels were skating, the car going straight ahead across the corner of the junction, sideways. Then complete confusion. His head was all over, his hands off the spinning wheel, his body jerking forward against the seat belt. The car was juddering, bouncing, making a noise like tearing metal. He heard glass breaking, felt something hard and sharp hit his face. He shouted out in shock, got his hands to his face, then the world was tipping in slow motion, his body sliding to the left. He thought the wheels must have gone sideways into the ditch at the other side of the junction. He saw the world slantways, moving too quickly across the windscreen. Then the windscreen shattered and he couldn't see anything. The car bounced again and his head smashed off the driver's window, then the roof. It was rolling, but there was nothing he could do. He could see trees in the windscreen, a fence, a deafening scraping and clashing noise, then sudden terrible silence and everything very still.

The silence lasted half a second. His ears cleared, his eyes opened. He was on his side, panting and gasping for breath. The engine was revving furiously, the horn sounding in a single incessant blare. He struggled to find the seat belt release, got his hand to it and pressed. His body fell against the driver's door. He tried to open it but it was jammed fast. The car was lying on the driver's door, the roof buckled in towards him. All the glass was shattered. There was actually grass against his face where the driver's door window should have been. He moved an arm and the horn stopped, then reached up in the darkness and found the keys. He cut the engine, then scrambled into a half kneeling, half standing position, straining up towards the passenger seat and the passenger door.

He pulled the release catch, praying it would open, but the door was already out of the frame, bent and twisted. He pushed both hands against it, exhaling loudly. It moved an inch or so. He got a foot onto the partition between the seats, standing on the side of the gear stick mounting. His shoulders were up against the door now. He heaved it open, his head coming out into fresh air. He took a lungful of it. He could hear a siren, very close. He turned to look and found a brilliant, dazzling white light in his eyes. He looked away and saw his own car beneath him, on its side, in a field. The roof was so crushed he could barely believe he was climbing out unhurt. He brought a hand up to shade his eyes from the glare and looked again. It was the headlights of the police car. There were at least two men running from it, coming towards him. They were shouting at him. He had a ringing noise in his ears and couldn't make out what they were saying. He eased himself out onto the rear passenger door, then jumped off, landing on soft grass and mud. He turned quickly to see the two men rushing at him full speed. He had time to shout a protest before the first one hit him, launching straight into his chest in a massive rugby tackle.

32

Lara was gone. Pasha sat with his head in his hands in the back of the Land Cruiser, his mind filled with images of her. Beside him in the rear of the car sat Salim Feroz, the guy who Raheesh Khan contracted to manage his security. Pasha was trying not to give too much away, not to react so that Salim would suss how afraid he was, how little control he had. Ordinarily, he liked Salim – he'd known him since just after leaving school – and Salim frequently used his connections to do things for Pasha, but Salim was certainly Raheesh Khan's man, and would report everything back to Khan, word for word. Including the entire account he had just given Pasha and to which Pasha had listened with a feeling of near desperation.

Had he lost Lara?

Salim had come thirty minutes ago to the Whalley house with documents Pasha had requested earlier that day – false ID for Caserne, and a ticket for him to fly to Pakistan, via Glasgow, leaving at six tomorrow evening. Salim was good at organising that kind of thing quickly, and good at following the rules, which included no questions. So he didn't have a clue who the docs were for. So far so good.

But Salim had arrived at Whalley to the sound of police sirens. There had been police all over the house. He'd observed them from a safe distance, from the road embankment above the fields, and – as it happened – thought he might have recognised a DC who was on his grace and favours list. It was dark, so he couldn't be sure. The DC had been conducting a search of the rear garden.

Salim had driven off and called the DC. It was him, and he had eventually told Salim that there had been a fatal shooting in the house – a white guy had been killed. From what was said Pasha realised it had to be Don Mack, the man he'd left watching his sister. Worse than that, witnesses were reporting at least three people leaving the house after shots were fired, one helping a young woman who had looked injured or sick. Her description matched Lara. She was being half carried by a guy who could only be the man called Paul Curtis, who had showed up at the Richmond property earlier in the day and been easily followed back to Camden. With them was someone who could have been that little runt Napier. Salim had found out all this, called Pasha and driven here to pass it on, in the car park of the restaurant they had just used, in a village about ten miles from Whalley.

So what the fuck was going on? Had Lara called Napier, somehow? Had there been a fight and she'd been hit? The mere idea made him want to scream at the top of his voice, like a madman. He put his fist in his mouth and bit down on it so that his knuckles bled. *That fucking idiot Don Mack.* Had he shot his sister? He started saying a kind of prayer, over and over again, in his head. *Please don't let her be hurt. Please don't let her be hurt. Please.* She had been half walking, he told himself, so whatever had happened it could not have been a gunshot wound.

'That's your sister, right?' Salim asked. 'They've taken your sister.'

Pasha nodded. 'I think so.' He just managed to say the words without gagging.

'Do you know who they are?'

Pasha looked up at him, took a breath, took his hand from his mouth. He saw Salim look at the blood. He reminded himself: *Everything is going back to Khan. Everything. Salim Feroz is not your friend.* 'Of course I fucking do,' he hissed. It was partially true. He knew the man's name was Paul Curtis. He knew that name rang some kind of bell. But he didn't know where from.

'And the dead guy?'

He looked Salim in the eye. 'One of mine.'

Salim frowned. 'And your sister is meant to be meeting Sham Asuri on Sunday, right? Here?'

Meaning in the Whalley house. 'Yes.'

'Fucking hell, Pash.' Salim looked suddenly very scared. Scared for *him*, for Pasha, scared on his behalf. 'So what the fuck do I tell Raheesh?' he asked.

'Tell him the truth, of course.'

'But will it be sorted?'

'Of course it will be fucking sorted.'

'You can guarantee that?'

'I can guarantee it. Obviously we won't be meeting Sham there. I'll talk to Raheesh about it first thing tomorrow.'

'Don't wait that long, man. I'll be seeing him in under an hour. You need to be with me, I think. You need to explain.'

Pasha shook his head. 'I'll call. As you can imagine, I've things to look after here.'

'You need help?'

He shook his head. 'You can go, Salim. Thanks. Your help has been invaluable. As usual.'

'And the house? Is there anything compromising there? I might be able to sort some inside assistance . . .'

'There's nothing. It's clean.' If the 'staff' had followed his instructions it was clean. If they hadn't left anything lying around, as they were so stupidly fucking wont to do. There was his laptop. It was his clean laptop, but you could get his name and some normal details from it. He tried to smile at Salim, weakly, but Salim just stared at him. Was he looking at him differently already? Pasha thought he could see something there in his eyes – the beginning of disengagement, a drawing back from him, like he had the worst kind of disease, the diagnosis written on his forehead. The look betrayed the thought – *how long will Pasha be alive?* That was what Salim was thinking now. *And will I have to kill him?*

He was halfway out of the car when Pasha asked for the documents.

'Oh. Yeah. Sorry. I forgot.'

Like hell. Pasha waited whilst he fished them out and handed them over. Their eyes met again and Pasha could see he was considering asking who they were for, whether they were connected to all of this. But he didn't. Pasha leaned over and shut the door on him.

He waited until he'd driven off, then got out and walked over to the two cars that contained his five 'staff'. Ram Ali was in an identical Land Cruiser. Pasha got him out, walked off into the darkness with him and told him what had happened. Ram looked unfazed. That was because he didn't know the significance of anything. 'Where's Billy?' Pasha asked. 'Billy' was Don Mack's nineteen-year-old boy, who Don had insisted on bringing in, on 'training'. The family business – being a hood. Billy was a fucking liability, too keen on guns and violence, a chip off the old block. And now his dad was dead.

'In the other car,' Ram said.

'Don't tell him here. Get Rash to take him back to his mother's. Tell him there. And warn him to sit tight. If he looks like he's going to compromise anything you'll have to subdue him a bit. Got that?'

Ram nodded.

'Then I want the rest of you combing hospitals in the area. In case my sister was hurt. Cover every hospital within a couple of hundred miles, closest first. Clear?'

'*Every* one?'

'Use your head. Not the geriatric homes, not the kids' hospitals. Go back to your place and get a list off the net. Share it out. This is fucking serious. We have to find her.'

'What are you going to do?'

'Try some other angles.' He would look too, try to work out a more intelligent way to contact the hospitals, in a shorter time frame, then try to work out other possible angles. Plus, within a few hours he had to get over to North Yorkshire with the travel documents, get Caserne on his way. He'd told Caserne to go to the place he was in the middle of buying from Philip Rathmore – Lara's place – that's how he always thought of it. The house she had dreamed of owning. The place she had spent weekends at, with Napier, when she was a kid. He was trying to get it for her, using one of his companies. Rathmore had tried to back out, of course, once he'd found out who was behind the company. That had required some threats – to expose the existence of his bastard son, or kill him. Rathmore was a politician, vulnerable, so he'd rolled over easily enough. The sale would go ahead, soon, if he could plug the gap in funding caused by Ross, get himself out of all this shit somehow.

Meanwhile, the house was half dilapidated, empty, not even alarmed. An abandoned mess. A nice place to hide. He had keys for it already – because he'd been many times, with builders and architects. It was perfect for Caserne to lie low in. No one was going to look there. But he couldn't leave him there for long. It was a priority to get to him, and something only he could do. No one else knew about Caserne. No one else knew about Mark Johnson, or any of that side of things.

'I'll be in touch,' he said to Ram. 'You ring me if you find her. Immediately, without doing anything else.'

He saw a trace of worry flit across Ram's features, an inkling of the gravity of it perhaps finally sinking in.

33

Paul drove. His head was reeling now. He couldn't just sit in the passenger seat because he would either spew or fall asleep, so Jules sat beside him and Chris and Lara sat in the back. As they set off Lara was in tears, sobbing quietly on Chris's shoulder, refusing to answer any questions. Everyone else was silent. It was like a funeral run.

Paul knew how it went. He'd killed before, and worse than this. Once – in some shitty mud brick village in Helmand – he'd strangled a man. That had taken a long time, all of it staring straight at the guy's face. So he knew how the reactions would hit him. But this was different. This was England, not a distant combat zone where no one asked any questions. This was going to have to be explained. He hadn't seen anyone watching as they had exited, but he was sure they would have been there. Four gunshots wouldn't go unnoticed in a neighbourhood like Whalley. The good citizens of Whalley would have been behind the curtains, taking down the details, calling in his registration plate.

For the first ten minutes Chris sat beside Lara like an ambush survivor, eyes wide and shocked, face rigid, the bandage untidy, fresh blood leaking onto it from the patch where the hair had been torn from his scalp. It was Jules who had to ask Lara the questions. Jules had been punched in the mouth by the man Paul had just killed. She had a fat lip and loose front teeth, but she wasn't dwelling on it. Paul had room in his head to admire that. It was Jules who told him they had left the car and come to get him, only to find a man with a gun, who had actually fired the first shot at Chris. It was Jules who twisted in the seat and asked Lara all the questions Paul would have asked.

They had to find out what she had taken and how many. They were assuming she had overdosed – as opposed to Pasha drugging her, for example – and she wasn't correcting them. She wasn't answering at all, in fact. They would ask the same questions in casualty, and that was where Paul was going. The nearest big town was Blackburn, but he thought Pasha would look for them there immediately, assuming it had a hospital. Burnley was only slightly further away and it definitely had a hospital because he'd been there once, with his mum. That was where he was going to try. Lara had walked out of her brother's house – albeit leaning heavily on Paul and wobbling – so it was possible she wasn't that bad. But he couldn't chance it.

And after that they would have to decide what to do. The consequences were something none of them could get to grips with right now. But they were there, in the air between them all, unacknowledged and threatening. They had seen a man shot in the head. Paul had pulled the trigger. It was like a gaping rent in the fabric of normality, not something Lara, Chris or Jules were used to. They would be like this for a while, Paul guessed, just sitting there in silence trying to get their brains to accept it, not having a clue what it meant.

But Chris surprised him. 'I had him, man,' he said, abruptly, interrupting what Jules was asking Lara. 'There was no need to shoot. I had him.'

Paul frowned at him in the mirror. 'You had him?'

'Don't be stupid, Chris,' Jules said. 'He had a gun. He was going to shoot you. Paul had no choice.'

Paul nodded. 'I think that might be a better version, Chris,' he said. 'When the questions are asked.' His voice wavered, as if he were about to cry. He wasn't, not any more, but the adrenalin did that to you.

'It's the truth,' Jules said.

'I could have brought him down,' Chris said. 'You blew his head off, man.'

Paul nodded. No point in arguing that one. Chris wasn't listening, anyway. He was in a kind of trance. 'You were brave back there,' Paul told him. 'Thanks. You gave me a break, distracted him.'

Chris's eyes changed focus and found his in the mirror. Did he understand what Paul had said? 'I mean it,' Paul said. 'You went for him. And he could have killed you. Easily. He didn't kill any of us, but it wasn't for want of trying.'

Chris thought about it, then started to shiver.

'It's shock,' Paul said. 'The shivering. A kind of mental shock. It will pass.'

'Why aren't we going to the police?' Chris asked. 'Why didn't we just wait there, wait for the police? We did nothing wrong.'

'Didn't we? We were burglars. And, anyway, I didn't fancy risking Pasha getting back before the police.' He looked at Lara. 'As far as I know, Lara was there of her own free will.'

She moved her face a little and looked at her legs. She looked like she was slipping, like she would fall asleep. Paul felt an extra flutter of panic in his chest. How many pills would kill her? He had no idea. The whole car smelled of her vomit. The front of her clothing was still wet with it.

'Isn't that right, Lara?' Paul asked.

She shook her head. 'No.'

Good. She understood what he was saying, she could

speak. 'What did you take, Lara?' he asked again. 'I need to know what you took.' But she didn't reply. 'We'll get you to casualty,' Paul said. 'They'll pump your stomach, then we can think about the police. After we've talked this through.'

'Talk it through?' Chris said. 'I don't want to think about it, man. I can't get that image out of my head. I can't believe you did that. I just can't believe it—'

'He had no fucking choice, Chris,' Jules snapped. 'For Christ's sake. You'd be dead.'

'That we had no choice is no guarantee that we won't end up charged with something,' Paul said. 'We have to make sure we're all saying the same things before we talk to the police. We drove away from the scene because we were terrified Pasha would return, with more guns. OK?' He looked at Jules. She nodded, understanding. 'And I didn't go in with a gun,' he said. 'The gun was lying in the house. I picked it up. Understood?'

Again, Jules nodded, but Chris was thinking too much. Lara wasn't responding at all. Did she even realise what had happened in there? 'Where is the gun?' Chris asked.

'I left it there.'

'We can't go to a hospital, Paul,' Lara said. She had sat up a little and was wiping her face with her sleeve. Her eyes looked dopey, her voice was thin and uncertain. He could barely hear her.

'Why not?' Paul asked. They were just getting to the outskirts of Burnley.

'We have to get away,' she said, a bit louder. 'He'll come looking for me in the nearest hospital.'

Paul looked at her in the rear-view mirror whilst Chris stared sightlessly ahead.

'You mean Pasha?' Jules asked, turning round.

Lara nodded.

'What were the tablets?' Paul asked. 'I saw the capsules in your sick. What were they?'

'Just some sleeping tablet, a tranquilliser . . .' She looked down, like she was ashamed.

'How many?' Paul asked.

'I don't know. I was sick straight away. They all came back up, I'm sure. I'm OK. I don't need a hospital. We can't go to a hospital.'

'I have to,' Paul said. 'I have to have you checked.'

'Listen to me, Paul. He'll work out what happened. Someone will have seen, or he'll find the vomit. He'll come looking straight away. He needs me to be there on Sunday. He's desperate. On Sunday the Asuris come to look at me. He won't just let me run off. These are people he is really scared of. He says they will kill us if I don't go through with it.' She hesitated. 'I'm part of some debt he owes them . . .'

Chris was looking at her now, frowning intensely.

'You seem drugged,' Paul said.

'I took one to sleep, about an hour before. It didn't work, so I took more. That's all. It was an accident. Then I was sick. The one I took earlier is making me dopey. That's all. Everything came out. I was sick a lot. Then I drank water and was sick some more. I feel OK. I feel like I took a tablet to sleep. That's all.'

He thought about it. 'I can't risk it,' he said. 'We'll go to casualty. They can look at you and we can get out quick.'

She shook her head. 'Stop telling me what to do. I'm not a fucking child. I did this because I'm sick of people telling me what to do.' She moved away from Chris and stared out of the window.

'I thought you just said it was an accident?' Chris said, still frowning.

She ignored him. 'Go where you fucking want,' she said. 'But I'm not going into any hospital.'

34

He drove across the South Pennines, to Halifax, to his
mother's place. The journey took just under forty minutes
because it was after midnight now and the roads were
completely clear. They saw no police cars. On the way he
called his mother and told her he would arrive with a few
friends. He tried to sound normal, but she picked up his
thick voice and asked him what was going on. He did his
best to reassure her. She wasn't going to be at the house
until after nine the next morning. She was a nurse, working
a night shift in casualty in Halifax. She would have been
able to check Lara, change Chris's dressing, sort Jules's lip.
That was why he had decided to come to her. But it was
good she was working, perhaps, because now he wouldn't
have to answer all her questions until after he'd had some
rest. Rest was what his bruised brain most needed now.

The house was a semi, within walking distance of the
hospital she worked at. She'd moved from Manchester five
years ago, getting a promotion of some sort. He had visited
whenever he was in the area – which had worked out about
twice a year – but the new house still didn't feel like home
to him. It wasn't the place he'd grown up in, the place
he knew every corner of (she'd sold that without even

consulting him), not the place he was used to his mother 'fitting' in to, as if she were a part of it – the house and the mother an intimate package of memories that couldn't quite survive without each other. It was like she'd changed into a different person when she moved, turned into something more independent than he was used to.

The house was spartan, modern, clean. He was used to his mum being quite relaxed about mess, but now she tidied everything up too quickly, tried to keep things in their places – the state of the garden was the only reminder of the way things had been before, and she told him she had plans to get a gardener to sort that. The furniture was all shiny and angular, from Habitat, he thought. Was that the style she had secretly liked, all those years living with the cheap, warped Formica his dad had provided?

He showed Chris and Lara to the room next door to his mother's. There was a double bed and a bathroom in there. Jules he put on the top floor. He would sleep downstairs, on the sofa. He told them what needed to be done before they slept. He wanted Jules to try to clean her cut lip and Chris to change the bandage. He found fresh bandages and pain-killers. He didn't know what to do about Lara. As he left them she was sitting on the bed looking shell-shocked.

Alone, he went out into the little back garden and called Phil Rathmore on his mobile. It took Rathmore a long time to answer, and his opening line was, 'Do you realise what time it is?'

'I wouldn't have called if it wasn't urgent.'

'What's happened?'

'I told you we needed some place to stay. That's urgent now. I need a place to spend a few days, somewhere isolated . . .'

'What's happened?'

'We've had a couple of brushes with Pasha Durrani. It's going to have to go to the police unless you can provide somewhere where he can't find us for a bit. Then I can think of alternatives, maybe. But there may not be alternatives. I might have to go to the police—'

'That's certainly not what I'm paying you to do—'

'You're paying me to guard your son. Your son, like it or not, is in some deep shit. The only effective way to protect him might be to go to the police. It won't necessarily mean that your connection is revealed.'

'It most certainly will mean that.'

'I don't see it that way. Chris wouldn't want that—'

'Neither Chris nor you know the half of it.'

Paul shut up, tried to think about that line, and what it might mean, but his brain wasn't working well. 'Can you do what I'm asking, or not?'

'I'll call you back.' Rathmore cut the line.

Paul stood for a while staring at the phone, before replacing it in his pocket. He turned back to the house.

Jules was standing not three yards away, at the kitchen door. Close enough to hear.

'What's going on, Paul?' she asked, voice rigid.

How much had she overheard? He couldn't be sure, so he couldn't lie.

'Who were you talking to?' she asked. 'I heard you say you were guarding his son.'

He sighed. He didn't want to lie to her. 'It was Chris's father,' he said, wearily. 'I've been working for him.'

She frowned. 'I don't understand.'

'He asked me to get close to Chris. I guess he thought he was in some danger—'

'Hang on. Chris's father asked you to get close to Chris?'

'Yes.'

235

'When?'

'A week ago.'

'But you were already close to Chris . . .'

He didn't know what to say. He watched her struggling with it for a bit. 'Not then I wasn't,' he said, at last. 'Not when he asked.'

'So you got "close" to him – because his dad asked you to?'

'Yes.'

'Did he pay you?' Her voice was getting louder.

Paul could feel the blood rushing to his face now. He looked at the ground. He felt very uncomfortable. 'Yes,' he said quietly. 'He's paying me. I'm working for him, like I said. That's why I called him . . .'

'Because it's a job?'

'Yes. That's right.' He didn't dare look at her now. He knew what was coming. 'Sorry,' he said.

'Sorry for what?'

'For not telling you.'

'Or Chris. Or Lara. They don't know either, right?'

'That's what Rathmore wanted.'

'Jesus Christ.' She almost whispered it, then turned suddenly. To leave.

'Wait,' he said. 'Let me explain it all to you. I'll tell you what's happening.'

She turned, her face bright red. 'You can *explain* it? You can explain the lies?'

He started telling her about it, the full story. He tried to make it sound harmless, but he knew what she was thinking just by looking at her face. She was thinking that he had lied to them all, that he was with them all because he was being paid, that she had thought him a friend.

'It's a complete and utter betrayal,' she said, when he

stopped talking. She was shaking with rage. She didn't wait for him to respond, but stalked upstairs.

He followed her, wondering if she would go straight into Chris and Lara, tell them. But she didn't. He thought he should go up to her, try again to explain, to give her his perspective on it, but he didn't have the energy. He walked into the front room, sat on the sofa and rubbed his eyes. He felt completely drained. He closed his eyes, thinking he would go up to her in a minute or so. But within seconds he was sleeping.

35

Andy sat in a single cell in Huddersfield police station rubbing the grooves on his wrist where the handcuffs had been. They had taken everything from him – his wallet, his ID, his mobile. They had taken samples of the blood on his hands, swabbed his nails, seized his clothing and given him a white prison jumpsuit to wear. He sat on the blanket on the wooden bench and endured a blind, useless rage he could not recall ever experiencing before with such intensity. He had fought the guy who had tackled him, struggled on the ground with all his strength, screaming at the man that he too was police. But the man had only wanted him subdued and quiet. The other one had quickly joined in. But even after they had cuffed him, belly down, arms behind his back, he was still kicking and screaming at them. When they stood him up he had to stop himself spitting in their faces. They were fucking idiots. It was all crucial lost time. They hadn't even listened to his warnings about Durrani, about the need to get to Mark's offices and home fast.

In the custody suite they had inspected his face – there was a bruise and a scrape – and stood him in front of a doctor they'd called out. The doctor had said he was fine, 'extraordinarily lucky', and had tried to cleanse the scrape, but Andy wouldn't let him touch it. So they'd swabbed and fingerprinted him, dumped him in a cell and left him to his ire. That was almost an hour ago. He had been sitting here by himself for that long now, waiting for the fury to subside. Sleep was out of the question. For perhaps the tenth time he stood up and yelled at the door '*I want my fucking phone call. I want my phone call.*' The sound bounced back at him. He sounded like all the frustrated defendants he had ever heard in the cell block. If he wasn't careful he would end up banging his head off the walls, like the worst of them. He sat down, tried to breathe steadily. He needed to make that call to Snowden. Snowden would sort this in moments. But the fucking idiots were treating him like anyone else they abused. No phone call, no solicitor.

He heard the door lock scraping and stood up. The door opened and the custody sergeant came in.

'Man to see you,' he said.

'Who?'

'Detective Chief Superintendent Foster. An SIO.'

'I want my phone call first.'

'You'll get it.'

He suffered the sergeant to cuff him again – he was an escape risk because he'd driven away from the pursuit car – then walked through to the booking area. There was a mid-forties, tired and drab-looking man in a raincoat standing at the counter, no one else. On the board detailing the occupants of each cell Andy could see they were having a quiet night, apart from himself. The man in the raincoat turned and held his hand out, like he was a friend.

'I'm fucking cuffed,' Andy said.

'Get those off him, Sergeant,' the raincoat said.

'With respect, sir. This man drove at speeds of—'

'Don't be silly. He's SO15. You know that. Get the cuffs off him.'

The sergeant didn't want to do it, and strictly, it was his choice, but he complied. The raincoat held out his hand again: 'Jim Foster, SIO. I thought we should have a talk.'

'I need my phone call.' He stared at the hand without touching it.

'Of course. Will you use your mobile?'

'They took it. Obviously.'

'We'll sort that out immediately.'

Andy began to feel himself calming fractionally.

'You'll want to call your people, I expect,' Foster said.

He sat in a small interview room, alone, with his mobile. He spent nearly twenty minutes trying every number he had, from Snowden to Stanesby, but no one was answering. Then he tried Control. They took his name and told him Snowden was unavailable, Stanesby was unavailable, Hemmings was off-duty, Pearce was off-duty, Luntley was on-duty, in Acton, but not answering. He sat gloomily in silence, his heart rate slowing, thinking about it. Then he started to think about Mark, remembering things they'd done together, way back, as probationers in Southall. There wasn't much emotion to the thoughts, because he couldn't even get near to believing that Mark was dead. When Foster came to the door again he looked up at him and asked, 'Is Mark dead? Is that definite?'

Foster didn't react as if the question were absurd. 'I'm afraid so,' was all he said.

'I can't get anybody,' Andy said, holding up his phone.

'No. We tried as well.'

'I don't know what's going on. I should be able to get them. They could explain.'

'I think you're going to have to explain. You want to

sleep first?' He was quietly spoken, polite, patient. Andy felt like hitting him. He shook his head.

'I've organised a solicitor . . .'

'I don't want one . . .'

'I think you should think about that—'

'Let's just get going. You'll understand when I've spoken to you.'

There were three of them in the little, windowless interview room, but Foster didn't introduce the other two – a younger man and a female about Foster's age. They both had note-books and blank faces. Foster started talking to him without issuing a caution.

'Wait a minute. Wait a minute,' Andy said. He sat in the chair they'd given him, at the other side of the metal table, shifting from side to side, restless. 'What's my status here? Why no caution? I've just spent an hour in a fucking cell, an hour I could have been putting to use trying to trace the man who killed Mark Johnson. So what's my status? Am I arrested, or not?'

Foster shook his head, the expression on his face suggesting the idea was absurd. 'Arrested? Did they arrest you?'

'Of course they did. They took me to the ground in a rugby tackle—'

'But did they actually arrest you?'

'Did they say the fucking magic words? Does it matter? They cuffed me and dumped me in a cell.'

Foster shrugged. 'You know how it is, Sergeant Macall. Look at it from their point of view. You fled the scene. You were so anxious to evade capture you rolled your car. The car, by the way, is now—'

'I don't care about the car. Am I under arrest?'

'Not as far as I'm concerned.'

'Right. So I can get up and go. Right now?'

Foster smiled a little. 'Naturally. But I'm sure you wouldn't want to do that. I'm running a murder enquiry. I have questions. And if you did opt to leave now I might *then* have to arrest you, which I don't want to do, not until I have some clear sense of your involvement. If you're a key witness to a murder case then it will look terrible if you are arrested by the enquiry. It will look terrible in court, I mean – it won't help your credibility there, as our witness. So I wouldn't want to arrest you until I was certain that you're a suspect, rather than a witness. You understand that, I assume?'

Andy bit his lip and looked away. 'Are you taping this?'

'Not yet.'

'Right. I'll make this quick. I'm a DS with SO15. You've checked that by now. Mark Johnson – the murdered man – was an informant I was controlling—'

'You told the officers who brought you here that he was a friend.'

'That as well. My best friend. My oldest friend. So forgive me if I seem a little distressed, confused and fucking angry—'

'It's hardly in accordance with PACE to be the informant handler for a friend. In fact, we've been told you are not responsible for informants, that you are not a dedicated human intelligence source handler. And certainly not the controller. We're told there's an entirely different department to handle human intelligence sources.'

'This was an exception—'

'To the law?'

'Yes.'

Foster took time to glance at his colleagues.

'Give me a break,' Andy said. 'We're talking about the

Police and Criminal Evidence Act regulations. It's not a fucking criminal offence. It's a set of rules about how you handle intelligence that governs admissibility of evidence in court. We're SO15, not a local force. We're looking at terrorists. People who are plotting mass, indiscriminate murder. We're trying to disrupt them. About five per cent of what we do gets anywhere near a court. So if my superiors tell me to do it that way, I do it. Understand?'

'How did you come to be there, in those woods?'

'I went there to meet Mark – his codename was Simon Parker. I went there to meet him and found his Range Rover parked up, and empty . . .' His voice started to break, so he stopped. He wasn't actually feeling anything but anger, so it was peculiar that his legs started to tremble.

'Take your time,' Foster said. Andy glared at him. 'We understand how shocking it is,' Foster added.

'The car was empty . . .' He stopped again. The words were cracking like he had a bad head cold. He cleared his throat. 'I went into the trees, to look for him . . .' His hands were shaking so much he had to squeeze them together. He looked down. 'I'm sorry,' he said. He realised with astonishment and shame that there were tears in his eyes, a lump in his throat. 'I don't know what it is. All I'm feeling is angry. Angry to be here. I need to get out. I need to find who did this . . .'

'That's our job now,' Foster said, gently, then turned to the younger man. 'Can you get Mr Macall a glass of water, please, John.'

The younger guy stood up to leave.

'It's OK,' Andy said. 'It's OK. I don't need water. Let's not waste any more time. There's nothing else I can tell you, anyway. Not until I've spoken to my boss.'

'*Nothing* else?'

The younger man sat down again.

'I can't tell you anything about why I was meeting Mark, or who killed him. Not until I've spoken to Snowden.'

'You know who killed him?'

'Yes.'

'Pasha Durrani?'

Andy frowned. 'How did you get that name?'

'That's what you told the officers who brought you here. You said you needed to get to Mark Johnson's offices before "Pasha Durrani". You said that's why you were driving so fast, not stopping . . .'

'Right. I'd forgotten I said that.' He rubbed his face. 'I shouldn't have said anything.'

'Mark Johnson's offices are in Manchester. Am I right?'

'Yes.'

'And you were driving south. Away from them, in other words.'

'I was lost. I was panicking.'

'Had you met Mark there before?'

'Yes. Once.'

'But you were lost?'

'It was dark then too. I have no idea where I am up here . . .'

'You have a satnav in the car?'

Suddenly Andy remembered something. 'Who called you? Have you thought about that?'

Foster nodded. 'Yes. We have. We're working on that.'

'Someone who knew I was there. Someone who tried to set me up for this.'

'If that's true then your evasion of the officers at the scene was unhelpful. The officers assumed *you* were the person who called it in. Hence they didn't look for anyone else. Not immediately.'

Andy winced. He shouldn't have fled the scene, of course. What had he been thinking? He stared at his hands. They were still trembling.

'Why did you want to go to Mark Johnson's offices?'

'To make sure I could get something from there. Something Mark was going to give me. I thought there would be a copy at his offices. Look, I really don't feel happy giving you these details without speaking to Snowden . . .'

'But why the rush? Why were you rushing to get there?'

'I needed to get there before the perpetrator. He would have the same idea. At least, that's what I thought then.' He saw now it was a ridiculous idea. If Pasha Durrani had anything to do with killing Mark then Mark's offices would be the last place he would be.

'You could have told us all that. We could have had Manchester officers there much quicker.'

Andy shook his head, feeling increasingly desperate. To explain himself he would need to tell them about the leak, about HAKA, everything. But he wasn't sure whether he could do that. He needed Snowden to make a decision on that, to sort it. 'I need to call my boss,' he said. 'I can't say any more. I have to speak to SO15.' Or Fletch, he thought. But could he trust Fletch?

They put him in another interview room and he tried Snowden again. Again no success. He was using emergency numbers, but no one was answering him. Control couldn't help. He told the woman on the switchboard that he was a murder suspect, but she had no advice for that. She sounded bored.

Foster came in. 'You get anywhere?'

Andy shook his head.

'Keep trying. I'll leave you here. I have to be back at the

scene. I'll come back in an hour. It's very important you contact your people. You shouldn't underestimate the problems you're facing here. You understand that?'

Andy stared at him. 'You want me to wait here for an hour?'

'That's right.'

'You don't believe what I'm telling you, then?'

'You haven't told me anything.' He looked at his watch. 'It's not personal, Sergeant Macall. So no need to look so irritated with me. I'm just doing my job.' He smiled. It was a nice, friendly, open smile. 'I don't care who you are,' he said. 'I don't care if you work for SO15, or the prime minister. You understand? I follow an impersonal process. It's like a little list of tick boxes. And you're ticking a lot of them right now.'

'Meaning what?'

'Meaning, you either get your people to co-operate within the next hour or I arrest you for murder.'

36

As soon as Paul opened his eyes he had the feeling that something was wrong. He sat up quickly. He was in his mother's living room, on the sofa there. His head felt pressurised, his mouth sore. But that wasn't it. Had he heard something?

He stood up and moved to the door, glancing at the mantelpiece clock on the way. Ten past two. He had been asleep for about an hour, then. Not enough. His legs felt weak. He put a hand out to the wall to steady himself, then listened. The house was silent.

He walked through to the kitchen. Nothing there, but he remembered the conversation with Jules, the fact that she had caught him talking to Rathmore. He got his phone out. Rathmore had said he would call back. He hadn't.

He walked up the stairs and immediately saw that the door to the room he'd put Chris and Lara in was standing wide open. He went over to it, whispering their names. But as soon as the words came out of his mouth he knew he was talking to himself. The bed had not been slept in. It looked like they'd been sitting on it, but that was it. He went to the little en suite bathroom. They weren't in there. Chris's old bandages were lying in the sink.

Heart thumping he went and looked out at the street. Jules's car was gone. He went back to the kitchen, searched for a note, checked upstairs. They'd left nothing. They'd gone and left nothing. He got his phone out and called them. Lara's number was unobtainable. Chris's and Jules's went through to answerphones. He left messages asking them to ring him urgently. But he knew they weren't going to.

He knew exactly what had happened. He went into the living room and sat down heavily. He rested his throbbing head in his hands. Jules had come back down when he was asleep, gone in to Chris and Lara and told them.

Then they'd all left. Without him.

37

At quarter past two, Luntley answered his personal mobile.

'It's Andy.'

'Oh.'

'You sound surprised.'

'You're calling my personal mobile, boss.'

'So what? What the fuck's going on? I can't get anyone to talk to me and I'm in trouble . . .'

'We've heard about it.'

'What?' He shouted the word. 'You've heard? From who?'

'We've heard.' Luntley dropped his voice to a whisper. 'We're not meant to talk to you, boss. That's the instruction.'

'What? Why? Instruction from who?'

'From Snowden.'

'Is he there?'

'Not here. Somewhere in the building though.'

'Get him. Tell him to fucking call me now. Tell him if he doesn't then I will tell West Yorkshire Police everything. You understand? HAKA, the leak, everything. All the names and details.'

It was clear what they wanted. Stanesby, Snowden, Fletch. They wanted Durrani at large, no matter what the consequences. Because they were playing a numbers game with the dead bodies. Durrani had killed John James Ross and Mark Johnson. But Ross and Mark didn't weigh much when put in the balance against all the terror deaths that could be prevented by having a man that highly placed on the inside, passing crucial information back to British intelligence. Justice wasn't what they were chasing. Justice didn't stop atrocities. Highly placed informants did.

Maybe he could have gone along with it, if it were only Ross. Maybe he could put Ross's death in the scales and discount it. Ross had asked for it, after all. He'd diced with the devil. But not Mark. Mark was a good guy, his friend. Mark had not deserved this. He couldn't let Mark be written off as a death worth ignoring. So he had to buck the system, kick against it, force it to operate like it was meant to. And all he had to do to achieve that was find Durrani and arrest him. If he arrested him they would have to action it, take it further, follow it through. Because he was a police officer. If he arrested someone, it counted. It was like Foster had said – enquiries were impersonal – if he brought Durrani in, then samples would be taken, questions asked.

The forensics were time-critical. The quicker you caught the suspect the more chance you had of recovering damning forensic traces from their person and clothing, traces that could place them at the scene. Probably it was already too late to get much that would link Durrani to Ross's death. But certainly whoever had done that to Mark would be dripping in forensic evidence. It was even possible Mark had fought back, wounded Durrani. Which meant Durrani's blood would be at the scene too. He just had to be swabbed, sampled and questioned. But to get that far he had to be found and arrested first. And Andy couldn't do that whilst he was trapped in this fucking police station. He had to get out.

Snowden didn't call him. Instead, at half past, a DC came in with his wallet and ID. 'You can have these now,' he said.

Andy took them off him. 'What about my clothes?'

The DC shook his head. 'You'll have to ask the boss about that.'

'Foster, you mean? Is he here?'

'He's coming. Just wait.' He went back out again.

Ten minutes later Andy opened the door and looked. He was in a room on the public side of the station, not within the cell complex. He could see a corridor leading towards where the main public entrance would be. But no one standing guard on him.

Why had they given him his wallet back? It was like inviting him to run.

He stepped out and closed the door behind him. He'd had enough. Something was going on. He hadn't a clue what. But he wasn't waiting around any longer. He would force the issue. He walked quickly down the corridor.

He found the door leading out, clicked the door release through to the front desk, opened it, walked through. There was a civilian behind the counter, an empty waiting room. She nodded at him, then looked at the jumpsuit and frowned. He thought about lying to her, coming up with an explanation, then decided against it. He was walking out, no excuses given. If they wanted to stop him they could arrest him. That was that.

Then he was out in the street, in the chill night air, walking quickly to the right. He'd got about fifty yards before he realised no one was coming after him. He stopped, completely puzzled. What was going on? He waited. He watched two uniforms come out after him, the way he had come, then turn left and walk off. Then a marked car came from the yard entrance.

No one was looking at him. He started walking again, taking out his mobile.

He called Luntley again and was surprised when he answered. 'Did you speak to Snowden?'

'Yes.'

'So what's happening?'

'They think you could be the leak.'

Andy laughed, but nervously. Luntley said nothing.

'You believe that?' Andy asked.

'No. But I'm nobody in here. My view doesn't count.'

'You still have a team on Chris Napier?'

A pause, then, 'No.'

'Come on, Mike. Don't give me the silent treatment. You know I'm not the fucking leak. You know what happened tonight?'

'With the informant, you mean?'

'Yes. With the informant. Except he wasn't just an informant. He was a friend of mine. He was hacked up, Mike. Hacked up.'

Silence.

'You hear that?'

'Yes. I wasn't aware you knew him. Nobody has said that here. I'm sorry.'

'What are they saying – that I killed him?'

'No. But they're coming up there to speak to the locals. They've asked the locals to hold you until then. I think they might be aiming to nick you up there, in connection with the leak. The local SIO isn't playing though. He's refusing to arrest you without the full facts. He has strong evidence that someone else was at the scene. That's what I heard. He thinks you're a witness and wants the full story. So Stanesby is coming up personally to convince them, and to speak to you. He's trying to arrange an RAF helicopter, to get there within an hour.'

'He's too fucking late.' Andy almost laughed.

'What do you mean?'

'Never mind. It was Durrani who killed Mark. I'm one hundred per cent on that. I'm going to find him.'

'What would be the use of that?' Luntley hissed the words in a kind of frantic whisper. He sounded worried. Worried about Andy's mental health, maybe.

'So I can arrest him.'

'Arrest him? Arrest him for what? Have you lost it, boss? That's not your job.'

Had he lost it? Maybe he had. The blood was flushing through him. He felt feverish.

'And anyway, what would be the point?' Luntley asked.

'To force some action against him. Stanesby and Snowden want him loose and free. If I don't arrest him no one will.'

Luntley was silent again, thinking about it, no doubt, trying to work out if it could be true. 'The locals know what they're doing,' he said eventually. 'You should leave it to them.'

'I can do it quicker. Besides, Stanesby will close them down.'

'You sure about that?'

'Why do you think he's coming up here?'

Another silence.

'But I won't lie back and take it,' Andy said. 'I can find Durrani if I can find his sister. So I'm asking you, have you got a team on Napier and Lara Durrani?'

'No. They evaded it. The sister left after midday, hasn't been seen since. Then about nine hours ago we thought Curtis left alone, in a car, so we kept the team on his flat. Turns out Napier and Julie Clarke must have been hiding in the car with Curtis. That's all I can tell you, boss. I have to go now. OK?'

'Wait.'

'I can't.'

'Give me a mobile number for the sister.'

'It's out of order. We've tried it.'

'Give me Napier's mobile, then.'

'We don't have it yet.'

'Curtis's mobile. Give me that.'

'We haven't got that either.'

Was Luntley lying? 'Is Curtis back in the London flat?' He saw a sign for the railway station and followed it. Would there be any trains at this hour? He had no idea. He was walking through the streets of Huddersfield, he guessed. He'd never been here before. He saw very few people, but those he did pass were looking at him as if he might be something dangerous, or unhinged.

'We don't know where any of them are,' Luntley said. 'It's all fucked, boss. You know that.'

He remembered something about Napier and Curtis. They still had family up here. The family would have contact details. 'Can you give me an address for Napier's family here? And Curtis?'

'OK. But I can't do any more.'

'That's it. I promise.'

He stopped in the street and typed the addresses into his phone as Luntley read them off. When he was finished Luntley cut the line without warning.

The address for Napier's mother was in Altrincham, near

Manchester. But Curtis's mother's address was in Halifax, not too far away. There was a landline number too. He thought about ringing it. Then thought she might just panic. Better to go there. He looked down at himself. He was shivering. The cell clothing was painfully obvious, thin, uncomfortable. But it was the middle of the night. There was nothing he could do. He saw a rank of three taxis outside the railway station. He walked up to the first. It was an Asian driver. He wound the window down and Andy read off the Halifax address. The man just nodded. No strange looks, no comment about the clothing, or the hour. Andy got in the back.

It was three twenty by the time the cab stopped outside a semi in Halifax. The curtains were all drawn, the windows dark. Andy paid the driver and walked up to the door. He'd had time to cool now, in the back of the cab, time to remember that he had a wife and children, that they were expecting to see him that morning, at the other end of the country. He would get a mobile number for Paul Curtis here, he thought, call him, see where that went. But then he would have to come back to earth, think about his position more carefully.

He walked up the short garden path and stopped outside the door. Curtis's mother would be asleep. He would have to use his ID, spin some kind of story that didn't give too much away.

He was standing staring at the door, considering this, when something shifted in his mind. It was like a solid weight lifting. Suddenly he could see clearly. What he was doing was absolutely useless. Even if he could get a number for Paul Curtis, there was nothing he could do after that. Not if his own side were shunning him. Without resources he was stranded. He had no car, no proper clothing, no computer, not much money. It was the middle of the night.

The truth was his friend had died miserably and there was nothing, absolutely nothing, that could reverse that.

He sat down on the step and started to cry.

He cried quietly for about ten minutes, just letting the tears come, not really thinking anything. He watched the tears dripping onto the cell shoes, sterile white moccasins that fitted him badly. He saw an image of himself as anyone else might see him, wandering around in institutional clothing like an escapee from an asylum. The best thing he could do would be to go back to Foster and explain everything, try to get his help.

He heard a noise behind him and turned to find that the front door had opened and a massive guy was towering above him. He stood quickly and moved back, wiping his face. The guy must have been all of six foot five. Had he seen him somewhere before? His face was cut, bruised, swollen, but he didn't look aggressive. He was squinting down at Andy, asking him something. 'Do you need help, mate?' That was what he was asking.

The penny dropped. 'Paul Curtis,' Andy said. 'You're Paul Curtis.'

The man nodded, looking puzzled, but not threatened. Andy sighed, his spirits suddenly leaping. 'You have no idea how glad I am to see you,' he said.

38

Jules put the hazards on, pulled the car over and took out the map again, taking deep breaths to try to stop the panic overwhelming her. It was ten to five, but the low sun was a diffusion of surreal red and pink, filtered weakly through a blanket of thick fog that meant she could only see about ten yards in any direction. She could see the road, the hedges, the towering outlines of black, sudden trees that hung over them, sometimes an area of wet, grey field, but never a horizon. Never anything that would orientate her. They were lost.

She had no idea where they were. She looked out of the car windows and had a terrifying feeling that she was not on earth at all, or not the earth she knew. This was a living nightmare. The atmosphere in the car was the same. They were a breath away from screaming at each other. She had a dull headache across her eyes, and a persistent thought that she wasn't seeing things properly, that she was missing something vital that would turn all this horror into something safe.

'We're lost,' she said, struggling to control her voice. She had been driving round these country roads for nearly fifty minutes, following the useless, vague directions Chris was giving her. They kept turning, doubling back. They were probably going over the same route again, but since it all looked the same she had no way of knowing. She was desperately tired.

'Keep going,' Chris said. 'It's here somewhere. I'll recognise it. It's near here. I'm sure.'

'We've been here before,' she said. She was going to explode with frustration and fear, get out, walk away from them, leave them to it. Chris was in the back, with Lara, who had said virtually nothing since they had left Paul's mother's house. Her eyes were sunk back in her face, dull. It wasn't the Lara she knew.

'I don't think so,' Chris said. 'I don't think we've been here before.' He was leaning forward peering through the space between the front seats. Lara was slumped back in the corner.

'It's all the same, Chris,' Jules said. 'We must have been here before. We're going round in fucking circles. There . . . look . . .' She pointed to where the fog was parting around a road sign. There was a village eight miles ahead. 'Framlingham,' she said. 'We've seen that sign before. We should go there. There might be a police station there.' It was perhaps the fifteenth time she'd said it in the last two hours.

'No. No police.' It was Lara who spoke.

'We have to, Lara,' Jules said, turning to look at her. 'A man was killed. We have to.'

Lara shook her head vigorously. 'Leave me. Leave me here if that's what you're going to do . . .'

'Let's not have this fight again,' Chris said. 'We agreed we'd find Rathmore and sleep. We're too tired to think straight. Let's just do what we agreed.'

Jules felt Lara's hand on her shoulder. 'I'm sorry, Jules,' she said. 'You don't need to be involved with this. We can get out and walk. You can go to the police and tell them what you want. But I can't go with you. I'm sorry. I would have to tell them everything then. Everything I know about Pasha, about what he's doing. There's no point in going to them otherwise. And I can't do that. I'm sorry. I can't. He's my brother. So just leave us here. I can take care of this. I know what I have to do . . .'

Jules heard Chris snort with frustration. He was as keen to get the police involved as she was.

'You can go too, Chris,' Lara said, very quietly. 'I don't expect you to stay with me. Besides, there's no point now. So you can go too. Go with Jules.'

Chris shook his head, more angry than shocked, Jules thought.

'And leave you where?' Chris demanded. 'Here? In the middle of nowhere? Are you mad, Lara?'

'I know what I'm doing. You can leave me and go. It's only me Pasha wants—'

'Don't be stupid, Lara.' Jules heard herself saying the words. 'I wouldn't do that. I can't leave you like that.' She brought her hand up and held Lara's. Lara looked at her, then started to cry. Suddenly, she was the same little frightened kid Jules had met all that time ago in school. It was the same thing pulling at Jules's heart, the same mix of pity and awe and attraction that she had never understood.

Chris put his arm round Lara. 'I'll call my father,' he said, sounding miserable, distressed. 'I'll have to—'

Jules scowled at him. They had walked out on Paul, at Chris's insistence, because Paul was working for Chris's father. So that had been a waste of time if all they were going to do now was ring his father in desperation.

'We shouldn't have left Paul,' Lara whispered, voicing the thought. 'He was trying to help.'

'He was lying to us,' Chris said firmly, but he didn't any longer look convinced. He'd had time to calm down. 'We should get to Rathmore and sleep. We can think about everything, even calling Paul. But not now. I have to sleep.'

She started the engine and pulled out. 'One last try,' she said.

After a couple of minutes following the road a lane led off to the right. Chris told her to take it.

'It's a dirt track,' she said.

'Good. That's what it's like.'

The car started to bump and bounce along, going gently uphill, still sunk in the mist.

'Bear right,' Chris shouted, as a fork came up. 'This is it.'

After a couple of minutes the road improved. It became a gravel driveway moving through trees. Then ahead she saw the trees fall back, and the shadow of a building start to materialise.

'We're here,' Chris said, not excitedly, but obviously relieved. 'Well done, Jules. Go round the house to the—'

He stopped. They could see the house now, in the mist, but also something else. There was a car parked outside it, a big black Jag.

'Someone's here,' she said. 'Your father?'

'Maybe.' He sounded gloomy about it.

'You won't need to call him, then.'

She pulled the car alongside the Jag. She could see the big house clearly enough now. It looked ruined, dilapidated. 'You sure this is it?' she asked. The image didn't match what Lara had told her about the place.

'This is it,' Chris said.

'You want us to sleep in that?' she asked.

'No. We'll go down to The Boat House . . .' He shut his mouth. They had both noticed Lara's face at the same time. She looked stunned, but she wasn't looking at the house. She was staring at the Jag.

'What's up, Lara?' Jules asked.

But before she could say anything the front door to the house started to open.

260

39

As Paul came off the tops and took the turn out of Silton it was almost five o'clock. If he was right, and Chris and Lara had come here, he guessed they were between half an hour and an hour ahead of him. He had driven dangerously all the way – well above the speed limit – in an attempt to close the gap, but now, as they sank towards the coast, the first streaks of grey fog swirled around the car and he had to slow dramatically, switch the fog lights on and pray that he was wrong.

'How far now?' Macall asked, stifling a yawn beside him. There was no urgency in his voice, because he didn't know what Rathmore meant. If it had been left to him they wouldn't be driving here at all. It was Paul, not Macall, who had the immediate conviction that Chris and Lara would be here as soon as Macall had mentioned Rathmore. Like a light going on. Both Chris's and Jules's phones seemed to be switched off, suggesting that they might well be asleep. But the idea had come to him like a charge of emotional energy, something he couldn't ignore. And with it had come the fear that somehow he was driving towards something terrible, that he needed to get there fast.

'Fifteen minutes, at this speed, if I can remember the way,' Paul replied.

He had paid little attention to the man sitting beside

him. Andy Macall had the air and appearance of someone about to lose his sanity. A feverish breathlessness, a twitchy way of constantly moving as he had paced up and down in Paul's mother's living room explaining why he was there, trying to paint a picture that Paul would believe. He was a policeman, he claimed. Paul thought it must be true. He had the ID to prove it, he had information only the police would have, but his story was full of odd details. And he had been arrested for something, something to do with Pasha.

Paul had taken in only so much of the detail. His head had already been swimming. He had given Macall minimal information in return – certainly nothing about the killing – but he had included the fact that he had been employed, in a security role, watching Chris Napier. And he had told Macall that it was Phil Rathmore who had employed him. He hadn't disclosed that Rathmore was Chris's father, but his silent response to Macall's questions as to why Rathmore was involved must have led to some elementary arithmetic. Macall had continued his pacing in silence, thinking, whilst Paul was slumped on the sofa, waiting to see where it would all lead.

It had led to a question: 'Did you know that Rathmore is selling property to Pasha Durrani?' That was what Macall had asked him. It had been like sloshing icy water across his face.

'What?' he had asked, incredulous. 'Phil Rathmore is selling property to Pasha Durrani? Are you sure?'

'As sure as the fact that you live in a Camden flat belonging to Rathmore. I know the reason for that now. But I can't put the pieces together on the other thing – why would Rathmore be selling a six million quid Yorkshire pile to Pasha Durrani? Given everything we now know, why would he being doing that?'

'What's it called?'

'Rathmore Hall. It's in North Yorkshire. It's near to—'

Paul stood at once. 'I know where it is,' he said. He remembered that he had asked Rathmore if he still owned it. Rathmore had said it was sold long ago. A lie. And now he was being told by this man Macall that there was a direct connection between Phil Rathmore and Pasha Durrani, through the sale of Rathmore Hall. It was enough to make him call Rathmore again, at once.

But Rathmore hadn't answered. And into the gap left by Rathmore's evasions and lies fell all his fears.

Phil Rathmore still owned Rathmore Hall. Chris would know that, of course. *Therefore*, it seemed suddenly obvious that Rathmore Hall was where they'd be. Macall had tried to explain to him that it was very far from obvious, but Paul wasn't listening. He was listening to something deeper. An instinct.

So he had taken his mother's car and brought Macall with him, because Macall had insisted, because it would have wasted time to put him off.

'I can't see any reason they would be here . . .' Macall started again now. He sounded gloomy, depressive. During the last hour his jittery demeanour had given way to an exhausted look. He had more than once taken out his mobile, looked at it long and hard as if considering making a call, then replaced it. Once he had said, out of the blue, 'I have two little kids. They're waiting for me in Brighton . . .'

'We're wasting our time,' he said now. 'I've lost him.'

'You need to be quiet,' Paul said. The fog was getting thicker, reflecting back off the headlights, confusing him. He could only crawl forward. To his left he thought he could glimpse the outline of the buildings that made up the potash mine, towering up through the mist. That was about two miles from the house. 'I need to concentrate,' he said. 'If that's the chemical works over there then we're less than ten minutes away.'

40

When he heard the noise of tyres on the gravel Pasha was bent over Caserne, wrapping an inadequate bandage around his left upper arm. The bandage had come from the first aid kit in his Jag. It wasn't enough, but he hadn't brought more because, when they'd spoken by phone two hours ago, Caserne hadn't told him he was injured, hadn't said any-thing at all about the fight with Mark Johnson.

When Pasha arrived he'd found the front door wide open – the locks broken – and Caserne out cold on the floor in the room beyond, lying in a pool of his own blood. He had managed to revive him, managed to get him sitting up and speaking, but it was clear he needed hospital treatment urgently. He could move slowly, he could talk, but he was only going to get worse without treatment.

Pasha had extracted the story from him. Caserne had failed to kill Johnson cleanly, and there had been a fight. Johnson had been carrying a knife, it seemed. Moreover, he had been suspicious enough to hear Caserne's movement in the woods and come looking for him. As a consequence, Caserne had two knife wounds and a mass of cuts and bruises. He had managed to get away from the scene unhindered only by actually calling the police to deal with the man who had arrived to meet Johnson, DS Andrew Macall – the same man Pasha had stood behind in the petrol station. Perhaps that showed some imagination on Caserne's part, perhaps not. Certainly Pasha was sure the police wouldn't be sidetracked for long. Caserne must have bled all the way out of the woods and back to his car. There would be a trail of his DNA lighting the way to him like a homing beacon.

The man allowed Pasha to inspect him with reluctance. There was a wound to his torso, just below the ribs on the left side. It looked bad, and had bled a lot, all over his clothing, but Pasha could see that it was a flesh wound, a gash through fat, skin, muscle, not piercing anything below. The arm wound was worse. It was a deep puncture which had severed something big, an artery or a vein, and maybe smashed the bone. Caserne had improvised a tourniquet and had stopped the bleeding, but as soon as Pasha loosened the tourniquet the bleeding started again. Caserne had no sensation in the lower arm now, no movement, but a lot of pain from the wound. His fingers looked grey and lifeless. Pasha tried to relax him, but the man was clearly in distress. He wouldn't let go of the knife he held in his remaining good hand, no matter what Pasha said. So Pasha sat him up and bandaged the arm whilst Caserne glared at him, the knife held at his side.

He had good reason to be frightened, of course. Pasha was cursing and swearing as he went to and from the car, getting the first aid kit. He had exploded twice as Caserne told him about the cock-up with Johnson. Pasha said nothing about it, but it was clear they weren't going to get the man on an aeroplane in this condition, so Pasha's first thought on examining the injuries had been how he could kill Caserne. That was what was going to have to happen. It was the only safe way to deal with the problem. The other options just meant massive exposure to unwarranted risk.

But could he do it? He calmed himself and tried to talk reasonably and comfortingly to Caserne whilst he wrapped the bandage round the arm. What was needed was to get him off guard and drop a rock on his fucking head. Or get the knife off him and cut his throat. Yes. He could do it. Better still, get the gun out of the car and shoot him. That was easiest. He could do it because every minute he spent here was time against him, because his absolute priority still had to be to locate his sister and try to keep to his plans. Caserne didn't matter. He was worse than an animal. He would be no loss to the world.

Pasha was thinking all this, just finishing the bandage, and at the same time spinning Caserne a story about how he should sleep a bit whilst Pasha went for 'safe' medical assistance, when he heard the crunch of gravel outside. Then the engine. It was a car, approaching along the drive. 'Have you called someone?' he asked, at once.

Caserne shook his head.

'So who the fuck is that?'

He ran to the boarded up window nearest to the door and tried to peer through the cracks, but there wasn't a clear angle. He moved to the door itself and tried to open it an inch. He could hear the car slowing outside. Whoever it was they would have seen his Jag already because, stupidly, he hadn't put it round the other side. 'Where's your car?' he whispered back to Caserne.

'At the other side.'

'Good.' He turned back and looked at Caserne, still clutching the knife. 'Give me the knife,' he said. He shouldn't have left the gun outside. Too late now.

Caserne said nothing.

'Get over here and give me the fucking knife now,' Pasha hissed. 'You can't deal with this, so I have to.' He got the door open enough to see. The car had stopped right along-side his Jag. He could see a woman at the wheel. He couldn't see if there was anyone else with her. The girl was talking he thought, looking in his direction. Could she be on a radio? There was nothing held to her mouth. He realised Caserne was right behind him, breathing heavily. He stepped back and took the knife from his hand, then pulled the door open and walked out, knife behind his back. He was staring intently at the girl, waiting to get close enough to her to be able to see inside the rest of the car. But then he saw the panic on her face. At exactly the same time he spotted movement behind her and another face. He couldn't believe it. It was Napier. It was Christopher fuck-ing Napier.

He started to run towards the car. The girl was trying to start it again, clumsily. He got to the door and wrenched it open. The girl screamed as she saw the knife. He pushed it into her face and reached in to get the keys.

'*Shut up. Shut up and get out,*' he yelled. He got his hand to the keys and got them off her, then stepped back and peered past the girl. Napier was starting to open his door now. The fucker would be trying to make a run for it. In the back seat Pasha saw someone else. Just sitting there, face white with shock, staring at him. His sister. Lara.

His jaw dropped. He stood by the open door, the keys in his hand, and blinked rapidly. It was enough of a pause for Napier to get the door open. He was shouting at Pasha as he got out, threatening him, but Pasha could see the fear in his eyes. Pasha stepped forward and pulled him out of the way, then bent in and looked at Lara. There was a sudden lump in his throat. 'Christ, Lara. I thought I'd lost you,' he said. 'I thought I'd fucking lost you.'

She started to cry then, not even looking at him. She was

shaking her head from side to side. Pasha stood back, pulling up to his full height. He took a deep breath and looked at the sky. '*Thank you*,' he whispered to himself. It was the first thing that had gone his way.

He walked round to his car without paying much attention to them. They were his now, all of them. They didn't know how to deal with violence, or the threat of it. They weren't going to try anything. All the same. He got the gun out of the passenger glove compartment and heard Napier start stuttering about it. He was standing by the open door, looking useless, looking like the useless fag Pasha had always thought he was. Pasha pointed the gun at him, watched him flinch and duck behind the car. Pasha walked round until he was in sight again. He was on the ground, cowering, begging him not to shoot.

'Get in the house,' Pasha said. 'Stop whimpering and get in the house.'

He told the girl in the driver's seat to get over to the house too. She had more spirit though. She wouldn't leave Lara, she said, her voice warbling like a little bird's. Pasha walked round and opened the rear door where Lara was. He asked her to get out or he would kill her friends. That made it simple enough. While Lara was moving he leaned in the front passenger door. The other girl was still behind the wheel. He gave her the keys and told her to move the car round to the other side of the house. He gave her his own keys too – for the Jag – and told her to come back and do the Jag next. He thought about making the threat explicit, but there didn't seem to be a need. She was shaking like a leaf, couldn't take her eyes off the gun.

'How did you know we would come here?' Lara asked. She sounded exhausted.

'I didn't,' he said. He moved a little closer. 'This place is mine,' he whispered. 'I own it. That's why I'm here.' It was only half a lie. Not even that. It would be his soon, if he could hold things together, and there was a chance of doing that now. He saw her frowning. She looked at him with incomprehension.

'Why?' she asked.

'For you, Lara,' he said. 'I bought it for you. It was the place you always wanted. I'll do it up – it will be magnificent. It will be your home. You marry Shamsuddin, but you live here. I will live here with you.'

'You bought this place?' Lara asked. She sounded dumbfounded.

He stood right in front of her. 'I bought it for *you*, Lara,' he said again. 'Do you understand?' It wasn't how he had wanted to tell her. But maybe she would get it now, maybe it would get through to her.

'You're fucking mad,' she said. She was still frowning, still staring at him. 'I wouldn't want this place. It's a collapsing dump.'

'It won't be—'

'I never wanted . . . are you mad, Pasha? Are you fucking mad? You bought . . . I don't believe it.' She started shaking her head.

'But you used to talk about it,' he said. 'You made it sound so beautiful. You came here when you were sixteen, with Napier. You told me all about it, how you would have wanted to live in a place like this. I even came here, without telling you, to see it. Eight years ago. So I would know where it was. I swore to myself that someday I would get it for you . . .'

'This wasn't the place I was talking about!' she said sharply. 'We never came here. We went to the *other* place . . .' She waved her hand off in the direction of the sea. 'You're an idiot, Pasha. You bought the wrong place.' She started to giggle, a mad cackle, her face screwed up, her hand over her mouth, tears still coming out of her eyes.

The wrong place? He felt stunned, suddenly struggling with a confusing surge of emotions. Embarrassment, anger, disbelief. He didn't know what to make of her words.

By now the other girl had moved the cars and come back. She was standing by Napier, waiting. He walked over to her in a daze, took the keys off her. He told them again to get up the steps and into the house. He waved the gun and they stumbled up the steps. He walked after them, then shouted back at Lara, 'Inside, Lara. We have to work this out. Inside.' She looked at him with a peculiar expression that he hadn't seen before. He realised what it was. It was pity.

She stood hesitantly and took a step towards him, then followed. The other two were through the open door. He went in after them and they all stood in the centre of the empty room – what counted as a reception area. It was as large as the entire ground floor of the house he'd been brought up in. Caserne was standing against one of the walls, gawping at them, still covered in his own blood, an image from a horror film. Pasha threw him his knife. It clattered across the floor and stopped quite near his feet, but Caserne didn't stoop to pick it up. Pasha turned slightly and saw that Lara was right in the door now, looking round the room. She didn't seem to see Caserne. She was looking at the ceiling, as if she were trying to remember it. 'No,' she said. 'No more, Pasha. It ends now.'

Then suddenly she was gone. He shouted after her and stepped into the doorway. She was walking across the gravel, heading for the back of the house. He screamed at her, telling her to get back. She glanced back and he took a step towards her. She started to run. He screamed again. But then she was out of sight, round the wing of the house.

He turned back inside. 'Watch these two,' he shouted at Caserne. 'Kill them if they try anything. Pick up the knife. Now.' But he couldn't wait to see it happen. He had to get Lara quickly. He turned and sprinted after her.

41

It was pure luck that she didn't slip and fall. She knew that. She ran too fast for it to be safe. She was shaking inside, her heart very loud in her chest, still unsure how many tablets might be inside her, and the fog was thick, so that everything came at her suddenly, dashing out of the mist, whipping into her face before she had time to react. Branches, long grass, bushes, a chain fence with a 'no entry' sign that had not been there eight years ago, barring the route from Rathmore down to The Boat House. She went under it, down on her belly in the dirt. She had flat shoes on and jeans – nothing to hold her up – and she knew he would be behind her, so at the other side she ran like she had never run before.

Down through the woods in near darkness, barely able to see five feet in front of her, gasping for breath, chest tight. As she made up her mind, she felt something like relief.

She knew the way, because everything about this place was etched into her memory. She could see nothing for the mist, but she knew there was only one path from the house through the woods and down to the cliffs, so she must be on it. She looked for things to recognise, for some clue that *this* was where she was again, in Rathmore, where so much of her was anchored, but as she ran, and as nothing seemed familiar in the fog, she realised that she wasn't *there* at all –

not in the Rathmore she knew. Because that place existed in an impossible, unobtainable realm: in the past. *That* was the Rathmore she knew, the real Rathmore. This place was nowhere, an illusion.

As the trees vanished she had the feeling she was running down a steep slope with grassy, overgrown fields to either side. She let go. She had run here eight years ago, just like this, running to The Boat House, to Chris, to Paul. She even put her arms out as she had then, and felt the wind on her face, the mist stripping past her. She was going so fast, her hair blown out behind her, that she had a momentary sensation that she was flying. Then it all caught up with her and she tripped, lost her footing, came crashing down onto her head, then over, rolling along the path and then off it into tall, wet grass. She lay for a moment panting like a wounded animal, taking note of the pains in her elbows and her knees, the new throbbing where her head had hit the path, the blood coming from her nose. Then she was up and off again. And this time, as she started, she could hear him shouting in the fog behind her. Shouting after her. Shouting her name.

The cliffs were there suddenly, the path ending at a fence, the sensation of dizzy, plunging space in front of her, the noise of seagulls out in the mist, and waves crashing far below, the rich, rotting smell of the sea filling her nose. She thought it strange that now, of all times, she was experiencing what it was to be alive, taking everything in, noticing. But it didn't last long. Because she had to get onto the steps, and she could hear him, his running footfall on the path behind, closing quickly.

She set off, taking the rickety, broken steps two at a time. Not far to go. She knew the place. A platform where the steps switched back on themselves. She remembered it. She had stood there with Chris, arm in arm, staring at the view. The sea. And the house – The Boat House – directly below them. But she couldn't see anything now. Just fog pressing its wet breath against her face. Sounds, smells. She almost fell again, caught hold of the rail and felt it creak and give. But it didn't matter. She stood straight. She was here. She had returned.

She looked at the wooden boards and tried to get some sense of herself, as she had been, standing here eight years ago. She looked at the wood and saw all the detail in the grain. She looked back at the cliff, streaked with seagull droppings and lichen. The air was dank, chill, the place dark in the sinking layers of fog. Not how she remembered it.

She realised then that she could never get back, never return.

She had been completely happy here. There had been a kind of perfection. Not always a heady, ecstatic feeling, sometimes just a long, warm contentment. Her and Chris, and Paul. She had thought the time spent with them here was just a part of her life, a staging post on the way to somewhere. But now she saw with brutal clarity that it had been her life. All of it.

She grabbed the rail as she heard Pasha's feet clattering down the steps. In a careful, sure movement she swung herself over the edge so that she was on the outside of the rail, hanging out into the drop. She looked down only briefly, and only briefly thought that it helped, the mist, because she couldn't see anything below her, couldn't see the distance at all. Then she looked up and saw him stopping himself on the platform, arms outstretched towards her, gun in hand, eyes wild with fear, screaming at her to stop.

*

'*Do something! Do something, Chris!*'

Chris could hear Jules screaming at him. She was half crouched on the floor, her face streaked with tears. He could see her and hear her, but he couldn't move.

All his life he had been like this – frightened of fighting, frightened of violence, unable to act. He had been bullied mercilessly at school because he had never been able to just forget the consequences and fight. But if he didn't do something now, right now, then he was going to be killed. He watched the man moving his eyes from the knife, then back up to him, watched him trying to position himself against the wall so that he could stoop to get the knife, and he knew that it was *right now*, or never. Once the man had the knife in his hands, it would be too late.

'*Move, Chris. Move!*'

The man was covered in blood, his breath rasping, his eyes half closed, obviously injured in one arm and somewhere down his left side, too weak and confused to simply bend over and get the blade. But still Chris couldn't move.

'*Do it, Chris! Do it now!*'

Shut up, Jules, he thought. *For Christ's sake shut up.* She was going to panic the man. The man was leaning back against the wall – about four foot from the open front door – like he would collapse if he stood up straight. He had managed to shuffle along the walls towards the door, kicking the knife in front of him to get into the position he was in now, blocking their exit, but he hadn't been able to stoop and get the thing. He had been told to kill them – Jules and himself – if they tried anything, but Chris wasn't sure he would be strong enough to do anything without the knife. The knife was at his right foot. His right foot was actually touching it. Jules was about eight foot to the left of Chris, slightly nearer the door, but the man wasn't watching her at all. His eyes were on Chris only.

'*We have to do something, Chris*,' Jules was yelling. '*Pasha's gone after Lara. We have to stop him. He could kill her . . .*'

The man shouted something at her. Chris saw him shift his weight. She was scaring him. All the shouting. He was going to have to get the knife . . .

Chris started to scream. He opened his mouth and out it came. He stood with his feet rooted to the floor and screamed with all his might, his face twisting up, his hands clenched tight in front of him. It was a howl of frustration and rage. It was twenty-four years of suppression bursting out of him. It sounded like some kind of barbarian war-cry, erupting from his heart, a pent-up bloodlust set free. He saw Jules start to move towards the man because that was what she thought it was too. The beginning of something. He saw the man's expression change and his legs bend. His eyes were down. He was moving towards the floor and the knife – because a scream so aggressive must lead to violence. He thought Chris was rousing himself, funnelling his strength into some explosive release.

Only Chris knew – as he stood there yelling at the ceiling – that there was nothing in it but helplessness, and fear and frustration. His legs wouldn't move. And even if he forced himself forward he knew he would fall. Because that was the way it always was with him. Because he couldn't fight, couldn't handle this, couldn't do anything. He was screaming because if he didn't let it out somehow he would collapse onto the floor, roll into a ball and start to cry.

He stopped only as Jules started to stand. He started to shout at her, to warn her not to do anything, to tell her that he wasn't with her, that he couldn't help. She was going for the door, he thought – hoping to get through it and out as he did something to distract the man, as he *dealt* with him. She was moving too quickly though, too fast to stop.

She was about five foot away from the man before he saw that she had something in her hand, something she must have picked up off the floor. He saw what it was as her arm drew back to throw it. A stone, about the size of a half brick. He had seen it as they had come in. A single stone lying on the floor – something they used to jam the door, maybe. And now she had it in her hand and was throwing it. She wasn't going for the door at all. She was going for the man. Something changed in Chris. The panic became movement. Desperate, insane movement – something completely out of his control. His legs started to move. He wanted to stop himself, but he couldn't. His head was pounding with blood, his vision constricted. He was going forward, fast, screaming again, fists clenched . . .

The man wasn't even looking at her as she threw it. He was stooping towards the knife. She released it with a grunt of effort, hurling it down at him. The man had his one good hand already on the floor beside the knife when it hit him. Chris heard a crack like a branch breaking. Very loud. The man's head jerked off sideways. His jaw did something peculiar, like it had actually come away from his face. Then he was rolling backwards across the floor and Jules was right over him, yelling something at him.

The man began to howl like an animal. Chris felt pee spreading down his legs. The man came up into an unbalanced crouch, moving with unexpected speed. He had the knife in his good hand. His jaw was hanging sideways, out of joint, but his eyes were on fire, and he was suddenly alive, dangerous, enraged. He was going for her. As Jules tried to stop herself from running into him he came up and caught hold of her clothing. He was using the same hand that held the knife. She pulled backwards, trying to get away from it. The man went over, still holding her. Chris was right there beside them as Jules came down on top of the man, then rolled away, kicking and shouting for help. Chris saw the man release her and draw the knife arm back.

For a second Pasha froze. He had caught up with her, found her. But as he jumped onto the narrow platform she was sliding over the edge, moving over the safety rail. He stopped himself and found his voice. He screamed at her. She looked up at him like she was startled, surprised to see him, then shifted her weight so that it was firmly placed on the outer edge of the wooden platform. She had both hands on the safety rail. 'Get back!' she shouted. 'Stay there.'

He took a step towards her, taking a big, deep lungful of air to try to get his breath back. He had run all the way.

'Keep back!' she shouted again. 'Stay there!'

He was no more than six feet from her. He could lunge, arms out and he would catch her. But what if she slipped? 'What are you doing, Lara?' he asked, hissing the words at her. 'What are you doing?' He bent carefully and dropped the gun to the wooden boards so that he would have both hands free.

'Stay there Pasha. You try to touch me and I'll let go. I'll do it. Believe me.'

'Don't be silly. Don't be stupid . . .' He tried to speak quietly, tried to control the anger he felt. He took another step forward, then the fear burst out of him '*Get back over here! Get back here now!*' He screamed it at the top of his voice. But she didn't even flinch. She was staring right at him. He screamed it again, took another step towards her.

'Shut up,' she said quietly. 'I won't have anyone talking to me like that now. Not any more. It's all over, Pasha.'

'Nothing is over, Lara. Please . . . please . . .' His voice cracked and he stretched his arms towards her, imploring. 'Please come back over. Please. You've made your point, so now please just come back before you slip . . .'

She laughed. 'Before I slip? Can't you see what's happening?' She shook her head, like she was sad about something. 'I've been running from you all my life,' she said. 'Running from your . . . intensity.'

'Lara . . . I'm begging you . . . please just come back over. We can talk this side of the rail. We can—'

'I hadn't realised how much the threat of you had twisted everything until today. This has been going on all my life. You've been going on at me my entire life. Wanting me, trying to control me. It stops here, Pasha. I'm sorry . . .'

He lost his temper again. '*Get fucking back over here now. I'm telling you. Get back now!*'

She smiled at him, an odd smile.

Then suddenly she was pushing backwards, moving, letting go.

He dived straight away, arms out and reaching for her. Her hands moved as he came towards her. He slammed into the metal railing, felt it move and give, then had both hands on her right arm. He closed his fingers over her and tried to get his feet forward, to brace himself, to stop himself going over. She still had her feet on the boards, but was leaning out, trying to pull away from him. He heard her start to say something as his whole upper body was wrenched forward, over the rail. He was leaning out, one leg up to balance himself. But he had her. *He had her.* She was shouting at him, screaming that he should get off her. She was in mid-air, dangling out, with him hanging on fast against the railing, leaning over, straining to keep his fingers tight on her arm.

It was a split second of time, suspended, so that he could see every detail of it. Then his body twisted with her weight and one hand tore loose.

He couldn't hold her with only one hand.

An instant later his fingers were empty.

He screamed out loud, turned and looked, but she was gone. There was nothing there. Nothing but his hand stretched out into empty air. Below, in the mist, he could hear nothing but seagulls and waves. No shout, no scream, no impact. It was as if she had never been there.

Jules saw the knife arching up towards her head as Chris started to punch the man. She *thought* he was punching him, but the knife dropped immediately, and the man fell to the floor like he'd been poleaxed. Then Chris was over him, one arm swinging at him, screaming at the top of his voice. He had the stone in his hand – the one she herself had just thrown. He hadn't punched him, he'd hit him with the stone. She scrambled backwards out of his way. He was striking the man with the pointed end of the stone, bringing it repeatedly down into his head and face. One of the man's hands was up above his head, uselessly trying to ward off the blows, but Chris was going berserk, smashing past the hand, ramming the rock into his face, down on the back of his head, hitting him anywhere he could see in a frenzy of energy and movement.

The man managed to turn onto his knees and start to crawl away. There was blood flying into the air every time Chris hit him, the head recoiling viciously, the man making a low, guttural moaning sound. And still Chris was screaming, still going for him. She pushed herself to her feet and ran to him. She got hold of his shirt and yanked him back.

He fell backwards off balance, then screamed at her to get out.

'Enough, Chris!' she shouted, right into his face. His eyes were wide, the lips drawn back, spittle all over his chin. 'Enough. Let's go!'

He jumped to his feet and turned away from her. The man was still crawling, heading for the doors at the other side of the room. Chris dropped the stone and picked up the knife.

'No! Chris. No!' She shouted it at him four or five times. But he wouldn't stop. So she ran to him again, caught hold of the arm with the knife, dragged him back. He started to struggle with her.

'We can't risk it . . .' he was hissing. 'We can't leave him. Get off me. I have to finish it. Get off . . .' She slipped to the floor and wrapped her arms round his legs. Past him she could see the man pulling himself along the floor. He was on his belly now, making no noise at all, but still going.

'Let him go!' she shouted. 'Let him go. You'll kill him . . .'

'I want to fucking kill him. I want to finish it . . .' He shook his legs, trying to get her off, but she held tight. He started to walk, dragging her after him, then fell forward and lay panting and exhausted. From the other room they heard the man shouting something incoherent.

'He's still alive,' Chris gasped. 'He could have a gun. Get off me, Jules. I have to check . . .' He kicked at her, quite deliberately, catching her in the chest, hard enough to wind her. She lay back and he pulled himself to his feet. She heard him walking through to the other room. She tried to get up but was shaking too much. She got as far as a crouch, then heard noises. Dull blows. Sharp breaths, gasps of pain.

She got up and stumbled through. The man had got as

far as a big arched window with cracks in it. She could see the fog beyond it. The man was flat on his belly, one hand clawing at the glass. Chris was standing over him stabbing down into his torso with the knife. She turned away and started to retch.

He came past her moments later, still carrying the knife. 'Something snapped,' he said in a hoarse whisper. 'I couldn't stop.' His voice sounded weird, cold, not like him at all. 'I'm going after Lara,' he said. She couldn't look at him. 'You go out and find a phone signal. Call the police.' He sounded like he was going to cry. He waited a moment, beside her, and she heard him sob, just once, but still she couldn't look.

She heard his footsteps through in the other room, then looked back at the man. He was lying where she had last seen him, but perfectly still now. She crawled as far as the wall and hauled herself to her feet. 'Chris!' she shouted, but her voice was feeble, too feeble for him to hear, because when she looked through he was already gone.

She pulled her phone out and switched it on. They had come here with their phones switched off, to avoid contact with Paul. But if Paul had been here he would have stopped all this. She waited for it to boot, not daring to look at the man now. The phone fired up and she saw there was no signal. She ran through the other room and outside, staring at the signal indicator. Nothing. She looked into the fog, then looked back at the house. Pasha had taken the keys to her car. So she could either run back up the path they had driven down, waiting for a signal, or follow Chris and try to find Lara before Pasha did.

She put the phone in her pocket and started to run in the direction she guessed Chris had gone.

42

'This is it,' Curtis said. Andy opened his eyes and saw that the trees flanking the lane had gone and they were approaching a large country house, built of white stone. He couldn't see much detail in the mist but noted there were no cars parked outside.

Curtis stopped in front of the place and opened the glove compartment in front of Andy. There was a torch in there, which he took out. Then he got out quickly, without saying anything. He looked nervous, though Andy couldn't see why. He was moving with too much energy for Andy to match. Andy opened his own door and got out. He leaned on the roof of the car and watched Curtis scanning the woods to the side of the house, then scrutinising the front of the building. There were two big ornamental columns either side of the front door, and steps leading up to it. Above the door a stone was engraved with the words *Rathmore Hall, 1826.* The place seemed very deserted and looked dilapidated. There was graffiti on some of the stonework down by the door, plants growing out of the window ledges. 'They're not here,' he said to Curtis, stating, he thought, the obvious. 'No one's here. The place is deserted.'

But Curtis shook his head. 'The car could be round the other side,' he said, for some reason whispering. 'You check.

I'll do the house.' He marched off towards the house, limping slightly.

Andy sighed, watched him climb the steps and pause, then push at the front door. It was already open. He considered shouting a warning to Curtis – to be careful of falling through the floors – but Curtis was a very big boy. He could look after himself. Instead, he set off for the side of the place, as Curtis had asked him to.

There was a path round the side, skirting overgrown flower beds which bordered woods. The woods were of conifer and oak, and the trees very high. Andy stared into the dark spaces without much interest. He could hear nothing moving, see nothing to be worried about, but the memory of pushing through the woodland to find Mark's body set a chill in his spine, so that he began to shiver.

The fog was so dense that he could see only about twenty yards ahead. So he was right past the wing of the house before he got a view of the space behind, before he saw the three cars parked there. Then he felt really frightened. Just seeing cars there, in the fog, was unsettling enough – knowing that they were not, as he had assumed, alone here. But then he took in types and plates. One of them he recognised immediately – it was Pasha Durrani's Jag. The second came to him a moment later – it was the car belonging to Julie Clarke. 'Jesus Christ,' he whispered. 'Jesus Christ. Curtis was right.'

Paul found the body quickly, through in the back of the building, flat out in a still spreading puddle of blood. His first thought was that it would be one of them – Chris, Lara or Jules. When he got up enough courage to approach it and saw that it was no one he knew, he felt a moment of relief, an absurd and disgusting joy. It didn't last. The body

– when he touched one of the hands – was warm like his own.

He ran quickly back the way he had come, through the two rooms marked by traces of violence and distress. He was panicking now. He had found them, but he was certain Pasha had too. They were at The Boat House. He was sure of it.

As he came out of the front door he shouted for Macall, then heard him yelling from the pathway that led down the side of the building. He sprinted there, almost running into Macall as he turned the corner. He stopped in front of him, staring past him, into the woods, trying to listen.

'Durrani's here,' Macall said. 'You were right. He's fuck-ing here . . .' He was breathless, talking excitedly. 'His car's round there. And the car belonging to Julie Clarke . . .'

'I know. They're all here.'

'Where? In the house?'

'No. There's a dead man in there. But no one I know.'

'Fuck. I'll call it in. I'll have to—'

Paul brought his eyes down to look at Macall. 'Not here you won't. There's no signal.'

'Then let's get out. Drive back to the road—'

'I can't do that. I have to get to them. There's another place, down through woods behind you. It's called The Boat House. That's where they'll be.'

'How do you know?'

'That's where we always came. I'm going down there. It's about a mile through the woods. I have to run . . .' He was stepping past him already.

'I'll come with you,' Macall said.

43

Pasha came down the stairs in a blind, mad rush, tripping many times, in the end jumping seven or eight stairs at a time and slamming into the cliff face at the bottom. He had been here before and knew that the stairway twisted up the cliffs so that for most of the way it was right above the house, but he didn't know which parts were above the house, which hung out over the beach and rocks. So when he got to the concrete embankment at the bottom he looked up frantically, trying to judge the position of the platform, but he couldn't see anything for the fog.

Heart in his throat, he ran to the retaining wall and stared out at a thin, cold strip of rocky beach with a white mist hanging over it like smoke. The tide was strong, the waves crashing explosively into the pebbles. He couldn't see any sign of her.

He turned back to the house and ran up the stone, whitewashed steps that led up to the flat roof. As soon as he turned onto the roof he saw her.

She was at the edge nearest the cliff. He ran straight to her, only pulling himself up as he saw how badly twisted her body was, as he took in the long tongue of blood running away across the dirty, weathered white paint. He cried out her name, then stopped beside her, hands in the air, not sure how to touch her. All sorts of thoughts flitted through his mind, about spinal injuries and keeping airways clear. She was on her side, a leg twisted beneath her, arms pulled in towards her chest. The head was rolled backwards at an unnatural angle.

He took a step closer, forcing himself to look properly. He started saying her name, whispering it. He saw the blood was running away from her head and her chest was completely still. He crouched suddenly and gently pushed his arms beneath her. He pulled her towards him and her head rolled backwards, limp. He sobbed. He moved his arms so that he was cradling her against him, then bent his face close and started talking to her. 'Don't leave me,' he whispered, voice cracking. 'Please don't leave me.' He could feel her warmth against his chest, like she was alive.

He began to cry out loud. Then stood up with her held against him. He didn't know what to do. There was blood running out of her mouth but she wasn't choking.

He started to howl into the night air, head back.

When he stopped he heard a noise above him and realised it was footsteps on the stairs, far above, a dull, heavy thudding. Then a voice, male, shouting Lara's name through the mist. Pasha turned at once and started to run. He didn't want anybody to see her. He didn't want them anywhere near her.

He carried her back down the stone steps and found the rear door to the place. Everything was dark, the door locked. He kicked it twice, still holding her. The locks broke second time. He barged in and watched her head lolling around over the edge of his arm, like the snapped neck of a pigeon, the blood streaming out of her mouth and nose. She was completely slack, a dead weight.

He moved into the room behind the door, heedless of what he found. It was a kitchen. He went through it into the

288

next room. There was a massive window with doors and a view out to a kind of short pier jutting out the front of the house, lost in fog.

He placed her carefully on the floor, trying to arrange her smashed limbs so that she looked normal. He was snivelling and gagging, his eyes streaming. He couldn't even see her clearly. The shouting was very close now. Whoever it was started to whisper her name. Pasha heard him enter the house, heard him hiss her name then bump into something in the kitchen area. Pasha knelt on the floor beside Lara. He could feel something coiling inside. He knew who it was now. He recognised the voice.

A light came on in the kitchen then the door between swung open and Napier almost fell into the room. He was holding a knife. He stopped when he saw them. Pasha watched his eyes move from himself to Lara, back again, watched him take in her condition, the trail of blood. Then his face twisted with grief and he started to mouth something. Pasha pulled the gun from the back of his trousers and stood. It felt like his blood was boiling. He slipped the safety off and pointed the thing directly at Napier. But Napier didn't move. His eyes were on Lara. 'You killed her,' he stuttered, his voice a coarse noise. 'You killed her . . .'

'No. You fucking killed her.' He fired, aiming for Napier's head. He fired three times in quick succession and each time Napier flinched but didn't move. The noise was deafening. Pasha saw bursts of plaster and brick behind Napier's head and to the right of him, in the ceiling. He fired again. But they were all misses. Napier was no more than ten feet away, but the gun was kicking his arm back, firing high and wide. And his eyes were full of tears, so he could hardly see to aim.

He brought the sleeve of his other hand across his eyes. Napier was coming for him now, the knife up, his face red with rage. Pasha fired again, desperate, trying to hold the gun down with both hands. Napier recoiled backwards like some massive fist had punched him in the chest, then collapsed to the floor. Pasha fired twice more, but thought he missed again, both times.

Then he walked over to Napier, the gun held out, intending to put it right against his head, to make sure. But Napier was just lying there. He was on his front, blood coming out from under him. His eyes were wide open, staring at Pasha, blood running out of his mouth. Pasha pointed the gun at his head. Napier was trying to say something, the lips moving. He started to cough, and then choke. The eyes looked fraught, confused.

Suddenly, Pasha heard a noise and looked up. There was a girl standing in the kitchen, looking right at them. Pasha stepped towards her. He could hear other noises outside now – the stairway reverberating again as someone else came down it. He would have to kill the girl, he thought. Kill everybody. It didn't matter now. None of them mattered. The girl was a friend of Lara's. He had met her. Julie something.

He brought the gun up to shoot, but at that moment she bolted through the open kitchen door, back outside. He fired and the shot put the kitchen window out. He ran immediately, chasing her. Outside she slipped and fell. She had turned onto the pathway that ran towards the front of the house. He pointed the gun at her, then suddenly his brain cleared. He changed his mind. He lunged after her and caught her by the hair as she pushed herself up. She screamed at the top of her voice. He pulled her to him and jammed her head against his chest, then slapped a hand over her mouth and told her to shut up, shouting the words right into her ear. She kept screaming under his hand.

He pushed the gun back down his trousers and felt the hot barrel sear his skin. He had to get away from here. He couldn't get back up the stairs, so he would have to walk round the cove, swim if the tide was in. The girl would do as protection until he got there.

44

Paul had been trying to get down the stairway without any noise, because he could hear footsteps on the levels below. He had stopped many times to peer over the side, to try to see who it was, but the fog was too thick. There was a chance it was Pasha, though, and it was possible he was armed. If Pasha heard their descent he could wait and pick them off with ease. They couldn't take that risk, so they had come down carefully, slowly, making as little noise as possible.

They were just past halfway when Paul heard the shots. Three at once, a pause, then another. The sound was dulled – a muffled crack – coming from inside the house below them. He stopped and looked over the safety rail. He thought he could just see the roof of the house below, see a light filtered through the fog. Macall caught up with him. 'What's up?' he whispered. But right then there were two more shots.

Paul started to run down, taking six steps at a time to keep his momentum going and stop himself going head over heels. He forgot about Macall, forgot about the noise. He thought he heard another shot after a moment, then a scream. He had maybe forty feet to go, he guessed, but there was no time to look over the side and check. All his concentration was on the steps and keeping his balance.

He got down without falling and in the shadow of the cliff face went into a crouch to look towards the house. He saw an open door – the kitchen door, if he remembered correctly – with light streaming out of it. He could see right along the narrow concrete walkway which led around the side of the house to the jetty at the front, but could see no one moving on it. To his left the beach was stony and steep, falling down to a choppy sea and breaking waves, wreathed in mist. Macall came into a crouch just behind him.

'I'll go in,' Paul whispered. The last thing he wanted was Macall with him. 'You go round the front.' He pointed to the walkway. 'You'll get to a kind of jetty which comes right out the front of the house. There's doors in the front there, just past the jetty. Keep an eye on them, but don't do anything. And keep your head down.' He started off as Macall was replying, and didn't pause to listen. No time. He had to get in.

He made the kitchen door at a run, then edged his head past the frame and back again, quickly. An empty room, a floor strewn with broken glass. He crouched and went through, again at a run. The door to the next room was wide open, and the room beyond in darkness. He moved to the wall immediately to the side of the door, going very quietly, then took another rapid look through. Immediately his heart was thundering, his nerves on edge, adrenalin flooding through him. Two bodies on the floor. No movement. He would have to go in, quickly. He dived through, going sideways, waiting for a shot to ring out. It was like clearing houses in Helmand all over again – the same functional fear, the same focus, the same absence of opportunity for thought. Before you could consider things it was over. Except this time he had no gun. He rolled painfully across the wooden floor, came up into a crouch, ready to move again, fixed his eyes on the first body, then the second.

There was a moment of frozen time. He was waiting for noise, or movement, or something to change. Someone to shoot, or go for him. At the same time it was sinking in. What he had seen. What he was looking at.

The first body was Chris, the second Lara. He reeled backwards like he'd been hit by something. He actually went over backwards onto the floor, one hand out into something wet. He couldn't believe it. He could feel a strangled whine starting in his throat, feel his whole body bunching up, every muscle tightening into a gigantic cramp. He was too late. Too fucking late. He gritted his teeth, looking frantically around the shadows. It was the room he remembered, the one with the piano, where Chris had sat and played. There was the cocktail cabinet they'd used, there were the big, glass sliding doors out to the jetty and the sea. He pushed himself towards Lara and looked, on his knees right beside her. He thought his heart might stop. He started to gasp for air. He stuck a fist into his mouth and bit down onto it, then smashed his fists repeatedly into the side of his own head. He knelt staring at her, unable to move.

He turned slowly towards Chris. He didn't want to go over. He legs were like jelly and he couldn't get to his feet, so he crawled over, too slowly, his throat so thick he could hardly get breath through it. The light from the door was right across Chris's face.

'Oh Christ,' Paul said.

Chris was alive. Chris was staring at him, the lips moving, the eyes full of fear and uncertainty. Chris was still alive.

He went into a kind of emergency routine, the way he had done in more than one firefight, when someone was hit. He moved Chris's arms carefully away from his body, trying to keep the head and neck still, looking for the wounds. Chris's T-shirt was drenched in blood, but Paul couldn't see where it was coming from.

He started talking to him, slowly. He was trying to tell him he would be OK. He stroked his face, told him help was coming, then thought about that and got his phone out. There was a signal. He dialled 999 and asked for the ambulance service. He ran his hand through Chris's hair as he spoke. Then he put the phone on the floor and started to tear at Chris's T-shirt. He had to get to the wound. He told Chris what he was doing, kept telling him to be calm, that everything was OK. Chris's eyes were on him, but he thought they might not be focused. They weren't moving. He was slipping. The lips were still now too, blood bubbling through them.

He couldn't hear Chris breathing. In between speaking to him he kept saying their location in the direction of the phone, telling them there was no easy vehicle access if the tide was in, that they would need a boat or a helicopter. He hoped the operator could hear. He told them what he was doing as he did it. He described Chris's injuries as he found them. Then stopped, paralysed with the realisation that none of this was going to work. There was a massive, ragged exit wound in his back, blood coming only weakly out.

It was too much. On the battlefield he would have dressings, injections to keep Chris going, the whole range of options the kit provided. And still he would have expected someone with this kind of hit to die.

He started to tear off his own T-shirt, thinking he would roll it and stuff it into the wound. But that wouldn't stop the internal haemorrhaging. Nothing that he could do, right here, right now, was going to stop that.

He gave up, took a huge breath, then leaned over so that he was in front of Chris's eyes. 'It's OK, Chris,' he said. He forced the level of his voice down. 'Everything's OK. It's just a flesh wound. It feels worse than it is.' He remembered Rob Ogle screaming as he bled out. But Chris wasn't saying anything. 'There's an ambulance coming. You're going to be OK. Just a couple of minutes and they'll be here. You're in The Boat House. You remember the place, remember when we were here, remember what we did? Me, you and Lara. You and Lara, really. I was just there because you took pity on me, invited me along.' He had to pause, thinking about himself back then. 'I was a big, unhappy, lonely lump,' he said, slowly. 'You two were like stars. Beautiful people, gifted. But you were generous to me. You treated me like a human being, you made me your friend, you took me out of it, made me feel alive. Both of you. Did I ever thank you for that? Not enough.' He laughed, the words catching in his throat. 'I'm thanking you now.' Chris's eyes moved, he thought. Or something changed in them. Did he understand? 'You had the best time of your life here, Chris,' he said. 'You and Lara.' He took his hand from Chris's head, where he'd been smoothing the hair, next to the now redundant, dirty bandaging. Chris's eyes were still open, still fixed ahead, but there was nothing there any more.

45

Paul brought his head up, got to his knees, stood. There had been a noise from outside, he realised. A fraction of a second later he recognised it. A shot. Then another. His brain kicked into gear. Jules was out there. And the policeman. He pulled his eyes from Chris's body. He had to get to them.

He turned towards the glass doors out onto the jetty and picked up a low armchair from near the wall. He stepped calmly forwards and hurled the chair at the glass. It went straight through, the glass shattering in thousands of fragments, the cold morning air rushing in with the sound of the sea, a girl's voice screaming. He ran towards the hole, jumped through and out onto the concrete.

Everything was happening too quickly for Andy. The second shot sounded like it should have blown his head off. He slipped in fright and fell to the pebbles. Then scrambled flat out, trying to keep moving. He couldn't feel any impact, any injuries, but he could hear the girl screaming again. They were up ahead of him, on the beach, Durrani and the girl. The tide was about thirty feet out, the beach steep and slippery. Everything was freezing, streaked with wet mist, bathed in half-light. Somewhere up above him seagulls were screeching. Out beyond the mist he could hear waves thrashing across rocks. He was about twenty feet from the house.

He came to his feet and ran in the direction of the noise, not even looking. Durrani was shouting, warning him off. Andy kept his head down, started to zig-zag. They were only ten to fifteen feet away from him, he thought. The mist closed, then parted. It was moving quicker now, a breeze in the air. The figures materialised out of it, taking shape like something alien, detaching themselves from the grey rocks and pebbles, becoming human.

The third shot must have hit the pebbles near to his feet. He heard the bullet strike, felt shards of stone thrown up into his leg. He skidded sideways again, then came up at once and looked. He could see them clearly now. Durrani was moving backwards, pulling the girl with him, trying to shoot at the same time. Andy took a breath and went for it.

He was almost on them when the gun fired a fourth time. He felt something sear his face, his head snapping sideways, then he was diving into Durrani, arms around his chest, rolling across the pebbles with him.

Durrani started hitting him with something. Hitting his head, his face, his body. The blows were heavy, stunning him as each one landed. He couldn't hold onto him. There was a moment when he was desperately dragging at Durrani's legs, then Durrani was somehow above him, kicking out at him. Andy brought his hands up to cover his face and saw the gun come down to his head. He twisted, lashed out with his arms, screamed and shouted. Behind it all he heard the dull click of the mechanism striking an empty chamber.

Immediately Durrani was running, the gun thrown down. Andy got a leg out and tripped him, but Durrani was up again at once. Andy got to his knees and looked. Saw the girl to his left. Durrani was running without her. She was OK. Andy sank back down, shocked, dazed, too befuddled to give chase. The girl was staring at him. His head felt like someone had split it with an axe. 'Are you OK?' he managed, feebly. Off in the mist he could hear Durrani's footfalls. The girl didn't say anything. She looked like she was in shock.

Andy sat himself up and tried to find his mobile. He started going through the pockets of the jacket Curtis had given him, feeling his rasping breath easing. He got the phone out, but right then Curtis was crouching beside the girl, hugging her. 'Where is he?' he was asking. 'Where is he?'

'He's gone,' Andy said. 'He ran out of ammo.' He pointed back along the beach, into the mist in the rough direction he thought Durrani had gone. You could hear nothing but stony surf there now.

'Are you hit?' Curtis asked. 'There's blood all over your face.'

Andy shook his head.

Curtis stood. 'I'll go and get him,' he said. 'Wait here with Jules.'

Paul ran into the fog, listening. The sun was higher, the pink tinges disappearing, but the fog wasn't anywhere near lifting. He veered towards the incline leading to the sea and ran until his feet were sinking into the piles of shingle and pebbles, slipping towards the waves. He knew this beach well. The shelf was steep and could produce a vicious undertow. The water was freezing too. Was Pasha up to that? Was he really going to try to swim around the point?

Paul couldn't see what else he could be intending. The steps were blocked, which just left the route around the point. There was a road there, of sorts, when the tide was completely out – enough of a track to get a four-wheel drive up to the house – and you could walk it easily, but that route wouldn't be available now. Paul couldn't see the cliffs sticking out to the north, but he knew they were there, and he knew from the position of the water that the only way round would be to swim.

Could he hear something, out there? He slowed down, listening, sticking to the shoreline, his feet washed by the incoming waves. The gulls up on the cliffs were loud, the waves constant, the mist dampening everything. But he thought he could hear a steady splashing, like someone swimming. He saw something at the water's edge, about ten feet in front of him. It was a pile of clothes. Jeans, shoes, socks, a T-shirt.

He started to strip, taking off everything except his underwear. The tide was coming in. The currents would be against him swimming out, but at least there was less chance he would be swept away. He waded in, up to his thighs, carefully feeling his way down the slope. The temperature was maximum ten or eleven degrees. Low enough to sap your strength and kill you if you were in it long enough, low enough to tighten your muscles into a cramp.

He looked out across the surface. Past the line of breakers the waves weren't so high. The sea condition was relatively calm, compared to what he had seen here a couple of times, eight years ago. Nevertheless, he started to shiver almost at once. Then heard someone coming along the beach behind him, a voice calling out. Macall. He ignored him, trying to gauge the distance to the cliffs and the point. Could Pasha already have got round there? It was possible.

He dived in.

He struck out with strong, even strokes. The cold closed around him immediately, encasing his chest in an icy grip. He dipped his head under and pulled through the breakers holding his breath, his swollen eye – now partially open – stinging fiercely. He was waiting for the undertow to pluck at him, waiting to react to it, but nothing happened. Instead he was suddenly alone in a flat, swelling expanse of calm water, with almost no current, bounded on all sides by slow moving fog. He could hear the surf behind him. And his breath. He kept pulling, getting faster. Then he trod water and listened.

He thought there was a sound ahead and off to the right. In the wrong direction. Straight ahead he could see the sun burning through the fog, a pale orange disc. There was a shadow off to his left which he thought might be the point and the cliff there. But he couldn't judge the distance. The noise came to him again. If it was Pasha then he was headed straight out to sea.

From far away a foghorn boomed. The chill really started to set in, so he started to move again, shivering badly, his teeth chattering, his muscles constricting. But now he could definitely hear a splashing noise. And something else. Someone shouting? He struck out in that direction. Then, suddenly, he could see him. Or see his head. His head was moving up and down, going under. The arms were thrashing, but he wasn't making any headway. Paul changed to freestyle and headed straight for him. At some point he must have passed the line of the cliffs, because the water suddenly became much choppier and much colder. He lost sight of the head, but kept going, as fast as he could.

He swam straight into him. His arms struck something in the water, then his head, then Pasha was right there, his face contorted, his arms thrashing wildly, the hair plastered to his head. Paul rolled and kicked at him, pushing himself off. Pasha was gulping at the air, trying to grasp at anything, obviously in serious difficulties. He started to shout, begging

301

for help. '*I'm cramped*,' he yelled. A wave took him further away. He coughed as the water entered his mouth. His head was bobbing beneath the swell. '*I can't fucking float. I'm freezing. Help me.*' He had a stricken, terrified look.

Paul took two strokes back – out of the range of his flailing arms – and felt the icy weight creeping into him too. It was too cold. They were out in the middle of nowhere, in open sea, no one around them, no land in sight. He felt a twinge of panic. He should turn back right now. He was strong enough. He had his bearings. But Pasha was lost, he thought. He could reach over to him, help him. One arm would do it, maybe. Just support him and guide him in.

Instead, he watched the head bobbing beneath the waves, then coming up again. The frantic terrified gulping for air. Paul was only a few feet away, treading water. He could turn back at any time, survive. He was a long way from getting cramped. But Pasha was drowning. If Paul didn't do something Pasha was going to die.

He didn't want to watch that. So he turned and started to swim back in the direction of the beach. He counted twenty strokes then stopped and looked back. The head was still there, but even as he watched it vanished for too long. He counted the seconds he couldn't see it – seventy or eighty – then heard a strangled cry, a coughing and retching that was cut off. He turned his back and started swimming for real, wanting to just get very far away from it.

He made the beach within minutes. When the water was up to his chest and he could stand, he looked back again. It was difficult to see anything. The mist was like a wall. He thought Pasha was only about three hundred yards out. But that was enough. He would go under, drown. Paul was sure of it. He listened and heard nothing but the water and the birds.

46

It was twenty-six days before Paul went to see Phil Rathmore. He waited until after Chris's funeral – delayed because of the police enquiry. The funeral was in Altrincham, at a church near to his mother's house. Paul didn't go. He didn't go to Lara's or Pasha's either, the day after, in some public crematorium in Wimbledon. On both days he sat alone in his flat and drank a beer.

There had been so many police interviews he had lost count. The enquiry was being run by a Yorkshire force, but they sent people to London to interview him, usually at Holborn police station, so he wasn't too put out. He had told them the truth from the first interview, even about the shooting in Lancashire. He was awaiting a decision on that, but it clearly had helped that he had an officer from SO15 on his side. As a consequence of Macall's interventions, he thought, there hadn't been an issue about bailing him, but there was a condition on his bail that he shouldn't contact any other witnesses or potential witnesses. That included, he assumed, both Jules and Phil Rathmore.

The officer who did most of the interviews with him – a DI called Nuttall seemed more bothered that he had consistently refused to tell them who he had been working for,

303

rather than the fact that he had admitted killing someone. It bothered Nuttall even though he *knew* who had hired Paul, because Paul had told Macall, and Macall had passed that on, not being burdened with any peculiar morals about confidentiality. It bothered Nuttall because he was a policeman, and policemen didn't like it when you told them to fuck off.

There was a miniature heatwave in London that Wednesday, but you wouldn't notice that in Rathmore's air-conditioned flat. Still being in the flat was one of the things that made Paul go to Rathmore. That and a feeling that it was what he ought to do. Because Rathmore had paid him and he had failed. There was no getting away from that, no matter what the detail was, no matter how complicated the mitigation.

So he went to say sorry, to close the arrangement. It was a professional way to behave, he decided, and his dad had been full of admiration for that kind of thing. He knew that Rathmore had lied to him, of course, and that if he had been told the truth about Rathmore Hall it was just possible Chris might still be alive. So there wouldn't be much by way of real feeling behind the apology. Still less any empathy. But wasn't that the essence of professionalism – to go through the motions, to do the right thing anyway?

They let him in without argument. The same big house with the same empty room smelling of antiques and furniture polish, the deer's head on the wall above the door, the same room beyond, with the big tables and the low, uncomfortable chairs.

Not quite the same Rathmore, though. The man who came out to greet him looked frail. He spoke slower, moved slower. His face was the same bloodless white, but thinner. The white hair looked stiff and slightly untidy. One clump was sticking out at an angle above the left ear. He was wearing a dressing gown – a big, comfortable, quilted affair that wrapped around him – though it was past lunchtime. It looked like he would shiver without it, though the rooms were warm enough, and as far as Paul could make out he had on ordinary slacks and a white open-necked shirt beneath. A pair of soft leather slippers on his feet, with bare ankles showing. There was no smell of aftershave this time, no sense of energy or haste.

'I'm sorry, Paul,' Rathmore said, standing in front of him by the big table. 'I haven't ordered tea. Would you like some?'

Paul shook his head.

'I've been a bit unwell. Please sit down.'

'No. I won't keep you long,' Paul said, voice very low, eyes down. 'I'm not meant to be here. I have bail conditions not to contact witnesses . . .'

'I'm not a witness. I've told them nothing. I've had to resign as a consequence . . .' He looked off to one side, as if thinking about that, but he said it nonchalantly, as if the loss of position meant nothing to him.

'I only came to apologise,' Paul said. 'And to say that I would repay the money you paid me—'

'Don't be silly, Paul. I know what happened. It had nothing to do with you. There was nothing you could have done. I am to blame, of course. He was my son. There were things I should have told you. I'm not sure what difference anything would have made. But you should have known about Durrani, about the contact I had with him. And I should have taken your advice and notified the police. If I had done that, Chris would still be alive.'

'And Lara.'

Rathmore shrugged. 'I don't know about that. They have told me she probably killed herself. That was her choice.'

No love lost there, then.

A long silence. Paul stared at the floor, Rathmore stared at the long table. They were about a foot apart, on the same side of the table.

'I don't know what else to say,' Paul said, after a while. 'I'm very, very sorry. I should have stopped it. Somehow.'

Rathmore put a hand out, onto Paul's shoulder, then the other onto the table in front of him. 'It was a crime,' he said. 'My son was murdered. The man responsible is not in this room. Please sit down. If I stand too long I'm afraid I will fall.'

Paul sat on one of the straight-backed chairs. Rathmore sat on the one next to it, then angled it slightly, so he was facing Paul. He leaned an elbow on the table and rested his chin in his hand. 'I read your statements,' he said. 'You left him to drown. I'm glad you did it. I won't pretend otherwise. For that alone I would want you to keep the money, stay in the flat until our contract expires.'

Paul sighed. 'I left him because I didn't want to watch another death,' he said, but knew that didn't explain anything. 'And I don't want your money—'

'And for your honourableness. For that you deserve a fitting reward.'

'My honourableness?'

'You mentioned my name nowhere. You told them nothing about me. You were a man of your word, as I knew you would be. For that I am in your debt. Remember that. For that I owe you.'

'That was the job. That was our agreement. You owe me nothing.'

'I've done my best for you,' Rathmore said, ignoring him,

not looking at him, speaking quicker. 'I've spoken to those who needed speaking to. Nothing is going to happen now. You won't be charged. I have that on very good authority. In fact . . .' Suddenly his voice broke and he bent his head. Paul saw his shoulders start to shake. 'I'm sorry,' Rathmore said, the words muffled. 'You must know how I feel. He was my only son, but they were your closest friends. You're probably feeling all this yourself . . .'

Paul watched him for a while, watched him trying to control his emotions. A single tear dribbled down his nose, dripped onto his lap. *No*, he thought. *I'm not feeling any of that.* He looked at his hands, then moved them. Other things, physical things, were happening though. For two days now he had no sensation whatsoever in the tips of his fingers. He had woken up like that. 'I can't feel my fingers,' he said, hoping Rathmore would get it, hoping it would help, be a sign that he was, perversely, suffering something. But Rathmore was crying like a little baby now. He couldn't hear a thing.

At two thirty, Andy met Fletch in a pub in Victoria. A bad choice, as it turned out. In all the chaos and uncertainty of the last three weeks – with one investigation and internal enquiry after another – he had paid little attention to the really burning national questions, like the fact that England were about to play Slovenia in the World Cup. The pub was packed.

Fletch was already there when he arrived, sipping a pint of something in a corner, a newspaper in front of him, studiously trying to ignore the noise from the gathering fans, looking very much like an undercover policeman at a prison reunion.

Andy sat opposite him. He tried to keep his face calm,

tried to talk to the man as if they were on the same side, but it was difficult. 'I'm here because I was told to be here,' he said. 'What do you want?'

Fletch folded the newspaper slowly, that thin smile on his lips, then took his glasses off and put them in a case. Finally, he looked up at Andy. 'Ditto,' he said. 'You think I would wish to come here and talk to you?'

Andy shrugged. OK. Now they had their feelings for each other straight. Now the hostility was out on the table, right in front of them.

'I'm to give you an explanation,' Fletch said. 'That's what I've been asked to do.'

'An explanation?'

'Yes. Naturally there has been some focus on how Durrani knew where Johnson was to meet you, and you have made allegations concerning that which have caused some trouble internally. So I'm here to tell you what went wrong. Because distractions don't help, and because we all have to get on with live projects now. The world of terrorism hasn't stopped.'

'I don't need a speech from you. And we've had enough of a post-mortem at our end to know full well what went wrong. Your department was obsessed with turning Durrani. As a consequence I was arrested and placed under pressure. You wanted me off him. You made my life uncomfortable because I wouldn't toe the line. But that's by the by. That's just a little internal squabble. I'll get over it. They're even threatening to promote me to help me get over it. More difficult to ignore is the fact that there was a leak back to Durrani and that leak had to come from your side. That led to deaths and there is still a concerted effort to cover that, to avoid it, to not dig into it and not apportion blame. I won't go along with that. You should be warned. I won't stop pushing at that until someone is held responsible and the lessons are learned.'

Fletch sighed. 'How very courageous of you. But you'll wear yourself out, I fear. There was a leak. Yes. But it wasn't as simple as you think. I am authorised to tell you about it, providing it goes no further. Can you promise me that?'

Andy smiled. 'Of course. If you give me a proper explanation.' Fuck him, he thought. Tell him anything, do what you have to later. He owed him nothing.

'I told you it was a joint operation – the effort to get Durrani on board – a joint effort with our coalition partners.' Fletch dropped his voice theatrically. Andy was sure he was about to be fed another pack of lies. 'Well . . .' Fletch continued, 'it was and it wasn't, it seems. We've now been informed that Durrani was already on the US payroll. He's been working for them for the last six years. But when we went to them and told them we could hook Durrani, they didn't tell us that. They offered help and co-operation. They didn't tell us he was already one of theirs. There has been some pretty nasty flak as a consequence of that, I can assure you.'

'Wait a minute. He was working for the Americans and the Americans were working with you to turn him? I don't get it.'

Fletch frowned. 'We came to them with the prospect of turning Durrani, they went along with that rather than tell us he was already on board, rather than give that away. It's that simple.'

'And meanwhile they fed back to him what was happening?'

'So it appears.' He shrugged again. 'To protect him.'

'They fed back to him what we were doing in order to

309

keep it a secret that he was working for them? *That's* what you're telling me?'

'I'm afraid so.' He looked down at the newspaper, apparently unconcerned.

'People died. And that's what you're saying happened?'

'Yes. It's a cock-up. People have been dropped as a consequence. There's been an almighty diplomatic row—'

'And that's meant to keep Mark's widow and kid happy? To know that it was an all-American cock-up?'

'Mark?'

Andy clenched his fists. 'Mark fucking Johnson. The dead man. The man this little cock-up got killed.' He lowered his voice, tried to keep his feelings under wraps. People at the bar were staring now.

'Their error was to misjudge Durrani, obviously,' Fletch said. 'He was working for them, but he was working for himself also. He had his own agenda. That's the nature of the game we play. And Durrani was from the sub-continent, in spirit and character, at least. The Americans don't have much experience in dealing with that kind of mind-set. Not like we do . . .'

'So the Americans had access to the information you had?'

'Yes. Through the computer systems. Standard procedure on a joint operation—'

'Who?'

'Sorry?'

'Who was it? Give me a name. Who was it who told Durrani all these things – where I lived, where I would meet Mark . . . all of it. Tell me the name.'

Fletch looked pityingly at him. 'I can't do that. Obviously. This wasn't something criminal, Macall. People were doing their best. The stakes were very high. They made some judgement errors. That's all. We don't want to push at it any harder than we have. We're all in this together after all. We're all trying to stop the bad guys. Durrani was as well. In his own way. He was genuine. Over the years he provided invaluable information to the Yanks. He's saved lives. You should bear that in mind.'

Andy stood. His face was bright red. Fletch stared up at him, completely calm, waiting to see what he would do with about the same interest as he might watch an animal in a zoo.

'Fuck you,' Andy said. He turned and pushed his way out.

Paul called Jules as soon as he was finished with Rathmore. She answered, surprisingly. He told her about the bail conditions. Even more surprisingly, she agreed to meet him. That was it. No pleasantries, no attempt at conversation. He suggested a place and time and she just said 'yes'.

They met in King's Cross, in a coffee place right in the station. Paul had suggested it because he thought she would be able get back home quickly if she changed her mind. She must have caught an earlier train than he expected, because when he walked into the place she waved to him from a table near the back. He sat down opposite her. She stared at him. No smile, no greeting.

She looked bad. Thinner than before – and she had been thin already – face drawn, red eyes harshly rimmed with black, hair lying flat and lank on her head like she was ill. She had on a pair of jeans that looked loose on her, and a T-shirt. Her arms were resting on the table.

'Thanks for coming,' he said, then glanced at her. She had that intense frown he recalled, the same awful look she had given him the night she had found out he was working for Rathmore. He looked away.

'You weren't at the funerals,' she said. She sounded sad, her voice weak. She *was* sad, of course, but he had expected her to sound angry also.

'I couldn't do it,' he said. He wracked his brains for some fuller explanation, but he was so uncertain of his feelings he couldn't get his mouth to open and say anything else. He put his hands on the table and leaned on it, looking down. 'Have you been OK?' he asked after a while. He had to say something. 'I mean, are you managing?'

She nodded, then suddenly reached out a hand and took hold of one of his. He looked up at her, then opened his mouth to say something. She got there first though. 'Don't say anything,' she said, quickly. 'Don't say anything, Paul. Just hold my hand.'

So he did. They sat there in total silence. She was gripping his hand fiercely. After a few minutes of it he realised that tears were running down her face and she was shaking terribly. He moved his other hand and closed it over their linked hands. 'It's OK, Jules,' he said. 'It will be OK.'

She managed some kind of half smile. 'I know,' she said. She wiped her eyes with her sleeve. 'I know. But just don't let go of my hand. Not for a while.'